# Killer Run

**Books by Lynn Cahoon**

The Tourist Trap Mysteries

Killer Run

Dressed to Kill

If The Shoe Kills

Mission to Murder

Guidebook to Murder

# Killer Run

**A Tourist Trap Mystery**

Lynn Cahoon

LYRICAL PRESS
Kensington Publishing Corp.
www.kensingtonbooks.com

LYRICAL PRESS BOOKS are published by

Kensington Publishing Corp.
119 West 40th Street
New York, NY 10018

All Kensington titles, imprints, and distributed lines are available at special quantity discounts for bulk purchases for sales promotion, premiums, fund-raising, educational, or institutional use.

Special book excerpts or customized printings can also be created to fit specific needs. For details, write or phone the office of the Kensington Sales Manager: Kensington Publishing Corp., 119 West 40th Street, New York, NY 10018. Attn. Sales Department. Phone: 1-800-221-2647.

Lyrical and the L logo are trademarks of Kensington Publishing Corp.

First Electronic Edition: August 2015
eISBN-13: 978-1-60183-417-1
eISBN-10: 1-60183-417-9

First Print Edition: August 2015
ISBN-13: 978-1-60183-418-8
ISBN-10: 1-60183-418-7

Printed in the United States of America

*To the Cowboy: Thanks for letting me play with my imaginary friends.*

# ACKNOWLEDGMENTS

We authors tend to spend a lot of time in our heads. We think about scenes, characters, ways to kill people . . . and my husband, the Cowboy, is the best at giving me room to play with my South Cove gang. Even if it means he has to cook dinner. Big thanks to Laura Bradford, Megan Kelly, and my lala sisters. And of course, South Cove wouldn't be what it was without the gentle guiding hand of my editor, Esi Sogah, and the rest of the Kensington crew.

# CHAPTER 1

Modern wisdom says it takes twenty-one days to make a habit stick. Lack of exercise, eating too much, or even negative thinking are all habits that can be corrected in less than a month. My problem is, I don't seem to get past week one. Oh, my intentions are good. My heart's in the right place, but then the proverbial "stuff" happens.

Like the current Business-to-Business meeting where I presently sat, eating my second slice of Sadie Michaels's Black Forest Cheesecake, the newest selection from her bakery, Pies on the Fly. Each slice had enough calories to feed a small South American village for a week. However, Josh Thomas was off on a rant and the creamy chocolate dessert was the only thing keeping my mouth shut instead of pointing out the flaws in his reasoning. Today, the owner of Antiques by Thomas thought we should do something about the ocean smell that permeated our little tourist town. His idea was to have electronic air fresheners installed on each streetlight on Main Street.

I guessed the fact that South Cove was located on central coastal California, thereby, the ocean, hadn't been included in Josh's memo when he opened the store last year. I glanced over at Aunt Jackie and raised my eyebrows, a signal that she needed to control her tubby boy toy before someone pointed this fact out to the clueless Josh.

She ignored me.

As I eyed the last piece of cheesecake heaven, Bill Sullivan, owner of South Cove Bed-and-Breakfast, and our committee's chair, interrupted Josh's tirade. "I'm afraid I can't support your idea. Most of my guests book rooms with us specifically because of South Cove's proximity to the ocean. In my mind, the sea air is a selling point, not a distraction."

"You don't understand how damaging it can be to my inventory. I'm always having to dehumidify my shop. If air fresheners were installed, at least the smell wouldn't enter with my customers." Josh looked around the table. "I'm sure others on the committee feel the same way."

I saw ten heads shake as Josh tried to make eye contact with the other business owners. Even this month's representative from the local art galleries failed to meet Josh's eyes. Of course, that could have been because he was asleep behind the dark shades. Artists loved the grant money that being a member of the Business-to-Business committee gave them; they just didn't like the actual meetings. Or helping with community projects. Or even expressing a freaking opinion.

"Well, it looks like we can table this discussion for another time then." Bill took charge and glanced down at the agenda. "One more item, The Mission Walk sponsorship. Darla? Do you want to present or is Jill handling this?"

The Jill he was referencing is me. I'm Jill Gardner, owner of Coffee, Books, and More, or CBM according to the new logo on our last cup order. I'm also the liaison between the South Cove City Council and the business community. Which means I'm responsible for setting up the monthly meeting, publishing the meeting minutes on our website, and any other crappy job the mayor decides to assign me.

I nodded to Darla Taylor, the owner of South Cove Winery, and our local event planner extraordinaire. "Go ahead, you're spearheading this event."

The Mission Walk was South Cove's first entry into the world of the California Mission Society. The charity focused on the preservation of historic missions throughout the state. Now that the small wall in my backyard had moved up on the list from application to possible historic landmark, I'd been invited to help sponsor this year's 5K walk-and-run fund-raiser. Darla had jumped at the chance to plan the event, and I blessed her every time I got a new e-mail from her on one more task she'd completed that I hadn't even thought of doing.

I reached for the last slice of cheesecake, but Aunt Jackie slapped my hand, moving the plate off the table and onto the coffee counter. I refilled my coffee cup instead and sat back to listen to Darla's report.

"We're all set for next Saturday's run. The greenbelt has been measured and we've got parking set up for the start and finish lines. Greg hired off-duty police officers from Bakerstown to help with patrols that day. The only thing I need is a small group to walk the distance on Friday so we can make sure there aren't any surprises Saturday morning." She glanced around the table. "Who's going to volunteer?"

The room went quiet. I raised my hand. "You know Greg and I will be there, just name the time."

"Thanks. I'd like to do the run-through at 5 p.m. sharp. That way we'll know how long it will take our slower walkers so we don't leave anyone on the trail." Darla wrote down our names in her notebook. "Who else?"

"Josh and I will be there." Aunt Jackie lifted the coffee carafe from the table, taking it back to the pot to refill.

"Jackie, you know I don't . . ." Whatever Josh had been going to say was blocked by the scorching look my aunt gave him. Sure, now he shut up.

"Perfect. Matt and I will start timing you at the start line, and then we'll drive to the finish line to wait for you." Darla focused on me. "Do you want to ask Amy if she and Justin would come, too? I'd like some runners to see how quickly people can get through."

I held back my retort about me being chopped liver and nodded. Besides, if Amy and Justin ran, I could bring Emma and then Greg and I could have some quality time before the craziness of the weekend hit. We hadn't had much couple time lately, between the shop and his annual training requirements for the local police department.

Yes, my boyfriend was the local detective for South Cove. Greg King had just returned to the area when my friend, Miss Emily, had been murdered. When he'd started investigating her death, we'd started spending time together. I think he just wanted to keep his prime suspect close. He tells a different story. No matter what, we'd been a couple for over a year now. And we rarely, if ever, fought. Unless he thought I was messing with one of his investigations.

As Darla wrapped up the list of assignments for Saturday's run, the committee members filled their to-go cups with more free coffee and squirmed in their seats, ready for the meeting to be over. Fortunately, Darla was enough of a bulldog that she filled the final few volunteer spots before turning control of the meeting back to Bill.

"And that's everything." Bill closed the cover on the South Cove notebook where he kept the meeting notes. Mary, his wife and a marketing maven, hadn't attended the meeting, but she'd been working with Darla this last month to analyze the effect of the run on the city's business community. The couple's bed-and-breakfast had been filled for the last week with runners getting ready for the event. He waved as he left the shop. "See you all Saturday."

"As usual, they leave all the cleanup for the meeting to us," Aunt Jackie grumbled as she started moving tables back to their normal places scattered around the shop.

Josh inched toward the door. "Sorry, I have to open in ten minutes. Otherwise . . ."

We watched as Josh lumbered through the door, his next words lost to the wind. He scurried as fast as his close-to-four-hundred-pound frame would go toward his shop next door.

"I'm shocked, I tell you, shocked." Darla laughed as she placed chairs around a table my aunt had just moved. "Seems that Josh always has an excuse when there's actual work to be done. I don't think the guy has moved a box since Kyle started working for him."

"Being catty doesn't suit you, dear," my aunt chided Darla, her tone gentle. If I'd said that I would have gotten a lecture about being generous in spirit or at least in my words. Darla just got a verbal tap on the hand. I would have received a slap on the head.

My thoughts were interrupted when the door opened and a man and woman entered the shop. To refer to the pair as Ken and Barbie would be too generous to the dolls. Both of the new arrivals were actor-level beautiful. We had tourist traffic that came up from Hollywood at times, but typically they came later in the day and dressed in clothes a bit more casual, but just as expensive.

"I told you we were going to be late, Michael." The woman tossed back her blond hair with caramel highlights as she watched us moving the tables.

He sighed. "We would have been on time if you hadn't had to call your stylist about what outfit would be appropriate for a business meeting."

The woman smoothed down the blue jacket that hugged her curves. "Blame me for wanting to make a good first impression." She turned toward me and flashed a hundred-watt smile. "Forgive our bickering. I'm Sandra Ashford and this is my husband, Michael. We're the owners of Promote Your Event. We've been hired by the Mission Society to assist with their fund-raising events. We're checking in to see if you all are ready for the walk on Saturday."

"I'm Jill Gardner. I own the land where the South Cove Mission was found." I held my hands up and glanced around the room. "As well as this store. We've committed to be one of the sponsors for the event."

"Lovely." Sandra's gaze covered the shop's dining area and book department in less time than it took to read a road sign. A look of disgust flashed on her face for a second, her lip twitching like the smell from the coffee of the day was Stockyard Drip instead of Vanilla Bean Delight. Then her plastic veneer went back up and I almost thought I'd imagined the negative assessment. Until she spoke her next words. "I guess it will have to do."

Darla stepped next to me and held out her hand. "Darla Taylor, South Cove Winery, and *Examiner* lead reporter." She grinned at me before adding, "And South Cove Mission Walk chairman. I'm so glad you took time out of your busy schedule for us. Come sit, I've got the event plan right here. I'd love to have you go over it to make sure I'm not missing anything."

Michael stepped forward and shook Darla's hand. "I'm sure it's grand. You know, these events never could get off the ground without the tireless effort of volunteers like you."

As Darla stepped toward a clean table, I heard a sigh come from Sandra's direction. "I swear, if I have to do any more of these one-horse-town events, I'm going to scream."

Michael grabbed her elbow and leaned closer. "Be nice. Or pretend to be nice. I know it's hard to act like something you're not." The couple followed Darla, and as I watched, Sandra shook off her husband's grip.

*Those two have issues.* I knew what it was like to be in a marriage that wasn't working. Between my law practice and my own failed relationships, I'd had plenty of examples. The Ashfords were definitely dysfunctional and on their way to nuclear relationship blowup. I just hoped they'd get through Saturday. The Mission Walk was too important to be collateral damage from a couple's disintegration. I stood by the table as they sat on both sides of Darla.

"Before we get started, can I bring you some coffee? A carafe? Or something more decadent, like a cinnamon roll and a hot chocolate?" I wiped a circle from a coffee cup off the almost-clean table before Sandra could zoom in on the flaw.

"Bottled water." Sandra didn't even look up from digging in her leather tote.

"I'm good." Darla waved me to a chair. "Sit down and help me present our plan."

Michael turned toward me. "That cinnamon roll sounds amazing. Can you heat it with a little butter? And coffee, cream and sugar."

Sandra snorted. "No wonder you didn't want to go to the gym today. You were planning on blowing your diet."

"I'm not on a diet." Michael smiled up at me. "However, I should have accompanied my wife to the gym. Sometimes you just want that extra sleep."

*And time away from a witch from hell.* I started to walk to the counter, but my aunt waved me away. "I can handle this. Just sit down."

By all rights, Aunt Jackie should have been the one involved in the discussion. She had a knack for marketing. I just muddled through before she'd come to help me run the shop. I slipped into the last chair at the table and accepted a folder from Darla.

Listening to the plans and schedule, I knew that she had been the right choice to set up this event. She had thought of everything. As I looked through the maps, sign-up sheets, and lists of South Cove businesses from which she'd gotten donations, I was impressed.

Aunt Jackie set a glass of orange juice in front of me and looked over my shoulder pointing to an item on the list. "I didn't think Lille would be participating. That woman's always griping about giving away her profits."

Darla laughed. "When I told her you were sponsoring all the water stations and providing CBM cups, she decided she needed to do something. So she's hosting a small celebration circle at the end of the walk. Burgers and fries."

"Just what a health-conscious runner wants at the end of an exercise event." Sandra snorted.

Michael dug in to his cinnamon roll, holding his fork up to show his wife. "There's more to life than just health food."

"I hope you choke." Sandra glared at the man across from her.

Her response sent a chill through me. Seemed like we'd be lucky if they made it through tonight, let alone all the way through the Mission Walk.

# CHAPTER 2

When I met Amy for lunch the next day, I recounted the event, blow by blow. The couple had continued to snipe at each other all during Darla's presentation. What Michael exclaimed over as charming and innovative, Sandra called boring and too "small town" to bring in repeat walkers.

"When they left, I was drained. I went home and took a nap rather than taking Emma for a run." I dug into my large Asian chicken salad, looking for the perfect bite of crunch, salt, and sweet. Diamond Lille's might be a total greasy-spoon café, but Lille had branched out into weekly salad specials for the summer and I'd enjoyed every one I'd tried so far. Next week, Southwest Tilapia was on the menu.

"Sounds like a toxic relationship to me." Amy picked up her double-decker cheeseburger and took a bite, wiping the grease from her mouth with a paper napkin. I loved my friend, but sometimes, I wish I had her metabolism. The girl could eat anything and not gain an ounce. Of course, she surfed for hours most weekends. Except for my beach run with Emma and working at the shop, I tended to stay close to my couch. Especially with a book in hand. Of course, I called it "research." Bookstore owners had to be up on the current releases.

"Oh, and I volunteered you and Justin to run the course Friday evening so Darla can time the event." I took a sip of my iced tap water with a lemon slice and thought about the New York–style cheesecake sitting in my refrigerator at home. Since I'd run this morning and was now eating healthy for lunch, maybe a slice of that would be my dinner. With a fresh pear, of course. "Can you be there?"

"I think so. I'll text Justin right now. We put off our surfing date until Sunday so we could be part of the five-K. He's really excited about supporting the town and your mission project." Amy took her phone out of her purse and clicked out a message. Justin taught history at a local college so if he wasn't teaching, most likely he was in the library reading or sitting in his office, writing. The guy looked more like the carefree surfer he played on weekends than the stuffy professor, and his students adored him. "Now, tell me about your upcoming trip. A weeklong cruise to Alaska?"

Greg and I had booked the trip last month, kind of a celebration for dating for a year. Mostly a getaway from what had been a crazy-busy winter. Typically, the shop slowed down after the holidays, but not this year. So even though my aunt was griping about me disappearing during prime tourist season, nothing was going to stop our vacation. Well, I guess Greg could be called back to work if some freak weather event hit or worse, but I'd been watching the Weather Channel for a couple of weeks, and so far, we were good.

"I packed two digital cameras and extra memory cards. I've loaded my e-reader with books. And I've been running every day and eating salads to lose a few pounds before I'm on board with the buffets." I pointed down at the salad. "I could eat this every day."

Carrie, our waitress, stopped by and refilled our glasses. "I'll tell Lille. She's been all freaked out over some food critic who is supposed to be showing up this month."

"I didn't think they scheduled visits like that, or at least, didn't tell the restaurants when they were coming." Amy waved a French fry at Carrie. "Are you sure she's not just having a bad month?"

A grin covered Carrie's face as she leaned closer to answer. "Normally, I'd agree with you, but I guess Diamond Lille's was picked to be in some diner food contest for the paper. If we win, the diner will be on the front page. Lille's dreaming of all the new customers."

"Not sure where she'd squeeze in one more customer. This place is jam-packed every time I'm here." I appraised the lunch crowd. Out of all the booths and tables, only two were empty, and I'd watched both of the prior inhabitants get up and leave within the last ten minutes.

Carrie leaned over. "She's talking about buying the building next door and expanding. Her new boyfriend is a contractor, and he can get her a good deal on the remodel."

I thought about the building next door. Diamond Lille's sat on the corner of Main and Gull Street. The house behind the restaurant was Lille's home, a quaint gingerbread house. I doubted she wanted to tear it down. The only other option was The Train Station on the other side. Harrold Snider had run the model train store for as long as anyone in South Cove could remember. I watched Amy's face as she came to the same conclusion. "You mean Harrold is closing his business?"

Carrie shrugged, clearly uncomfortable with the way the conversation was heading. "All I know is what Lille lets slip. And Harrold hasn't been in for breakfast for over two weeks. I think they had a fight."

"There hasn't been any application to the city for a remodel permit. Maybe Lille's just looking to the future. You know, when Harrold decides to retire." Amy leaned back in the booth and grabbed her phone, keying in a text.

Carrie glanced over at the cashier's stand, where Lille stood, ringing up an order. "I don't know. I mean, he's pushing seventy now. Maybe he thinks he is retired."

"Well, no use worrying about something that hasn't happened yet. Right?" I took another bite of my salad.

"It sure would help me out. I'd love to be able to bring home more tips. These old dogs"—Carrie pointed at her feet—"won't be able to stand many more years working here. Maybe I should go back to school and learn a new trade? But who am I kidding? They'll probably have to carry my body out of here on a stretcher."

As Carrie walked away, I focused on my lunch companion. The meal had turned interesting. I loved having businesses grow and thrive in South Cove, but not at the expense of others. Harrold's train store brought in an eclectic group of tourists, ones looking to expand their collections. And they typically stopped in at my store, too, since I kept a shelf of handbooks on train collections after I'd seen the traffic increase. "You think Lille has plans to buy out Harrold?"

Amy finished her last fry before she answered. "I've never heard he wanted to sell. And if he's stopped coming by, that's a sign they aren't getting along. Harrold built that store from nothing with his late wife, Agnes. I don't see him closing down anytime soon."

After lunch, I visited The Train Station. Harrold had just opened, having shorter hours during the week just for drop-in traffic. Most of his customers came on the weekends, so he worked long hours on Saturdays and Sundays, then took his time off during the beginning of the week.

Harrold stood at the counter, studying a catalog. His long, weathered face broke into a smile when he saw me. Even in his advancing years, the man was attractive, especially when he smiled. His silver hair was cut into a short crew, and he wore a blue dress shirt and jeans. "Well, if it isn't the coffee lady. What are you doing in my shop? Looking to set up that boyfriend of yours with a new hobby? Or do you want my suggestions on new books to stock?"

"Neither. I'm just stopping in to say hi." Not wanting him to guess the real purpose of the visit, I fell back on my other job—South Cove business liaison. "I haven't seen you at a Business-to-Business meeting lately."

"You know I don't like all that committee stuff. You need something for the walk this weekend? I can't volunteer time, but I could throw some money your way. The shop is doing great since I added a website and began selling online. Christopher, my grandson, set up the whole thing. All I do is print out any orders that come in and ship them out." Harrold's face beamed with pride. I wasn't sure if it was about the store or his techy grandson. "You should have him do a page for your store. People are buying everything online these days."

"Actually, Jackie and I were just talking about that. I'm not sure I could compete with the big retailers, but maybe it would add in some revenue." A brainstorm hit me. "Could your grandson come and talk at the Business-to-Business meeting? I bet if he showed how effective his site has been for your store, he'd get tons of business."

Harrold grabbed a business card and wrote something on the back. Then he handed me the card. "Here's his phone number. If he says yes, I'll even come to the meeting."

"I'm holding you to that." I tucked the card in my purse and headed out the door. Harrold's business was thriving. Definitely not the time to close down and sell out. What was Lille thinking? Something was going on, although I had no idea what. Amy had promised to keep an eye out for any proposals to the council regarding Harrold's shop. I guess all I could do was wait to see if Carrie's rumors were true.

As I walked home, my cell chirped. Not recognizing the number, I answered. "Hello?"

"Good morning, darling. Are you counting the days until you and that man of yours disappear into the frozen north?" Rachel Fleur's voice oozed luxury and decadence even over the phone line. She ran a one-woman travel agency in Bakerstown where we had bought our cruise. The woman was a hard sell in a soft package.

I smiled despite my reservations about her. She and Greg had some history. But like his ex-wife, Sherry, that was then and I was now. No use getting all worked up about something in his past. Nothing like living in a small town where you see your ex-relationships every day. Sherry had even upped the ante by opening Vintage Duds at the first of the year here in South Cove. So I was lucky enough to see her often. Of course, most days she ignored my existence, which was the best I could ask for.

But Rachel lived in the next town over, and from what Greg had said, their relationship had been a few dates over several months. When they realized they weren't making seeing each other a priority, they decided to stop pretending. Besides, Rachel was great to work with. "Hey, Rachel. I think we're all ready. Did you need something from us?" Yes, I used the couple pronouns. I knew she understood Greg and I were a couple, but man, the girl was drop-dead pretty. It didn't hurt to make sure.

"No, Greg stopped by earlier this week and gave me a check for the balance. I couldn't get the guy to spring for dinner in the city and you're getting a weeklong cruise. I think you need to show me your tricks." Rachel's laugh bubbled over the phone line.

I couldn't help myself, I laughed. "No tricks. I'm just who I am, and thankfully, Greg loves me the way I am."

"Whatever. Keep your secrets close. I'm glad Greg found the one. We just weren't made for each other. It's sad when people hold on when they are clearly wrong for each other."

My recent encounter with Michael and Sandra popped into my head. Those two should be running to the divorce lawyers rather than fighting out their drama in front of everyone they met. I wondered if Rachel knew I used to be a divorce lawyer in what seemed like another life. Before I got a chance to ask, she spoke again.

"Hey, speaking of the love of my life, I've got another call coming in from him. I guess I'll see you when you get back. Have a great vacation." Rachel didn't even wait for me to respond, the phone reception went dead. So, Rachel was seeing someone. I'd have to ask around Bakerstown on my next visit and see who had the woman so worked up.

I stepped into my front yard and groaned at the length of the grass. Since the walk was taking up our Saturday, I realized I needed to pull out the mower and spend my afternoon in the fifth-worse chore on my I-Hate-to-Do list, yard work.

Emma barked at me as I walked through the backyard to the garage, where Greg had stored my mower. For the last few months, Greg had mowed the lawn before I could even consider doing it myself. I'd been spoiled and didn't even think of the task anymore. He said it relaxed him. One more reason I'd never really understand men.

By the time I finished the backyard, Greg sat on the porch watching me. I dragged the mower over next to the garage. I smoothed my hair, knowing it had to look like a witch's nest, and strolled toward him, taking the cold beer he held out to me as I reached the steps. Sinking onto the step next to him, I took a drink, feeling the cold liquid do its magic on my throat and thirst. "Thanks."

He pulled a piece of grass out of my hair. "I would have mowed tonight. In exchange for your spaghetti marinara." He took a sip of his beer. "But I have to admit, you have an interesting method of mowing. You plan on doing those little squares all over the yard?"

"Don't complain. It might not be in pretty little diagonal rows like you mow, but it's done. And I guess that means you owe me dinner." I pulled my sweaty T-shirt away from my body. "As soon as I get a quick shower."

"I'm broke. What if I grill something? You have any steak in your freezer?" Greg looked hopeful.

"Paying for a vacation will do that to a person." I shook my head. "No steak, but I have some frozen tuna you could take out. I've been trying to avoid shopping since we'll be on vacation."

"That will work." He frowned. "How did you know I paid off the trip?"

"Rachel called and asked me if I was looking forward to the cruise." I pulled my phone out of my pocket, checking for any missed calls while I had mowed the yard. I tried to sound casual. "Did you know she was dating someone?"

A smile crossed his lips before he answered, "For real, or to try to make me jealous?"

I hadn't considered that possibility, but I'd assumed her statement to be true. "I guess I don't know. Would she go that far, since the two of you haven't been a couple for such a long time?"

"I wouldn't put it past her. When it comes to Rachel and Sherry, they both like playing games." He kissed me on the forehead. "That's why I love you. You are what you appear."

"Sweaty and a hot mess?" I stood and headed to the back door. "Make my dinner, sweetheart, I'm starved."

"No, I like your sweet and selfless demeanor more." He followed me into the kitchen. "You have stuff to make a salad?"

I shrugged. "Not sure. I've been eating out a lot." My statement made me think of my lunch with Amy. I paused in the doorway. "Did you know Diamond Lille's is in some sort of best diner contest?"

Greg was already bent down, looking through the produce drawer. "If they taste her meat loaf, she should win, hands down. But this is the first I've heard of it."

I headed upstairs to my room and a quick shower. Greg usually knew all the gossip, since his dispatcher was also the town fortune-teller. I guess Esmeralda's nose for news didn't include the more mundane events of South Cove.

When I got back downstairs, a cucumber and onion salad sat marinating on the counter and Greg was outside with Emma, playing tug-of-war. Emma was winning. At just under a year old, my golden retriever was strong. She could outrun me when I let her loose on the beach. And, as I watched, she let Greg win one, because she was as much in love with the guy as I was. The dog had a big heart.

I slipped outside into the summer air. The day had cooled after the sunset, but still, the temperature felt warm and comforting on my bare arms. I'd thrown on a sundress and even a little lipstick before I came down. A girl had to try once in a while.

Releasing the chew toy to Emma, Greg answered his phone and went to the grill to flip the fish. As he listened to the other side of the conversation, the final question he asked made me take notice. "You sure everything's okay?"

I curled up on the porch swing, my feet tucked under me. I rated the possibility of Greg going out on a call fifty-fifty from that one question. He closed the grill lid and lifted his head. When he saw me, he used the slow, sexy smile reserved for when he wanted something.

I raised an eyebrow and he chuckled. "I guess I'll talk to you to-morrow then. Your other boss just gave me the evil eye."

"I did not," I protested, making Greg laugh again. "Whatever. Tell Toby I'll see him tomorrow."

After concluding his conversation, Greg took the other end of the swing. "You look amazing."

I stretched my legs out and rested my feet on his thighs. "Thanks for noticing. What's going on with Toby?"

Greg ran a finger down the bottom of my sole, and I about jumped off the swing.

"Stop tickling."

He ran the finger down my foot. "Then move your feet, woman."

I sat up and swung my feet toward the deck floor. "Better?"

"Not really, but at least I'm not tempted." Greg took another swig of beer. "Toby's over at The Train Station. Someone thought it would be funny to splash red paint on Harrold's window."

"Who would do that?" I thought about how old Harrold had looked when I'd visited earlier.

"Kids. At least that's Toby's take on the situation." He nodded to the grill. "I think the tuna's done."

I reached out and held his arm back. "I don't think this was a prank. I need to tell you what Carrie said this afternoon."

# CHAPTER 3

Greg had listened to my recounting of the story, then had called Toby back and relayed the same information to him. Of course, the story didn't change anything. Whoever had thrown the paint was long gone, so determining if it was a local teenager or Lille's new boyfriend wasn't something that could be handled before morning.

We ate dinner, then Greg kissed me and left to visit Toby at the station. In the past, I might have ignored my niggle of worry and chosen not to pass on gossip. Greg and I had argued enough times about me playing investigator—his words, not mine—so I decided that oversharing would be my new go-to process.

I'd already run and was walking into work when my cell rang. Glancing at the caller ID, I saw the name flash on my display. How in the heck had she already heard about the vandalism? "Darla, what's going on?"

"I'm calling to ask you the same thing. You didn't call me to say whether Amy and Justin were on board for Friday's trial run. And will Greg be there?" I could tell Darla had me on speakerphone.

"You already at the office? I didn't think the winery opened until eleven on weekdays." I slowed down my walk, taking in the red paint splattered on The Train Station's window. Luckily it blended in with the brick surrounding the window and nothing had hit the large wooden door. Harrold could scrape the damage off with a putty knife mostly. I sighed in relief. After Toby's call last night, all I could think of was how I'd feel if someone had attacked Coffee, Books, and More.

"It doesn't. I just like to get my contacts and to-do list done early before I open. You never know what your day will bring." Darla paused a beat. "So, did you talk to Amy?"

I put The Train Station and its newly decorated window behind me before I answered. "I did and they'll be there at five. Justin has a late Friday afternoon class. And Greg cleared his schedule."

"Perfect." I could almost hear Darla checking our attendance off on her list. "Now, one more thing. Tell me everything you know about the vandalism."

It took me the rest of the walk to convince her that I had no inside knowledge, even though I was dating the local police detective and had hired another one of South Cove's finest to work part-time at the coffee shop. By the time I got to the store, Sasha Smith, our intern-turned-real-employee was waiting at the door. During the summer months, Sasha worked with me and Toby two days a week, then switched to a later shift starting on Friday. I'd worried that we wouldn't have the business to hire her on full-time when she first started, but besides the normal seasonal increase in traffic, I'd had a huge uptick in locals on the book side of the shop, mostly, I thought, because of the new book clubs that we ran out of the store. Thursday afternoon was Sasha's after-school bunch, then Friday nights was Aunt Jackie's mystery group. Sasha was leading the Friday group this week, too, so my aunt and Josh could help with the walk.

Sasha tucked a paperback mystery into her purse. "If you'd been a few minutes later, I might have figured out the killer."

I grinned. My staff always knew how to fill a few extra minutes. And their referrals were gold to my hard-core book customers. "I'm sure you'll have time to finish today. I don't have a lot of prep to do."

"I'm not so sure. Last night, Jackie texted me a list of things that needed to be taken care of before this weekend. I guess she couldn't reach you." Sasha flipped on the lights and marched to the back of the shop, disappearing into the back room. She came back a few seconds later without her purse, brandishing a sheet of yellow paper in her hand. "Here it is."

I should have been happy my aunt had taken the time to make a list of the work needed to be done before the walk on Saturday, but honestly, I wanted some reading time myself. Diving in to a good book was my way to escape from the stress of the world. And even though my own shop had been ignored by the vandals and their non-helpful painting style, The Train Station's attack had bothered me more than I let show. At least to Greg.

"You start on that list, I'll handle the daily prep and any customers who arrive." I washed my hands in the sink and then put on my apron, pausing for a second to breathe and feel my gratitude for Coffee, Books, and More's escape from the random damage to Harrold's place.

By ten, the prep work had been completed and both Sasha and I were sitting on the couch, deep in our books with cups of coffee within reach. We both looked up when the bell over the door rang. Josh Thomas lumbered into the shop. The book dropped out of my hand, and I scrambled to pick it up and shove a bookmark to mark my place.

He scowled at me. "Where's Jackie?"

I paused, taking in the new Josh. Instead of his usual funeral director look of suit and white dress shirt, he had on a navy blue tracksuit, complete with a company logo announcing to the world that he'd paid knock-off prices for the outfit. "*Neke*" didn't make running clothes, but that worked for this outfit because Josh didn't run.

When I didn't answer, I got a more determined glower, and I heard Sasha's tiny giggle behind me. I stammered, "Upstairs in her apartment?"

My aunt lived in the small apartment that took up the second floor of the building I'd bought six years ago to open Coffee, Books, and More. Before Miss Emily had died and left me her house down by the end of Main Street, I'd lived there, too.

"I tried her door, no answer." Josh glanced around the empty shop like maybe we were hiding my aunt from him in some kind of weird practical joke.

I shook my head. "I swear, I haven't seen her today."

And just then, mostly to prove my words a lie, my aunt sauntered out of the back office, her own tracksuit a bright pink with a designer label on the lapel. "Stop growling at everyone, Josh. I just came down to grab my backpack and fill it with bottled water."

Instantly, Josh's demeanor went from annoyed to welcoming. The boy had it bad for my aunt. Which probably explained the tracksuit. I couldn't help myself, I asked the obvious. "You two going running?"

I got a second glower from Josh, but Aunt Jackie ignored my pointed jab. "Walking, actually. We're going down to the beach for a few laps."

"I don't know why you needed to go so early," Josh mumbled. I guessed the activity hadn't been his idea.

Aunt Jackie came around the coffee bar and handed him the backpack. "Because I work at night and your shop opens at one. If not now, we'd never get time to do this."

Which I thought was Josh's plan in the first place.

Aunt Jackie stared at the book in Sasha's hand. "Did you get my text?"

Sasha flew up out of the couch, tucking the book behind her. "Yes, ma'am. I finished the entire list a few minutes ago. The boxes are all packed and ready to go near the back door."

Aunt Jackie's glance went toward the office door she'd just exited. Like she could see through the wall to assure herself that Sasha wasn't fibbing. "I'm sure I'll think of a few more things tonight, I'll leave another list for you on the desk."

"What, no 'thank you' or 'good job'?" I prodded. Sometimes my aunt could be a little pushy, especially with people who let her get away with it. Like Sasha and apparently, Josh.

"Sasha knows she's a valued member of the team. Saying thank-you would be an insult to her work ethic." Aunt Jackie strolled to the exit, and Josh hurried to beat her there so he could open the door for her. "See you tomorrow."

Both Sasha and I stood, watching until the couple disappeared down the street toward the beach entrance. Finally we sank back into our respective seats, but neither of us opened our books. "That was . . ." I searched for a word.

"Interesting?" Sasha prompted.

I shook my head. "No, I was thinking more like frightening. I hope Josh paid his medical insurance premium this month. I'd lay money on him not making it to the highway before he strokes out."

Sasha reopened her book and didn't meet my eyes. "I bet he makes the beach parking lot."

Walking home that afternoon, I didn't see Josh passed out under a bush or sprawled on one of the many park benches the city council had sprinkled through town for seating during our many parades. I'd stayed late to work on the books so that Aunt Jackie could take the mess to our accountant the next week. After playing with numbers all afternoon, I needed a diversion. I considered stopping in to Antiques by Thomas to see if he'd returned to work, but I couldn't think of a good excuse to do so. Saying "I wanted to see if you were still alive" seemed a little callous. And I didn't need more furniture, especially of the type Josh sold: old and expensive.

My phone chirped, and I saw I had a text from Greg. I paused on a bench to read the message before I got too far away. Sometimes we met for a quick dinner at Diamond Lille's, and tonight was pasta night. My hopeful thoughts were dashed with the first line. I read it aloud just to get the full depressing effect: "Stuck at work. Will see you tomorrow at the fake race."

I looked into the restaurant's windows. If Greg wasn't coming by, I might as well eat dinner early. I put the phone in my tote and jay-walked across the street. Let him arrest me, at least we'd be together for the booking. I giggled at the thought and went into the diner, bee-lining toward my favorite booth before anyone else could claim it. I hadn't needed to worry; the diner was dead. A few locals sat around one table, talking, but other than that, I had the place to myself.

Carrie appeared from the back and grabbed a coffeepot, then walked up to my table. "Greg meeting you?" She poured a cup and held out a second.

"Just me tonight." I tapped the menu. "Too early for the baked manicotti?"

She checked her watch. "I'll check in with the cook. We just finished our weekly staff meeting, so he's knee-deep in prep. But I'm sure John can do it. You might have a bit of a wait."

I pulled out a biography of Jacqueline Kennedy and laid it on the table. "I'm fine, I came prepared. Can I get a glass of water, too?"

"Coming right up. You want a salad with the pasta?" Carrie finished taking my order and before she disappeared into the kitchen, stopped at the other table and topped off their coffee. I leaned into the booth and tucked a foot up under me, preparing to lose myself in the early years when Jackie and Jack were dating.

Feeling a bit guilty about my dinner plans, I decided to call Greg and see if he wanted me to deliver something to the station before I went home. I dialed his cell, but it went straight to voice mail. Must be in a meeting, I mused. So I called the station, as Esmeralda would still be on duty until five.

"South Cove Police Station, what can I do for you?" Her voice sounded upbeat, like she'd been bored to death at her desk and hoped there was a major issue somewhere in town so that she could call in the troops.

"It's Jill. I was wondering if Greg called in a to-go order for tonight's dinner. I'm at Lille's now, so I could drop something off for when he's out of the meeting." Carrie brought my water as I waited for Esmeralda's response.

"He's not here, honey. He took off about three, saying he had some errands to run." She paused. "I thought he'd told you."

I thought about the message. I'd assumed he was at the station working late. "My bad. He did text me, I just assumed he'd be there." Now I sounded like I was checking up on him. Time to change the subject. "You running in the five-K on Saturday?"

The sound of her laughter soothed my nerves. "Me? Run? Jill, I haven't run in years. Besides, I've got a full day of readings on Saturday. People want to check in before taking off for vacation. Summer is my busiest time of year."

I thought about Esmeralda and her fortune-telling business. She'd done some readings on me that had totally creeped me out. Mostly because she didn't seem to remember what she'd said afterward. Either she was the real thing, or she was really good at playing me. I wished her a good weekend and put my cell away, returning to the book.

This time, I did get lost in the story. When Carrie brought over my salad, I didn't want to pull myself back to reality. I kept reading, absently eating, until I finished the first section and closed the book, and noticed my food was all gone. I paid my tab and tucked the book into my tote. Walking home, I kept thinking about Jackie's early years, and the hopes she'd had for her life. Some people might think being a First Wife was all about the glamour, but the woman was smart.

Harrold waved at me from inside The Train Station as I passed by. The paint had already been cleared from his window, and now I saw he was changing up the train sets displayed. The man loved his toys. And I loved my books. I hurried home, knowing that if I wanted to finish the book soon, I needed to do it tonight. This weekend would be filled with Mission Walk events and duties.

\* \* \*

Glancing at the clock as I turned out my light that night, I groaned. Two o'clock. Tomorrow was going to come too early, but I patted the cover of the book. I'd read straight through to the last page, and it would be worth the book hangover I'd feel in the morning. I thought about ways we could showcase different biographies in the bookstore window. As I drifted off to sleep, visions of First Lady covers floated in my mind.

My phone blared me awake. I felt for the cell and dragged it to my ear, sitting up as I did. "Hello?"

"Where are you? I've had the store open for twenty minutes." Aunt Jackie's voice blared into my ear.

I sank backward onto the bed. "It's Friday. My day off?"

"Not this week, it isn't. Didn't you read my e-mail to the entire staff? We have a full house this morning from runners who came in early. Sasha was waiting for me when I arrived." I heard my aunt ring up an order on the cash register.

"If Sasha's there, you can't need me." No way were there that many people visiting South Cove for a race. I listened as my aunt counted out change for the customer, and then she returned to our conversation.

"Come down here and say that." The line went silent for a second. "Look, I'm not going to beg, but we really need the help and I don't want to wake Toby since he just got off his evening patrol."

I pushed myself up on my elbows. "Don't call Toby. I'll be there as soon as I can shower." I glanced at the clock again—six fifteen. "Give me twenty minutes."

"You might want to come in the back, the line's already out the front door." And then my aunt hung up the phone.

I thought about how many people would have to be in line before it cranked out the entryway and decided against the shower. I'd come home early before the practice walk tonight. I ran downstairs to let out Emma and grabbed a cup of coffee to get me started.

Ten minutes later as I power-walked to the store, I realized my aunt hadn't been exaggerating. There were people all over South Cove. Diamond Lille's was packed for breakfast, and people sat on benches with those buzzers in their hands. Since when had Lille invested in a pager system? I picked up my pace, dodging and weaving between people on the sidewalk.

In the park in front of City Hall, someone had draped a *Welcome to South Cove* sign between two trees. From the time I'd left late afternoon yesterday to now, the town had turned into a hot tourist destination. Flags hung from the streetlights, welcoming runners. As Coffee, Books, and More came into view, I saw what had my aunt frantic for help. The line snaked down past Antiques by Thomas. A steady stream of customers was leaving the store with CBM cups and little white bags filled with pastries from the shop.

Squeezing in between the two buildings, I headed for the back door, pulling my keys out of my pocket as I walked. Throwing my light jacket on the desk, I grabbed an apron and opened the swinging door to the shop. The sound was deafening. People chatted, the coffeemaker churned, and Aunt Jackie rang up another order. I paused next to her. "Where do you want me?"

"Fill up the dessert case, we're almost empty." She nodded toward the glass case beside her. "Then bring out more cups. I knew I should have told Sasha to overstock."

For the next hour, we worked side by side. I refilled the dessert case twice and brought out cups three times. When the line ended and the only customers in the shop were the ones enjoying their breakfast treats at the tables, Sasha leaned toward me.

"I don't believe I'll need to stop at the gym tonight." She wiped the back of her hand across her head. "I didn't think runners liked treats and things."

"They have to keep up the calories before a run. They've probably been eating brown rice and chicken for the last month. Today, before the race, they get to carb load." I started cutting another cheesecake to put into the case. I was sure our lull wouldn't last long.

Aunt Jackie nodded her approval at my action. "You and Sasha get the place set up again. I'm going into the back to sit down."

I touched her arm with my hand, slowing her movement. "You okay?"

She swatted my hand away. "I'm not that old and infirm. My feet are just killing me. Give me a few minutes and I'll be fine."

Sasha watched as my aunt disappeared in the back. "I think she forgot to take her pain pills."

"What pain pills?" Now I was concerned.

Sasha shrugged. "No big deal. She has arthritis like my mama. We've talked about it before, and I gave her the name of Mama's doctor. He's really good with getting the pain under control."

I stared at my newest employee. Sasha had been a participant in the Work Today program during the holidays. Once we'd trained her, we didn't want to let her go, so Aunt Jackie and I carved out shift times for the young mother. "I didn't realize she was having problems."

Sasha stacked more cups near the machine. "She didn't tell me. I saw the way she walked and told her about my mama and her affliction. Took me a while to convince her to go."

"Looks like your wall project has finally borne fruit." Mayor Baylor stood at the counter, glancing at the full dining room. "I knew all along the sanctioning of the South Cove Mission would be a boon for the town. Glad you listened to my counsel."

Thoughts filled my head as I went through the multiple choices of how to call our honorable mayor a downright dirty liar without causing a scene. Finally Sasha stepped in between us. "You here for your regular, Mayor? What about Amy? Are you taking back a cup for her, as well?"

I bit my lip to keep from laughing. Not only had the mayor never come into the shop on his own to order coffee, he'd never bought one for Amy, his receptionist. Mayor Baylor waved away the notion. "I'm sure Miss Newman has already had her coffee. Besides, who knows if she's even still at the desk? According to her, you all are doing some sort of trial run tonight on the greenbelt?"

"I'm sure she hasn't left yet. We're meeting there at five. Darla wants a real-life test run. I'm sure she could use more volunteers to set up trash cans or water spots if you and Tina aren't busy." I started a large mocha with French vanilla pumps for the man.

He pulled out his wallet and handed Sasha a ten. "Sorry, Tina and I are hosting a small get together tonight for the California Mission Society staff and donors. Black tie over at the winery. Darla's closed the tasting room to local traffic, and the event staff is coming in from the city to work." He held his hand out for the coffee cup. "I guess they only invite people whose sites have been historically finalized. Maybe you'll be on the list for next year's event."

I handed him the cup with a sleeve protector and a napkin wrapped around it so the mayor's delicate hands wouldn't be burned by the hot liquid. And then I lied. "Oh, I was invited. I decided that it was more important to ensure that tomorrow's race goes off without a hitch than drink with people who are only there to be seen as involved."

Sasha gave the mayor his change. "I think they call that acting locally. Or at least that's what all the celebrities are saying. Nobody's going to parties anymore, they're all too busy doing events like the run." Her eyes widened. "Do you think we'll get any movie stars running? I've got Olivia set up with her grandmother tomorrow, so I may just show up early with a camera tucked away in my running shorts."

"People are not avoiding cocktail parties." Mayor Baylor raised his shoulders as high as his five-foot-two frame would allow. "Tina and I were at an event last weekend where plenty of actors and celebrities were in attendance."

Sasha had already stopped listening and was looking at her phone, searching out something. "Here's an article from the *LA Times* about the change in celebrities' social calendars . . . I hope the Mission Walk can get some good press that way."

"I'm sure there are still people who like to attend cocktail parties." I couldn't think of anyone, except maybe my former coworkers at the law firm, or low-level politicians like Mayor Baylor, but there had to be someone.

The mayor pointed at me with a finger. "You are going to wish you were there. I'll have my picture taken with all the famous people and e-mail you a copy for Monday morning. Then you'll be begging for an invite to next year's event."

He didn't wait for an answer to his threat or promise. Sasha sighed as we watched the mayor leave. "If I could find a babysitter, I'd crash that party tonight. I'm sure the mayor's right, there will be a bunch of famous people wandering through."

"Don't tell me you're starstruck." I nudged her with my shoulder. "What about all that bluster about the LA article?"

"That's mostly the older actors who nobody wants to see anyway. Why show up at an event to be ignored? At least this way, they get a bit of attention for the charity aspect." Sasha nodded to Toby, who had just entered the shop. "Why don't you head home? I think we can handle the crowds now that Barista Babe is here."

"Stop calling me that." Toby sent a pleading look my way. "Can't you tell her to stop? It's demeaning."

"And so true." I laughed. Sasha was fitting into the family nicely. "Children, stop calling each other names."

"Mama's boy," I heard Sasha mutter under her breath. Then she yelled as a towel snapped her arm. "Hey, that hurts!"

"I'm letting Aunt Jackie deal with the two of you. See you both tomorrow?" We'd closed Coffee, Books, and More for Saturday with a sign on the door saying we'd be selling on site for the race from 5 a.m. to 2 p.m., then reopening in the main shop on Sunday morning. We'd borrowed a food truck from one of Aunt Jackie's friends, and this was our first official off-site sale day. Everyone but Toby was working the truck. Toby was running the race as a plant for the police department, to make sure nothing happened during the run.

"Yes, ma'am," they both answered.

By the time I'd left the shop, I only had thirty minutes to grab something to eat before Emma and I had to leave. The race would start south of town, then wind north to the outskirts of South Cove, ending up on the beach parking lot, where Emma and I started our beach run. Greg's truck was parked at the edge of the lot. He climbed out of the cab and gave me a quick hug before taking Emma's leash.

"You want to walk to the beginning to meet everyone? We have an hour before Darla's due to arrive." His hand dropped absently to the cell phone at his side. "She tried to reach you a few minutes ago, but you must have already left the house. She said she had an impromptu booking she had to finalize."

I grabbed a bottle of water out of the zippered pouch I'd brought along. "Yeah, the mayor has turned the race into a photo opportunity for him and his cronies. I bet Darla's feeling like she's being torn in two."

"She has Matt to help. Besides, this race check won't take more than an hour. Don't worry, she'll make the best of this." He locked the truck and put his hand on my back, leading me toward the trail. "From what she said, she charged them a premium rate for such a late booking."

"Sounds like Darla." I relaxed as we walked toward the start line. Darla had had volunteers run rope along each side of the trail. Benches were set randomly through the path. The smell of honeysuckle floated through the early summer evening. "Hey, have you heard anything more about the vandalism? Darla asked me this morning."

"She tried to get information from me when she called. I'll tell you what I told her. The DA believes it's just local kids blowing off steam."

"Has he met our local kids? We don't have a bad one in the bunch." I watched as Emma chased a chipmunk off the asphalted path. "I swear sometimes that guy just looks for the easy way out."

"And sometimes you look for things that aren't there." He pushed a lock of hair out of my eyes.

We walked the length of the race path chatting about our day, our upcoming trip, and absolutely nothing. That was one thing I loved about spending time with Greg. He was just as happy to talk about the types of trees lining the path as he was the local sports teams. Don't get me wrong, the guy loved his ESPN, but he knew when to shut off that side of his brain for other topics. At least with me.

As we came up on the start line, Josh and Jackie met us on the path. "You're late," Josh grumbled. He had on the same knock-off tracksuit I'd seen him in the day before. My aunt had switched to a fuchsia-striped jacket with solid legging pants. For her age, I had to admit, she looked good. Emma sat at attention, a whine growing in her throat as she waited for Jackie to see her.

Greg glanced at his watch. "Only by five minutes. I take it you're the slow group?"

"If that's a reference to my age, Detective King, you'd better think twice about the next words out of your mouth." Aunt Jackie marched in place as she gave Greg a withering look. She reached down and stroked Emma's head without a comment. My dog melted.

"I'm just surprised they set the two of you with that group. I would have thought Darla would have tagged someone who needed it." Greg's words flowed over the perceived slight, and I could see my aunt's shoulders relaxing. My boyfriend had that effect on people; even nasty little men like Mayor Baylor, Greg could calm with a word or two. The man could have been a successful politician, but he hated the games. I bit back a smile.

"Almost a good catch," Aunt Jackie murmured. She kissed me on the cheek and pulled Josh forward. "We'll see you at the finish line. Maybe we should all have dinner at Diamond Lille's after this to celebrate."

"You know I hate that place," Josh said to my aunt as we parted ways. "I thought you and I could go to the city and try out the steak house."

"You could use some time with other people."

The rest of Aunt Jackie's words disappeared as they turned a curve away from us. I smiled up at Greg. "I guess we have dinner plans."

"I'd do anything for your aunt, but seriously, eating with Josh is a whole 'nother layer of commitment. You know he's petitioning the council for air fresheners on the street—"

I interrupted, "To keep the sea air out of South Cove? Yep, he pitched his idea at the Business-to-Business meeting this month. The guy is certifiable. I swear, I don't know what Aunt Jackie sees in him."

As we rounded the corner, we came up on the large entryway to the path where Darla had set up ground zero for the start of the race. We were right next to a large parking lot where people could shuttle in either from South Cove or one of the beach parking lots down the highway. The banner had already been set up, and Darla was snapping pictures of the area. Kind of a calm-before-the-storm snapshot.

"Hey, there you are." Amy stepped forward to greet us. She gave me a quick hug and then repeated the gesture with Greg. She tapped his chest. "I thought maybe something happened."

"Like a natural disaster or a riot in our little town?" Greg chuckled. "Nothing like that. I just wanted a few minutes to spend with my favorite girls."

Justin came around and slapped Greg on the back before kissing my cheek. "They do make it a little hard to get alone time around here, don't they?"

Amy punched him in the arm. "Stop being a baby. I told you we'd go surfing on Sunday."

"I appreciate your helping out with the Mission Walk," I added, upping the sugar level in my tone a few points.

Justin shrugged. "Just making sure everyone"—he paused and pointed at Amy—"understands the sacrifices we men make for the women in our lives."

"You're going to think sacrifice," Amy murmured.

Darla stepped in between Amy and Justin, her five-foot frame making a human *W* as we looked at the trio. "Since we're all here, let's get started." She checked her watch. "I sent Josh and Jackie out at six on the dot. You two"—Darla pointed at the couple flanking her—"I want you to start at six fifteen."

Justin set his wristwatch. "No problem."

"When do we go?" Greg and Justin were discussing Justin's new runner watch as I asked Darla for our directions.

"Six thirty. I'll leave here and drive back to the South Cove finish line to meet up with Amy and Justin. Then I'll wait for the rest of you." Darla made some notes on her clipboard. "Tomorrow we'll have an official race clock and timer, but tonight, it's just me and my Timex."

When Amy and Justin took off, it was just Greg and me. We sat on a bench and waited. Greg took my hand in his. "You excited about the wall being recognized?"

I thought about the question for a minute before I answered. "I know the race doesn't mean the historical commission will actually find in our favor, but it's a good sign. And I'm a little worried about the amount of work ahead of us if the wall is certified."

"You know you're doing the right thing." Greg squeezed my hand. "Even if it does ruin my plans for a sweet hammock and barbeque pit in the area."

"I know, right? Emma's going to freak every time someone walks near the fence. I'm going to have to change the fencing area if I want it to be accessible to the public." I thought about all the changes that would take place in my life if the wall was ever approved. Maybe Mayor Baylor would get his wish and the house Miss Emily left me would be turned into a gift shop and tour center for the Mission Wall. "I don't know, maybe I should have just kept things the way they were."

Greg pulled me into a hug. "You know life doesn't work that way. If the wall is historical, we'll deal with the problems that come along with having a tourist destination in your backyard. We have options."

I laid my head on his chest and watched Emma sit next to him and lean into his leg. Greg was a rock to cling to in a sea of storms. And for a few minutes, I felt safe.

# CHAPTER 4

The race trial went off without a hitch, with Jackie and Josh bringing up the rear in less than two hours. Darla, Justin, and Amy left first, apologizing for not being able to make dinner. Aunt Jackie pulled me aside as we walked up the stairs from the beach to the parking lot. "I know I suggested this double date, but honestly, I'm beat. I'm going to have Josh take me home, and I'll heat up some potato soup I have in the freezer and then turn in." She stopped at Josh's black sedan and slipped into the passenger seat. "I'll see you bright and early at the food truck."

"Are you sure everything's okay?" I thought about Sasha saying my aunt had visited with an arthritis specialist. Maybe she was pushing herself too hard.

Aunt Jackie waved my concern away with a flick of her hand. "Now, don't be treating me like I'm ready for some old age home. I just walked three miles. I think I'm due for some relaxation time."

I watched as Josh pulled the car out of the parking lot and back toward South Cove. Greg put his arm around me. "She's a strong old bird. She'll be fine."

"I just worry."

He led me to the truck, and Emma jumped in the backseat and lay down on the blanket Greg kept back there for her. "I know you do. But until she asks for help, you need to let her be." He opened my door for me, holding out his hand for support as I climbed in. "Hey, want to go down to that clam shack on the beach? We could share a bucket of clams and have shrimp po'boys and fries."

"Carb loading for the race tomorrow?" I leaned back into the bucket seat. "You know I'm not running, right?"

"We walked the path twice tonight, to the beginning and back to the end. I think we deserve a good dinner." He turned the key. "I might even let you kiss me when I drop you off at your door."

"Aren't I a lucky girl?" I reached over and took his hand, and after dropping Emma off at the house, we spent the rest of the evening together like any other normal couple.

Race day was predicted to be hot and sunny, but most of the racers would be off the track and back in South Cove by the time the sun really started beating down on the beach. I brewed a single cup of coffee when I rose and ate a toasted cheddar bagel. This was our first trial run in a food truck. I was on the fence about the opportunity. Aunt Jackie was sold on the idea and had been running numbers to see what kind of business we'd have to have to set up a satellite shop that could attend the local festivals and fairs on a regular basis.

I put Emma outside with a new bone and headed down to the beach parking lot to meet up with Aunt Jackie and Sasha. As I passed by her house, Esmeralda was out in the front yard, watering her azaleas. I really was going to have to up my game in flowers if my house was even going to compare to my neighbors.

"Good morning," I called over the fence, pausing to see if she wanted to talk or would just wave me off. You never knew with our resident fortune-teller/police dispatcher. Sometimes she was chatty; other times, she didn't really want to talk. I guess since she had two careers in which talking was her primary responsibility, I could understand. That was one reason I loved the bookstore part of Coffee, Books, and More. I could hide out and read a book and still consider myself working because I was "researching" new authors. I patted the tote I'd thrown over my shoulder that morning just to make sure I'd packed a book in case traffic to the coffee shack slowed down.

"Good luck with the run today." Esmeralda shut off the water sprayer and walked over to greet me. "Sorry I couldn't help this time."

"No worries. We all have to work." I didn't believe in my neighbor's psychic gift, but I didn't want her to think I thought less of her talent. To each their own, right? I nodded toward the black cat nestled on the porch in a wicker chair. "Maggie hasn't been over to visit lately. Maybe she's becoming a homebody?"

Esmeralda glanced over at the now-yawning kitten. "Apparently she feels you're safe right now and don't need her help."

*Yep, that is it. My life is going well, and the cat can sense my contentment.*

Maggie meowed her agreement, and Esmeralda laughed. "Don't worry, Jill. We know you're a non-believer. It just doesn't mean we agree with you."

"Well, I'm just glad she's staying out of the road. I would hate it if something happened to her." I stepped away from the fence and waved.

My neighbor called after me. "Send Josh over to me if he needs help adjusting."

I turned to ask her what she was talking about, but Esmeralda had already turned the water back on and wandered to the backyard. Maggie blinked her eyes at me and then curled tighter to return to sleep.

I power-walked down to the beach, determined to keep Esmeralda's weird announcements out of my head. The last time we'd talked, she'd admitted to being able to read people, and with the rumors that floated around the small town, she typically could nail a prediction without any help from the other side. But I didn't want to think about what she'd heard about Josh or maybe Aunt Jackie that was causing this kind of premonition.

Sasha and Aunt Jackie already had the food truck open, and the smell of coffee filled the morning air, mixing with the salty breeze coming off the ocean. Sadie's purple Pies on the Fly van sat parked next to the food truck, and I waved at Nick as he loaded up a stack of pie boxes to take into the truck.

Sadie stood outside the truck, talking to Aunt Jackie on the inside. She waved me over when she saw me. "We've decided to leave half the dessert inventory in my van during the event. That way I get some free advertisement out of the race, too." She beamed up at Aunt Jackie.

I translated the agreement for Sadie. "The truck's too small for all the pies, right?"

Aunt Jackie nodded. "We'd only be able to stock twenty percent of what she brought if we didn't have the van available. Now, we may not need as much as we think, but it's always better to be prepared, right?"

I nodded and Sadie laughed. "You really know how to sell, don't you, Jackie? Here I was thinking you were doing me a favor by getting my name out there."

"It does get your name out there. There's just a secondary reason why it's a good idea." Aunt Jackie handed Sadie a cup of coffee. "What does that boy of yours want?"

Nick poked his head around the counter. "Nothing. I've got to get to the starting line. I'm running."

Sasha handed him a bottle of water. "Then drink this, you need to stay hydrated."

Sadie left the corner near me and Aunt Jackie to tell Nick good luck. "She's a good mom," Aunt Jackie murmured.

"You wishing you and Uncle Ted had had children?" I took the cup of coffee my aunt held out the window to me.

She shook her head. "Nope. If we'd had kids, then I'd be off somewhere playing grandma instead of working a coffee shack on this fine California morning."

"I almost believe you." I sipped my coffee. "You want me in there prepping?"

Aunt Jackie shook her head. "Why don't you go relax for a while? Sasha and I have this. I'll call you if we need you. Just make sure you're here before the race starts at seven. Josh is picking me up, and we'll be driving down to the starting line."

"I still can't believe you got him to actually walk the race."

My aunt's eyes twinkled with glee. "I have that man wrapped around my little finger. You need to learn from the master."

"Greg and I are just fine." I turned and watched the waves come up on the beach. Even though the sun had just broken over the mountains, the crowds were starting to gather. The starting line area didn't have any room to set up booths or sign-ups. Darla had a shuttle bus set up to take runners down to the starting line. Runners were scattered all over the beach, stretching and chatting.

"Turn over the *Open* sign and go mingle with those society people while you still have time." Aunt Jackie handed me a cookie bar. She nodded toward the sign-up booth. "I think Darla needs some help over there. It looks like they are upset about something."

There were two men in suits in front of the Mission Walk booth. Darla's arms were waving as she talked, but I couldn't tell what they were saying. I tapped my phone. "Call me if you get in the weeds."

"As if." Aunt Jackie sniffed, then turned her attention to a couple who had come over as soon as I turned over the *Open* sign. "What can I make for you?"

I wandered over to the booth with the bright blue and white flags announcing the Mission Walk. I could hear the raised voices as soon as I got closer.

"You should have been told that all entries had to be finalized online and no one could enter on site." The taller of the two men was shaking a finger at Darla, who had her hands on her hips. "How can we control the funds when there's no accounting set up?"

"How about you trust me and my staff?" Darla sputtered. "I guess you don't know that I've run a business for the last ten years all on my own without having draconian accounting methods. What do you think, I'm going to run off with the profits?"

"Now, Mrs. Taylor, please don't take our concern for following our standardization and rules for events as a slight. We've been doing these events for over ten years. We've learned and implemented the best processes over the years. The PR company should have explained all of this before the event was even approved." The smaller man held his hands out in a gesture of surrender. "Since they seemed to have failed in their duties, we'll have to assign a member of the financial committee to sit with you today."

"What's going on, Darla? Is there a problem?" I went around the side of the booth and stood by my friend. Her face was beet red, and I thought she was ready to climb over the top of the table and throttle the guy.

"Who are you?" The taller man stared at me, like I was interrupting.

"I'm Jill Gardner, the owner of the mission wall here in South Cove, and owner of the coffee shop. Darla's the South Cove's community event planner, and she has been involved with this from day one. This is the first we've heard of only online entries. Not to complain about Sandra and Michael, but maybe you should talk to them, not us." I straightened the flyers on the table in front of me.

"You're right, we will be talking to the Ashfords. As for today, Adam will stay with you until the end of the sign-ups and take the money box from there." The taller man spun on his heel and threw up a small spurt of sand as he huffed toward the parking lot.

"I wouldn't want to be Michael or Sandra when Oscar gets ahold of them." The man now known as Adam held out his hand. "Adam Truman, so nice to meet you. The event looks amazing, especially since it appears you did all of this yourselves."

"The Ashfords came by this week. I never imagined there would be a company hired on to help." I shrugged my shoulders. "We would have followed the rules, had we known them."

Adam circled around and found a chair. "Not a problem. We dropped the ball here, not South Cove."

"We'll be right back." I pulled a very red Darla out of the booth and toward a grove of trees that lined the Mission Walk. When we were out of earshot, I turned her toward me. "Are you okay?"

"We never got any instructions besides the original letter. If I had known . . ." Darla blustered.

I held up a hand. "I know, and I'm sure the problem lies with the Ashfords. I mean, seriously, those two are a mess. I just want to make sure you are okay. That was kind of tense over there."

Darla took in a deep breath. Then another. "Yes, I'm fine. I just hate the idea of being questioned by suits." She glared toward the booth. "Although Adam *seems* nice."

"Let's just get through today. If we decide to commit to next year, we'll be wiser and know to get all the information up-front." I put my hand on Darla's shoulders. "Besides, now handling the money is one less thing you have to worry about, right?"

Darla nodded, then her face broke into a wide grin. "Exactly. I just got a new helper."

I threw my arm around her and walked back to the sign-up booth, where a line was starting to form and Adam stood shifting from one foot to the next, clearly uncomfortable. "He looks scared to death."

"I'm sure he hasn't worked a crowd for years, if ever. Suits, they think they know everything." Darla stepped behind the table. "Form one line, people. Fill out your registration forms here, then turn them in to Adam and I'll hand you your shirt and entry number."

I waved at Darla and stepped down to the Diamond Lille's booth. They weren't open yet, as they were sponsoring an after-race burger event, but Carrie and John, the evening chef, were in the booth setting up.

"Hey, Jill!" Carrie held up her cup with the CBM logo. "Thanks for opening on the beach this morning. I needed my caffeine."

"No problem. Here to help out the addicted." I picked up one of the to-go menus with a fridge magnet as a giveaway. "I should have thought of something like this. Cute idea."

"Lille had them made up." Carrie held up the magnet that had a picture of Diamond Lille's and a phone number. "She's all into promotion right now. I kind of miss the days when all I had to do was take orders and deliver food. Now it's all about the image."

"You're a great server, what else is there?" I stuck a menu and magnet in my pocket to show to Aunt Jackie. We could make some up and deliver them to the local B&Bs with a list of staff-recommended books. Or even some of the other businesses in town . . . My mind wandered around the possibilities until I realized Carrie had answered my question. "Sorry, what?"

"I thought you were drifting. My mom used to do that when I talked about my day at school. The vacant stare look is a dead giveaway." Carrie laughed and threw her hair back over her shoulder. "All I said was that up-selling may not be my strongest skill. Look, John's giving me the evil eye, so I'd better get busy."

I thanked her for the menu and left the booth. As I was heading uphill, a woman bumped into me, hard, knocking my coffee out of my hand. Her brown hair was pulled back into a ponytail, and she wore the typical runner's uniform. "Hey, watch it."

I looked up into Rachel's eyes as she focused in on me. "Oh, Jill, I'm sorry. Not paying attention, I guess."

The travel agent looked ready to bolt, but she was probably in the runners' group that was lining up to be shuttled to the starting line. "No problem. I have an in with the coffeehouse."

"What?" Rachel was looking past me into the crowd. "Sorry. I've got to go."

I watched her worm her way through the crowds, not toward the bus line, but instead to the grove of trees. She stopped in front of a man who was standing off on his own, smoking a cigarette. I shaded my eyes, trying to see if this was the new Mr. Right in Rachel's life. She sure was acting like a teenage girl in love.

The man turned away from me, and the two melted into the trees. Oh well, maybe I'd see them later. I headed back to the coffee truck and slipped into the van, washing my hands in the sink and donning an apron. "Hey, Aunt Jackie, Josh is sitting out on the bench waiting for you. Why don't you let me take over?"

"Does him good to have to wait for a while. Didn't I teach you anything about how to catch a man?" My aunt rang up an order and glanced back at me. "Don't tell me you run at the snap of Greg's fingers?"

"We're not talking about my love life." I sliced up another cheesecake and divided the pieces into boxes, restocking the fridge as I worked. "Sasha, you want to chime in on the best way to catch a man?"

Her laugh filled the kitchen area. "Who says I want to catch one? Right now, and probably until my college life is done, I'm more into the catch-and-release program. That way you don't have to worry about games or problems. Let a guy wine and dine you for a few dates, then move on."

"What about love?" I finished prepping another cheesecake and washed the utensils I'd used.

"Single moms don't have time to fall in love. We have too many other fires on our list to deal with." Sasha handed two mugs out the window to a waiting customer.

"Now, dear, that's not true. What about Elisa and Toby? They seem to be on the path to the chapel." Aunt Jackie slipped off her apron and checked her hair in the compact mirror she carried with her.

"Toby's one in a million." Sasha didn't look up as she started a new pot of coffee. "Not everyone can be as lucky."

Josh now stood at the door to the van, waiting. Aunt Jackie kissed me on a cheek and waved to Sasha. "You two have fun. I'll be back after two to box up the rest of the supplies, and Toby is transporting them back to the shop."

I was tempted to pry a little more about what Sasha had said, but a rush of people hit the food truck and we were instantly busy. The runners might be health-conscious, but the race observers and walkers sure enjoyed their cheesecake. The race had started, and the last group had been shuttled to the starting line.

I leaned over the counter and watched Darla and Adam talking at the sign-up booth. He leaned against the booth's table, apparently in no hurry to get the cash box to the bank. Darla, on the other hand, had turned the booth from being a place to sign up, into the winner's circle. She had ribbons and medals strung around the table, waiting for the first runners to emerge through the grove of trees and across the finish line. Mayor Baylor was supposed to hand out the first ten ribbons, then he had another pressing engagement. Just enough time for the press to see him supporting the event.

I actually was very pleased at our first attempt at a race/walk. Darla was amazing at these types of events, and she made the entire process seem easy, a descriptor I knew wasn't true. Today's little tiff with the Mission Society over the process was a great example of what could go wrong, through no one's fault. Although it did make me wonder about Sandra and Michael. Had the slow destruction of their personal relationship doomed their business, as well?

"Jill, you need to come with me." Toby stopped by the booth, all dressed in runner's gear, tight in all the right places.

"Are you already done?" I glanced over at the finish line and realized people were starting to move through, collecting their badges.

"Barista Babe in workout gear. Outfit sold separately." Sasha teased as she stood next to me. "What's going on?"

"There's been a"—Toby paused, searching for a word—"an occurrence. Your aunt needs you."

"Oh no." My hand flew to my mouth. "Is she okay? I should have kept her from walking."

Toby chuckled and shook his head. "Like you could have stopped her. Anyway, she's fine. She's just a little upset. Josh, well, Josh collapsed on the trail."

"Are they rushing him to the hospital?" I slipped off the apron and glanced at Sasha. "If you get overwhelmed, just shut down. I'll be back when I can."

"You just get to Jackie. Don't worry about me." Sasha tapped my shoulder with a hand.

Toby held up a hand slowing me as he met me at the food truck door. "According to the EMTs, Josh is fine. Dehydrated maybe, but fine."

"I don't understand. What's the issue, then?" I stopped at the bottom of the stairs and held Toby back, waiting for his answer.

"Josh fell on someone when he collapsed." Toby shook his head. "A very dead someone off the side of the trail."

# CHAPTER 5

Toby led me against the wave of runners who were coming up the path toward us. Several runners called out "Wrong way," as they passed by. A few, more direct, muttered, "Idiots." About a half mile into the walk, Toby turned off the main path toward a bench. Several people milled around the area, and I saw Greg talking to Doc Ames. Josh was firmly planted on the bench, his head in his hands. Jackie saw me and waved me over.

"I can't believe it." She linked her arm around mine and squeezed. "How's the truck doing? Pulling you away isn't causing a problem, right?"

Leave it to my aunt. "Don't worry about sales. What happened? Are you okay?"

Aunt Jackie stepped away from the group, leading me with her. "I'm fine, dear. Poor Josh was feeling a bit faint. I'm sure he didn't eat this morning like I told him to, but you know men. You can't tell them anything."

"So, Josh got faint and . . . ?" I rolled my hand, hoping my aunt would get to the point and tell me who was dead, since it obviously wasn't the antique dealer who appeared to be freaked out but fine. Or at least as fine as he could be after walking daily for the last week. My aunt's fitness craze could kill the guy.

"He fell on that terrible woman." Aunt Jackie rolled her eyes.

"What terrible woman? And he killed her by falling on her?" I'd never heard of death by fat guy, but I guess it was possible in a freak-accident kind of way.

"No, he didn't kill her. She was already dead. Sandra Ashford, the woman from that PR team. She's the dead one." My aunt looked at me like I was slow. But then a smile crept onto her face. "It reminded me of the scene in the *Wizard of Oz*—where the house falls on the witch? All you could see were her feet in those knock-off designer shoes."

Greg came up to us and put his arm around my aunt. "You okay there?"

I saw the tears fill my aunt's eyes and quickly get blinked away. "I'm perfectly fine. The question is, how is Josh?"

"I'm sending him to the hospital to be checked out. The EMT guys are a little worried about his blood pressure." Greg looked at me. "I'm trying to keep this off the grid until the race is complete. The official line right now is that two racers are being taken to the hospital."

"Two?" I looked at my aunt.

"Not Jackie. Doc Ames is taking the body out using the ambulance. We think it's the best solution to try to keep this under wraps." Greg lowered his voice. "I need you to take Jackie out like you two were walking the race and tell Darla what happened. I don't want her to be left in the dark in case the press grabs hold of this."

"We can do that." I peered around Greg as the EMTs loaded the body onto the cart, an oxygen mask set on the dead woman's face. "Are you sure they'll think she's alive?"

"As long as they don't see the high heels, we should be fine. By this time, the runners are through the course and the walkers are starting to feel the pain. They'll be focused on their own progress, not the fallen around them." Greg waved Toby over to his side. "Set these two back on the path, then help Doc get the body to the ambulance. We'll come back for Josh."

"I'm not riding in the same van as that woman," Josh muttered.

Greg rolled his eyes, then turned toward the antique dealer. "We've ordered a special bariatric-equipped ambulance from Bakerstown. You don't have to share your ambulance, but you do have to wait for a few minutes. One of the EMTs will stay with you until the second one arrives."

Toby started toward the race path, but I stayed next to Greg. "You're sure it's Sandra Ashford? I mean, why would she even be out here?"

"I don't think she *was* out here. Not for the race, that is. It looks like a body dump. But yeah, it's her. The local chamber in Bakerstown will have her fingerprints on file when they set up their business. Apparently a new process for those who are in a consulting type of activity." Greg nodded to the retreating Toby and Jackie. "Besides, she has one of those paper name tags plastered on her dress. From a meeting or something. You'd better catch up."

I nodded and quickly caught up to Aunt Jackie. We didn't talk at all on the way back to the finish line. Between Toby's determination and my aunt's focus, we were at the celebration before we knew it. Darla put a medal around both Toby's and Jackie's neck. When she reached me, she frowned. "I didn't think you were walking." She glanced toward the coffee truck, looking confused.

"Can you get someone else to hand these out? We need to talk." I took Darla by the arm and led her away from the path toward the back of the booth.

"Sure." She motioned to the woman standing in the booth. "Clarice, can you take over for a few minutes? I've got to deal with this." She handed off the medals and pulled me over to the side of the booth. "Well?"

"There was an accident." I stopped and looked at Toby, who had followed us. "Well, not really an accident—"

Toby interrupted. "Josh is having some medical issues and is being taken to the hospital."

I saw Darla visibly react. "Honey, I thought you were saying someone died on my watch. Josh going to the hospital is unfortunate, but not unexpected." She started walking back to the finish line.

Toby put his hand on her shoulder, stopping her. "Darla, when Josh collapsed, we found a body just off the path. I'm sure it has nothing to do with the race, and we're not stopping the walk, but Greg thought you should know. Please keep this quiet, though."

"I'm not running off to file an article with the *Examiner*, if that's what you're worried about." Darla shook her head. "I'm not an idiot."

Toby put his hands up. "I just wanted to be clear. You know how Greg gets . . ." He glanced at me. "Sorry, Jill, but it's true. I needed to say it or he would have had my hide."

We watched him sprint back into the crowd toward the scene. Darla sank into a chair. "I can't believe this is happening. What a day. First, the run sponsors are all over my butt because of a rule I didn't even know about, and now there's a death on the greenbelt? What's next, Diamond Lille's booth bursting into flames because of a grease fire?"

I held back a smile. "I'm sure we're fine." But my gaze instinctively turned to the booth that had a long line in front of it as the runners waited for their free food. "Look, I'd better help Sasha get things packed up. Toby probably won't be able to help close up with this."

As I stepped away, Darla grabbed my arm. Her eyes were bright and curious. "You don't know who they found, do you?"

After convincing Darla I had no clue, which was hard since I didn't even believe my own assertions of ignorance, I sprinted back to the coffee shack. Sasha had already closed up the outside, moving the *Open* sign to *Closed*, and, with Nick's help, was stacking things into the Pies on the Fly van. We'd leave the empty food truck locked up and parked here, and Jackie's friend would come and get the keys from me tomorrow. I was sure I was going to get a sales pitch to purchase the vehicle from the guy, and, before today, I would have jumped at the chance. Now, with Sandra dead, I realized maybe I needed to take some time with the decision.

"Is Jackie okay?" Sasha dropped the stack of boxes she'd carried from the truck into Nick's hands and ran up to meet me.

I took her inside the truck before I answered. Greg had asked us to keep this quiet, and although I was going to tell Sasha, we didn't need eavesdropping runners to hear. I leaned against the counter, suddenly tired. "She's fine. They're taking Josh to the hospital to be checked out, but I think he's okay."

Sasha pressed a hand to her heart. "I'm so glad to hear that. When Toby came to get you, I was scared to death."

I glanced through the window, but most of the crowd was still over at Lille's booth or crashed on the beach eating their burgers. "Actually, there's more. Josh kind of fell on a body when he collapsed."

Sasha's eyes widened. "Oh dear, God, please don't tell me he crushed someone to death."

I couldn't help it, I laughed. The vision of a cartoon Josh squashing Sandra came to mind and wouldn't leave. Sasha stared at me. Finally, I choked back my chuckles and wiped my eyes. "No. Well, kind of, but no, he didn't kill her. She was already dead."

"Who? Who is dead?" Sasha put her hands on her hips. "You're being a jerk."

"I'm not a jerk." I leaned closer. "You can't tell anyone." I went on to tell her about finding Sandra's body off the path.

"Are they sure?" Sasha squatted down, trying to catch her breath. "I mean, she looked amazing last night at the party. The dress she wore was killer."

"Wait, you went to the party?" I knelt next to her. "Did you see Sandra leave? Was she with anyone?"

Sasha sniffed. "I got my mom to babysit and Darla hired me to work as a server for the event. I needed the money, but I really wanted to see all the celebrities."

"But did she leave with anyone?" I pushed Sasha for an answer, knowing Greg would want to know.

"Nope. Michael stayed back after their fight. He sat at the bar and did five or six shots of whiskey. I can't believe anyone can drink that stuff straight." Sasha shook her head. "All he did was sit there and drink. I think Matt had to pour him into a cab later."

"Well, I guess the husband didn't do it. You know, statistically, he's the number-one suspect." I opened the last box of sliced NY cheesecake and offered it to Sasha. She took a plastic fork and broke off a piece.

"Greg won't want you playing investigator in this one." Sasha closed her eyes as she let the cheesecake taste take over her senses. "He gets a little touchy about you poking your nose in things."

I took my own bite of the treat. "Who said I was going to get involved? I'm just talking about the average murder suspect."

Sasha grinned. "A leopard can't change her spots. That's all I'm saying." She glanced at her watch. "I've got to get home and collect Olivia. We're going to the zoo tomorrow, and I don't think she has a clean outfit. I tell you, single parenthood has its joys, but hauling baskets of clothes and a three-year-old to the Laundromat isn't one of them."

"Do you need some help? I'm going to be home alone this weekend while Greg determines what happened to Sandra." I bit my lip. "We were supposed to be leaving on our cruise in a few days. I suspect that's off."

Sasha pulled her tote bag over her head and took out the keys to her well-loved, new-to-her compact sedan. A small wooden teddy bear with Olivia's name carved on the bear's tummy jingled with her keys. "If you don't need me to work as many hours next week, just call. I could use some time with the kid."

I shook my head. "I'm still taking the time off. If Greg cancels out on me, I'll dig in to the spare bedroom upstairs. I've been meaning to remodel that into a guest room since I finished the downstairs." I gave her a quick hug. "You're not getting time off that easy."

"A girl has to try." She waved as she left the truck.

I knew Sasha needed the hours, so there was no way I would step back from the schedule I'd already set for her. I locked up the food truck and gave Nick keys to the shop to put the leftover pies into the back refrigerator and the supplies into the office. Nick didn't have a lot of extra time to work for me along with his summer full-time job at Lille's, but anytime we did special events, he worked as many hours as possible to beef up his college fund.

Waving good-bye as he left the parking lot, I glanced back at the beach to see if Darla needed help breaking down the booths. I saw her at the finish line, still handing out medals and slips with completion times. There was still a line at Lille's booth, and a small band had set up on the beach, playing festive music. The area was crowded with people enjoying the day as well enjoying completing the event. If there hadn't been a dead body on the path, I would have called this a successful first Mission Walk for South Cove.

Now it was all about the cleanup. I walked over to Darla's booth and sat with my feet up, waiting to be put to work.

Three hours later, I was at home, my feet up on the coffee table and a book in my hand. Emma lay next to me, and her gentle snores were causing my own eyes to droop. Finally, I gave in and curled up on the couch for a short nap.

The ringing phone woke me. I grabbed my cell. "Hello?"

"Can you take me to the hospital to visit Josh?" My aunt sounded as tired as I felt.

I sat up, stretching my free arm and yawning. "Sure. When do you want to go?"

"Now, I guess. I'll buy us dinner in Bakerstown. I'm not feeling like cooking tonight."

I glanced at the clock; it was almost six. "I didn't realize they would keep him overnight for something like this." I wanted to say the word "trivial," but I didn't want Aunt Jackie to drive herself so it didn't pay to try to upset her.

"It's not the race thing. They're worried about his overall health. Apparently, the man is diabetic and he didn't even know." Jackie *tsk*ed over the phone. "He needs to lose weight obviously, but the man is hooked on candy. I've already gone over to his apartment and dumped out all the junk food. We need to stop at the store on the way back so I can restock with fresh fruit and vegetables."

"I'm sure he'll appreciate that." I grabbed my keys and let Emma out. I'd be back before it got too dark, but Emma liked being outside. Well, she really liked eating my sofa pillows, but I'd tried to break her of the habit by limiting her time alone with the off-limits treat.

As I pulled away from my house, Esmeralda's driveway was filled, and there were a few cars parked on the side of the street, as well. She had said her calendar was busy, but this was crazy. The good thing about my neighbor's in-home business, the clientele was polite and respectful. I think they were scared of the woman's power. No matter the reason, even with a large number of clients visiting on the weekends, I rarely noticed people coming and going unless I happened to be outside working in the front yard or running with Emma.

Tonight, getting out of my driveway was a little tricky, as I couldn't see around a large Ram truck parked on my side of the road. But I inched my way out, rolling down the window to try to listen for oncoming cars, and when I determined it was clear, I pulled out onto the road to South Cove.

My phone rang as I hit town, and I answered using my in-car Bluetooth. "Hey, what's going on?"

Greg's voice boomed through the car. "I'm just checking in. I'm still in Bakerstown at Doc Ames's place. Don't think I'll be over tonight."

"Kind of figured that. I'm taking Aunt Jackie into town to visit Josh. I guess they're holding him over for a night. He's diabetic." I pulled into the parking lot behind the coffee shop.

"I could have told you that and I'm not a doctor." Greg chuckled. "But I guess it was news to Josh?"

"Apparently. I'm sure I'll hear the whole story when we visit. Aunt Jackie's already cleared out all the candy and stuff out of his apartment. I'm sure we'll be seeing him in his knock-off tracksuit walking more often now." I waved at my aunt, who was locking up her outside door. "Look, she's here. Call me later?"

"Probably tomorrow. I'll be here until late, then I've got to prep for my first meeting with the DA on the case early in the morning." Greg paused. "Look, I need a favor and you're not going to like it."

I used my finger to disturb the dust on the display in my Jeep. "I think I can guess. I'm hoping I'm wrong, though."

"Can you call Rachel and cancel our trip? Sorry. There's no way I can get away on Thursday. I'm pretty sure we'll eat the cost, but see if she'll try to get us a refund."

"Greg, you have to be able to take time off sometime. I'm sure there's someone who can take over for a week." My tone was sounding childish even to me. And I knew I was fighting a losing battle.

"I've got to go. Just call Rachel. I'll make this up to you, I promise." Then he hung up. No "good-bye," no "love you," just a dial tone. I slumped in the seat and realized my aunt was already in the car.

"Trouble in paradise?" She clicked the seat belt and adjusted her suit jacket.

I started the ignition and pulled back onto Main Street. "We're not going to Alaska."

My aunt settled her purse on her lap. "I'm sorry. I know you were looking forward to the trip. But you know his job isn't regular hours. I thought you were fine with that."

"I thought I was, too. Now I don't know." I turned up the stereo as I turned onto the highway. Tears filled my eyes but I blinked them away. I'd known all along a weeklong vacation with Greg was a crapshoot, but I'd thought this time we just might get lucky.

*Lucky* was not my middle name.

# CHAPTER 6

By the time we'd reached Bakerstown, I was done with my pity party. As we turned down the street that would take us to the highway, I checked the time and clicked off the stereo. "I think we have a few minutes to catch Rachel at the shop. Her website says she closes at five on Saturdays. Do you mind if I stop by there now?"

"Go ahead. You know it's better to get these things done than sit and stew about them." My aunt studied my face. "Your mascara looks fine, but you may want to run this over your lips." She handed me a lipstick container.

"I'm just going in to cancel our trip. I don't think having on makeup will change anything." I swatted my aunt's hand away as I pulled the Jeep into the small parking lot in front of the travel agency. Like me, Rachel had bought the building along with the business, and she lived in the other half of the cozy little cottage. The front entry looked fresh and charming with a variety of flowers in different-sized pots filling what had been flower beds. The house/business was painted a bright white with red trim, reminding me of the pictures I'd seen of houses perched on the cliffs in Greece. Dating Greg, pictures might be as close as I got to real travel.

I took a deep breath and pushed away the *poor, pitiful me* thought. I glanced in the rearview mirror and realized I looked like a walking zombie, pale and hurt. I took the lipstick my aunt still held out and applied the shade onto my lips, smacking them together. The color did bring some life to my face, and as I handed back the tube, I said it before Aunt Jackie could. "You were right."

She tucked the tube into her purse, then smiled at me. "It's not about being right, my dear. I just don't want you to look like prey in front of the lions' den."

"I have no idea what you're saying or why, but I'm getting this handled." I opened the door and climbed out. "I'll be right back."

My aunt changed the channel on the stereo to show tunes as I took the few steps to the door. I guess she figured my "right back" might take some time. Turning the doorknob, I pushed on the door. Locked. Frowning, I glanced at the sign in the window that announced the open hours, and then checked my watch. Ten to five: The agency should be open.

A voice called out from the side of the building, and a woman with a water hose came into view. "Sorry, the travel agency is closed today. Rachel had a family emergency."

"Oh, I guess I should have called first." I dug in my purse and found a small notebook. "I'll just leave her a note. Do you think she'll be open on Tuesday?" Like most of the businesses in South Cove, Bakerstown Travel closed on Monday, which gave Rachel a real weekend from work.

The woman came closer, and I realized she was using a walker to assist her. "Honestly, I don't know. I'm Cathy Addy. I live next door and run the yarn shop. I probably shouldn't even be out here, but Rachel's plants looked parched."

"That's nice of you." I glanced at the yarn shop in the next little house. The number of plants and flowers surrounding the building made the travel agency look almost barren. "Your own flower gardens are lovely."

"Thanks. I was out watering this morning when Rachel left. That's how I knew she was gone. But I'd gotten the impression she might be back today." Cathy put the hose she'd been dragging into a new pot as she talked. "Impatiens are very fragile, especially in this heat."

"Do you need some help?" I'd finished writing the note. Then I folded it and tucked it into the mail slot. I'd call Rachel when we got to the hospital and leave a voice mail, too. Maybe she could make some calls Monday to get our tickets canceled. I stepped off the porch, turning toward Cathy.

She waved me off. "This is one of the few things I can do around the place. I have a house cleaner coming in once a week now, so watering plants and washing a few dishes are about all I get to do. I'll be fine."

I studied Cathy, who seemed to be the same age as my aunt in the car. Arguing with her would only upset her and probably get me in the doghouse with my aunt, as well. "It was nice meeting you. I'll be leaving you to it then."

"Stop by the yarn store next time you're in town. I've got some lovely new stock you might like," Cathy called after me.

"I'll do that." I waved and climbed into the Jeep.

My aunt turned off the stereo, which seemed to be playing a rousing chorus of "Oklahoma." "You don't knit."

"I could learn." I turned the Jeep toward the hospital. "Maybe it would be relaxing."

Aunt Jackie snorted. "What do you need to relax from? A hard day of reading?"

"Whatever." I turned the volume back up on the music, and we didn't talk again until we reached the hospital.

As I pulled up to the main entrance to let Aunt Jackie out, I leaned over. "I'll park, then leave Rachel a voice message. Then I'll meet you at Josh's room."

"Don't be long. I don't want to stay too long and tire him out." She straightened her jacket and smiled back at me. "Besides, I'm hungry."

I heard voices as I walked down the corridor toward Josh's room. The nurses' station was completely empty, and I could see patients watching me through their open doors as I walked the hallway. I'd only been in the hospital once, when my appendix tried to burst during my first and last date with Ken Forrey, my elementary, middle-school, and high-school crush. We'd gone to a movie, and I'd found myself throwing up in the ladies' room for a majority of the film. He'd dropped me off at the house, and my mom had rushed me to the emergency room. Besides a get-well-soon card his mother delivered to our house a few days later, I'd never heard from the guy again.

A nurse was standing by the bed, and Josh was railing at her.

"This isn't food." He waved a hand over his tray, which looked like food to me, even though it did look a tad healthy, without anything fried or covered in sauce.

"Mr. Thomas, you are going to have to change what you consider food if you even have a chance to lose weight. You have a green salad, a protein shake, and a side vegetable. That's more than enough food."

"You're trying to starve me." Josh whimpered. Then he saw me in the doorway. "I suppose you're enjoying yourself, watching my pain."

"Josh, stop being such a child." Aunt Jackie stood and stepped toward me. "I'm sure Jill isn't taking a bit of pleasure in your discomfort. I'll see you tomorrow and leave you to eat your lovely dinner."

"Can't you just stay a while longer?" Josh scooted his body higher in the bed. "I'm sure I'd eat better with you here."

"Your manipulations aren't working on me." She smiled at the nurse. "Thank you for taking such good care of Mr. Thomas. I'm sure he appreciates it, even if he's unable to express his positive feelings."

The nurse nodded and slipped out of the room. I followed, hoping I'd be able to bite back the smile before Aunt Jackie joined me in the hallway.

I leaned against the too-white wall, closing my eyes for a second trying to center myself. It had been a crazy day. I wondered, once the news leaked about the body being found on the trail, if the California Mission Society would feel differently about us sponsoring next year's walk. And apparently, we hadn't followed their rules to begin with. Two strikes against South Cove, and neither one was Darla's or my fault.

Aunt Jackie's hand on my arm brought me back to the present. "Let's get out of here before he throws another fit." She headed us toward the elevator. "I swear, that man is such a child at times. It's no one's fault but his own that he's in this situation. But no, tell him that and you'll get a list of other people to blame."

"Changing habits is hard." I pushed the button for the ground floor. "He's lucky you started pushing him to walk. If he hadn't collapsed on the walk, he might have never found out about the diabetes until it was too late."

"Exactly. It's a blessing in disguise. Now, getting him to see it that way, well, that's another story." Aunt Jackie leaned against the elevator wall, gripping the handrail. "I'm beat. Food, then I'm crashing. Do you think you can handle my late shift at the shop tomorrow? I hate to ask, but I really want to come into town to visit Josh again."

I held the elevator door open. "No problem. I'll work your shift. Now, where do you want to eat?"

We settled on a small mom-and-pop Italian restaurant that served the best gnocchi in town. Aunt Jackie drank red wine with her meal, I had a soda, and we both had coffee with dessert. I held up my cup in a toast. "Here's to a fairly successful first South Cove Mission Walk." My aunt clicked her cup with mine. "If you don't count poor Sandra." I nodded. "Especially if you don't count the dead body."

We sat for a while, enjoying the warmth of the room as we sipped the dark coffee. Aunt Jackie set her cup down by her half-eaten piece of chocolate cake, eyeing the cup warily. "I probably shouldn't be drinking coffee this late in the evening, but I'm not sure I'll be able to keep my eyes open on our way back to South Cove."

"It has been a long day." I finished the last bite of the molten lava cake on my plate, then picked up my own cup. I might just have to get a to-go cup to make sure I stayed awake during the drive. "All kidding aside, I did think Darla pulled off the race nicely. And the food truck idea was brilliant."

"Homer's willing to sell. I don't know the details, but you could talk to him tomorrow when he picks up the keys." Aunt Jackie pushed the rest of her dessert around on her plate. "I think it would be a nice addition to the business. There are plenty of festivals around where we could have a presence and draw customers back to South Cove. And we could add more hours to Sasha's schedule."

I shrugged, not wanting to think about expanding the business right now. It seemed like all I did lately was work. And now that my long-awaited getaway with my boyfriend was torched, work would be my focus for a while longer. I knew I was pouting, but I couldn't get past the hurt feelings, even though I knew Greg had no control over his workload, especially when someone had been murdered.

Aunt Jackie didn't seem to notice my lack of enthusiasm. "I'm surprised Rachel closed up shop. I didn't think she had any family in the area."

"You know Rachel?" Now, this got my attention.

My aunt sipped the last of her coffee and set the cup down reluctantly. "She's scheduled a few local trips for me lately. I'm talking to her about a short jaunt to the Greek Isles next winter, if I can get it cheap enough."

"Oh, I didn't realize." I didn't know why this surprised me. My aunt knew more people in the area than I did, and she'd lived there only a year. I guess being an introvert bookstore owner could account for my lack of local connections, but honestly, I knew my aunt had the gift of networking, something I'd have to work at for the rest of my life.

"She's such a sweet girl." My aunt put her napkin on her plate. "Are you ready to head back?"

I nodded, waving the ticket at the waiter. "So, do you know who she's dating?"

She paused in digging through her purse and looked up at me. "I didn't know she was dating anyone. What do you know?" She pulled out a lipstick tube and refreshed her makeup, using her knife for a reflective surface.

"Rachel said she was seeing someone a few days ago when I called her." I signed the credit card slip and figured out an appropriate tip. I almost pulled out my phone since I'd downloaded a tip app, but I thought my aunt might laugh that I couldn't do it in my head. I probably overtipped, but as tired as I was, all I wanted was to get home.

"Well, all I can say is I'm happy for her. She needs someone in her life. Everyone does." My aunt stood and took my arm as we walked out of the restaurant and to the car. "You and Greg will have plenty of time for trips. Just be patient."

I wasn't sure my aunt's wisdom was true, but I didn't correct her. We headed back to South Cove and our lives.

On Sunday I only had a few hours to get my life in order before I had to go in to cover Aunt Jackie's shift. And the food truck guy was supposed to show up to pick up his keys and a check for the rental before noon.

First things first, I took Emma for a run. The beach parking lot was empty except for the large van and a few cars. I glanced up and down the beach, but apparently, the owners of the cars were tucked in bed and would be retrieving them later. The beach looked pristine, with the waves gently lapping at the shore. No evidence of yesterday's mayhem was left except for the leftover vehicles. Instead of turning right toward the cove and our normal running path, I turned Emma left toward the entrance to the Mission Walk. Since the path was paved, both Emma and I preferred running closer to the water in the sand, but today, I wanted to check out the greenbelt.

When I got to the place where Josh had found Sandra's body, I pulled out a small digital camera I'd brought on the run just for this. It wasn't like I was going to be involved in the investigation, I assured myself. Only even I didn't believe me this time. I snapped several overall shots, and as I was focusing the shots, I realized the little outlet where Sandra's body had been found was just a few feet from the highway. And someone had carved a path through the shrubbery from the road to the greenbelt. I tightened my grip on Emma's leash and walked toward the road.

A small turnout that could hold a car or two greeted me as I came up the gully to the highway. This early on a Sunday morning, the road that curved up and down the California coastline was empty, but there had been people parked here yesterday, I could almost bet on it. I took a few shots and then turned back to the path leading down to the greenbelt.

A flash of white under a bush made me pause, and I reached down to find a soda cup from South Cove Winery. I tucked the cup into a sack I carried for trash pickup and returned to the greenbelt, this time letting Emma off the leash and running back toward our normal path. I don't know what I expected to find, but I felt a tad disappointed in the lack of any type of clue as to why Sandra was found on the greenbelt. Maybe I was losing my touch for this type of puzzle.

I brushed the idea away, and as we broke from the tree-lined greenbelt onto the sand of the beach, I picked up my pace. This was my time, and I wasn't going to let anything distract me.

By the time Emma and I had returned to the house and I'd showered and eaten a light breakfast, I had just enough time to start some laundry and check my to-do list for the day. I crossed off anything I'd written last week about the trip, like *Pack*, or *Cancel Mail Delivery*. I glanced at my phone: no return call from Rachel yet. No matter what kind of past Greg and Rachel had, I was positive a refund at this stage of the planning was impossible. I added a few things to my list for tomorrow, like a trip to Home Heaven, Bakerstown's hardware-slash-home-repair mecca to pick out a paint color and supplies.

After I returned home tomorrow, I'd clean out the spare bedroom, haul boxes down to the garage, and totally empty it out. I wanted a wrought-iron bed frame, so I added a trip to Antiques by Josh to my list, if he opened the shop this week. And I really wanted to find a homemade quilt and rag rug, but I'd have to locate a flea market to score those items. Good thing I had five days off starting on Tuesday. I might just get the room completed and still have time to sit on the beach and read for a day or so.

*Happy vacation to me.*

# CHAPTER 7

A knock on the door rousted me from my couch and the contemporary romance I'd been reading. I loved the way the author painted the Oregon coastline in this series, and the little town was one I'd move to in a heartbeat. Emma stretched and joined me at the door.

I peeked through the window and saw a man dressed in a Hawaiian shirt and khaki shorts. This must be the guy about the food truck, but just to be sure, when I cracked the door open, I asked, "May I help you?"

"Ms. Gardner? I'm Homer Bell. Your aunt said I could pick up the keys and my check today?" The man nodded his head in greeting.

I stepped out on the porch with the keys and an envelope I'd had ready on my foyer table. "Thanks for the loan of your truck." I handed him the items. "I've heard you're interested in selling. Do you have an asking price?"

The man broke into a grin. "Not yet. When your aunt asked me, I was a little surprised. I've had the notion to sell out for over a year. Now that I've made the decision, I get two interested parties in less than three days. I'm researching the truck's value and will call you late next week."

"Oh, I thought . . ." I paused, not wanting to say I thought he was giving us a deal just to get rid of the pink van. "I mean, that will work fine. Who is our competition, if you don't mind my asking?"

He tucked the envelope into his shirt pocket. "Actually, the other party has asked me to keep their interest quiet. I probably shouldn't have even said anything, but I was so excited when I got the call this morning. Your little town is full of surprises. I should have visited sooner."

I thanked him for stopping by to pick up the keys and then watched him return to a small compact car where a female driver was waiting. "Interesting," I said to Emma.

She let out a short bark, which could have meant, "You got that right." But probably, she just wanted to go outside. When I opened the back door, she bounded outside. So much for my mind meld with the canine family. I went to the fridge and grabbed the makings of an omelet and a fruit salad to eat before I went in to work. I turned on the small television I kept in the kitchen and listened to a cooking show while I made my lunch.

When I showed up at the shop, Sasha was sitting on the couch reading a new YA dystopian release. She'd hadn't ordered anything for the next month's book club yet, and I knew she was struggling to make just the right choice. I pulled on an apron and washed my hands before pouring my own cup of coffee, which I took over to the chair next to her. "You just need to make a decision."

"I know, but attendance is down, and I really want to bring the kids back this month." Sasha sighed and set the book down with a bookmark in the middle to mark her place.

"Attendance is down because it's summer. Aunt Jackie's mystery book group typically takes August off because there are so few of the members in town. You don't have to pack the room every month." I pulled the book she'd just closed toward me. "This is getting great reviews online. What are your other choices?"

Sasha grinned and pulled two books out of her tote bag. "I'm torn between this modern fairy tale, a book about a high school geek squad, and that one."

"Which one did you like the best?" I touched the cover on the fairy tale, loving the wispy blues running through the picture of the girl dressed in a long flowery dress.

"I loved that one, but I'm afraid the boys in the group will rebel." She leaned back in the couch. "It's hard to please everyone."

I pushed the books back toward her. "Then don't."

"I don't understand. You want me to give up on the book club?"

I laughed at the panic in her face. "No. Just let them choose any one of the three for next month. Have them put in their order at the next meeting."

"But how will we talk about three books?" Sasha shook her head. "It will be chaos."

I glanced around the shop. "Actually, you can divide it up into a group here, one in the dining area, and a third out on the sidewalk tables. You'll need a leader for each section, but if you don't get a kid to volunteer, you can have Toby or me come in."

"I like it, kind of choose your own adventure." She tucked all three books into her tote and checked her watch. "You're amazing, you know that?"

"I'm good at solving problems, that's all." I nodded to the door. "And you need to get home so you can have an evening with that amazing kid of yours."

The rest of the night was as slow as it had begun. A few stragglers from the race weekend stopped in for a drink to go before heading home. I e-mailed an order for Sadie's Pies on the Fly, ordered more books, and even double-checked the accounting program per my aunt's request. I had just finished the novel I'd been reading and was wandering through the stacks to see if there was something else when the bell rang over the door.

Darla and Matt came into the shop, holding hands. Matt had been Darla's intern last summer, and like Sasha, the winery had found a permanent employee through the jobs program. But there was another reason Matt was tied to South Cove, and that was the budding romance between him and Darla. She caught me looking at their entwined hands and blushed. I walked toward the counter. "Hey, you two. I didn't expect to see you out on your day off."

Darla slipped her hand out of Matt's and climbed onto a bar stool in front of me. "We were taking a walk when I got a call from Adam."

"The California Mission Society Adam?" I leaned on the counter and put my head between my outstretched arms. "How bad is it?"

"Why do you both think the worst?" Matt sat next to Darla. "Pour us two iced teas to go and box up a cheesecake. I'm barbequing ribs tonight for dinner, so we need something sweet to end the meal."

I lifted my head and nodded. "You're right. It could be good news. But if it was, Darla would have just called." I poured the teas and then opened the display case. "Chocolate or huckleberry?"

"Huckleberry." Darla sipped her tea. "I don't know if it's good or bad. The mission society board has requested a meeting with you and me tomorrow morning. Can you be at the winery at nine? Unless you'd rather have the meeting here?"

"The winery's fine. I don't want to appear to drive-bys like we're open. My local commuter traffic has been lobbying for open hours on Mondays." I boxed up the last huckleberry cheesecake and rang up the food and drinks. "The demands on a small business owner: be open twenty-four-seven, and carry everything the customer could ever want."

"You're doing great with the store. If they want coffee on Mondays, they can stop by Lille's. You supply their beans anyway, don't you?" Matt gave me a card, and I finished the purchase. It had been my largest sale since I'd walked in the shop at two.

"I doubt Lille's advertises that fact." I focused on Darla. "Have you heard anything about her expanding the diner?"

"Not a peep." Darla frowned. "What have you heard?"

Matt pulled her off the stool and aimed her toward the door. "Okay, Katie Couric, take off your journalist hat. It's date night, and I'm cutting you off."

I laughed and waved as the two left the shop. Just outside, Matt pulled Darla into a hug and planted a quick kiss on her lips. Sweet. At least someone was having a date night. I started the closing chores, and by seven, the shop's lights were off and I was power-walking my way home, a dozen chocolate chip cookies from the display case in tow, just in case Greg decided to stop by for a late visit.

Hope springs eternal and all that.

I still had six cookies the next morning when I made coffee since Greg hadn't called or shown up. If I didn't hear from him by noon, I would call to see if I could entice him to stop by for a quick dinner. Even detectives on murder cases needed to eat, right?

The phone rang as I took a bite of the first cookie of the day and I quickly swallowed. "Hello?"

"Jill, sorry I missed you." The female voice on the other end of the line was all bright and shiny, which made me sorry I'd answered the phone. Today was turning out to be anything but a fun day off. And *no one* should be happy on a Monday morning, unless it was someone who, like me, had the day off. The woman paused, waiting for my response.

"Who is this?" I knew I sounded irritated, but it was only seven thirty. I hadn't even taken Emma for her run yet, nor drunk a full cup of coffee.

"Rachel. From the travel agency? Sorry to call so early, but I'm still out of town and I wanted to let you know I'm trying to get your trip refunded."

Great, now I felt like a total jerk. The woman was only trying to help and I was snapping her head off. I took a breath and softened my tone. "I'm glad you called. Is everything okay? Your neighbor told me you had a family emergency?"

The line was quiet for a second. "Oh, you talked to Cathy? I adore her to death, but the woman can be a bit of a gossip. Actually, my cousin is having health problems and I'm babysitting her kids."

I hadn't seen Rachel as much of a mothering or babysitting type, but I'd only met the business side of her. "I hope she's getting better."

"Definitely. I'll be back home soon. And hopefully I'll have a check for you when I return. Sorry about the trip. I know Greg was really looking forward to getting out of town for a few days."

I shrugged, even though Rachel couldn't see my reaction. "Not your fault he has to work."

The line quieted, and I wondered how many times her plans with Greg had been cancelled because of his work. I guess I was preaching to the choir here. No use being the sore loser. "I guess I can't blame him. You know, the safety of South Cove is a high priority."

I felt the pause on the line. "So, did he say why he couldn't leave?"

Now I felt a pang of guilt. I knew, but until the death was announced to the public, I needed to keep my mouth shut. "Not a clue."

I heard someone on the other side of the line call out Rachel's name. A male voice, and I wondered about her claim to be out of town for family. Maybe this was a love shack getaway? "Well, I've got a meeting soon. Thanks for calling."

Rachel's good-bye was quick, and then the line was dead. Well, there went another happy couple for not just date night, but probably date weekend. Darla and Matt, Rachel and mystery man. Amy and Justin had gone surfing yesterday. Even Aunt Jackie and Josh had spent time together, although I couldn't say visiting someone in the hospital was my idea of a good time.

Emma put her nose in my hand and whined. "I know, girl, you love me."

She barked, then ran to the door. Clearly, she loved running and I was her companion. I tied my running shoes and devoured the rest of the cookie. Time to push out the pity party and run to clear my head.

I made it to the winery with five minutes to spare, only by driving instead of walking. I had to go to Bakerstown afterward, so it had only made sense. I pulled out my notebook and a pen and headed into the tasting room.

The room smelt like lavender and mint, and I realized the reason was the centerpieces on each of the small tables set up around the room. Unlike my shop, South Cove Winery was open seven days a week, even though they had shorter hours at the beginning of the week. Locals loved stopping by for a glass of wine or other adult beverage without the tourist crowd that would come later in the week.

No one was in the tasting room, so I wandered toward Darla's office, where I found Matt with a plate of fruit and a pitcher of orange juice heading to the small conference room next to the main office.

"Hey, Jill." Matt nodded toward the open door. "We're all set up in there. Can I get you something to drink besides OJ or coffee?"

I shook my head. "Coffee will be great." I paused at the door and took stock of the players already seated around the table. Adam and the other man who'd thrown such a fit about the mandatory online sign-ups were on one side of the table. Oscar, his name was Oscar. Michael Ashford sat next to Adam. Michael looked pale and disheveled, like he'd been in the same suit for the last week. Darla sat on the other side of the table, pen in hand tapping her notebook.

I dropped my notebook on the table next to her and went to pour myself a cup of coffee from the sideboard. When I sat down, I smiled and focused on the men across from us. "Good morning, everyone."

"We can get started?" Adam raised his eyebrows. "Are you expecting anyone else?"

Darla looked at me and we both shook our heads. "Nope. Just us." I focused on Michael, trying to catch his attention, but his gaze was downcast to the empty legal pad in front of him. "I'm so sorry to hear about Sandra. If we need to, we can postpone this meeting."

Adam put his hand on Michael's arm and patted exactly twice. "Well, yes, it's a tragedy, but we are all in agreement that we need to close the books on the Mission Walk this week. No use wasting time, especially since we're all here."

I sent Darla a *can you believe this guy?* look and then sipped my coffee. Darla stepped into the conversation. "So, what did you want to discuss? I don't have final numbers from the businesses on the effect of the race on South Cove commerce, but all in all, I thought it was a very successful event."

Adam looked at the other man, and I saw him roll his eyes. "Well, in several ways, it was successful. We just have a few notes about improvements for next year."

"Like, maybe giving us your expectations before the day of the race?" The comment was out before I could temper it. Darla had worked her butt off for this group, and they were listing off the things we didn't get perfect? Losers.

Michael squirmed in his chair and Adam nodded. "Well, yes, we acknowledge that the communication between us got a little lost. But we've talked to Michael, and he assures us that this lapse will not happen again."

"Sandra dropped the ball. She said she had talked to you and sent you the packet months ago." Michael finally looked up at us, his eyes bloodshot. His hand shook as he picked up his coffee cup. "I'm sorry. I trusted her."

Darla fluttered next to me. "Oh, please, don't worry about that now. It's all water under the bridge. I'm sure maybe she thought she'd done her job."

Yeah, blame the dead for all the problems. I couldn't help it, I was skeptical of Michael's claim. The only time I'd met the woman, she'd seemed on top of things, controlling, and in charge. If anyone had forgotten to send us the packet, I was sure it was the male partner of Promote Your Event. But I kept my mouth shut.

Adam continued, "So we're willing to give South Cove another shot with a race next year as long as you assure us that the rules will be followed." He handed out three-inch notebooks, one for each of us. "I'd like you to study the sections on fund-raising and race enrollment practices. This way, every racer is in our system days before the walk happens and can get updates from the Society on upcoming events they may be interested in attending."

Now I knew why they wanted only online registrations. It gave them a private mailing list for runners all over California. And I bet they didn't feel bad about selling their lists to companies who catered to the running crowd.

"So, that's it? We study the rules, promise to be good sponsors next year, and we're guaranteed an annual race?" I wanted to be clear on what they were offering. And we'd have to clear the pros and cons with the Business-to-Business group before we agreed to another race. Mary Sullivan would be able to quantify the additional business the race brought to the town.

"Almost. We want to make sure that the sponsor party isn't pulled together last-minute, like it was this year. We have a lot of prominent people who enjoy attending our race kickoffs who weren't even invited this year." The other man leaned forward. "I hope that won't happen next year."

Darla nodded, but I'd had enough. "Look, we didn't even know that we were supposed to set up an opening party. Remember? We didn't get the book until today. I'm sure your friends can understand missing out on one party in a year."

"Miss Gardner, there's no need to be rude. We've apologized for the lack of communication, and Michael has assured us this won't be an issue going forward." Adam glanced at the other man and he leaned back.

Now I got it. They'd brought Michael along to be their fall guy. *So sorry the dead girl screwed up your race. Just promise to be better next year.* I felt sorry for him. First, he lost his wife, and now these jerks were making him pander for his company's future. I closed my eyes and counted to ten before I responded. "We have the book, and we'll get back to you soon about dates for next year's race. I have to clear this with the business council and evaluate the advantages to the South Cove community. Is there anything else you wanted to say?"

Three heads shook across the table, and I realized our meeting was over. They'd tried to strong-arm us into feeling bad about the missteps for this year's race, but the only one I saw who got hurt was their list of possible customers who'd signed up the day of the race and weren't in their promotional machine now. They needed us, no matter what the notebook said.

"We'll be back in touch." I didn't stand as I watched the three men load up their briefcases and leave the conference room. After I was sure they were in the parking lot, I turned toward Darla. She was staring at me like I'd grown a third head.

"Look, you did an amazing job with the race. I'm sorry they didn't say that." I patted the notebook in front of me. "We need to look this over and see if we want to play by their rules for next year. Is it worth jumping through the Society's hoops to sponsor this race? Besides, Mary needs time to summarize the numbers for the town. Then we'll present our findings to the committee."

"You'd walk away from sponsoring the Mission Walk? Even though our participation might help with the final decision from the historical commission?" Darla shook her head. "We need to support your wall."

"Not if it means working with jerks like that." I shook my head. "Can you believe they brought in the grieving widower to apologize for their screwup?"

"Classy, right?" Darla sipped her coffee. "But it does tell us one thing."

I stood, my notebook in hand. "What's that?"

"Promote Your Event wasn't in the best shape as a company when Sandra was alive. Who knows what will happen to their business now that she's dead."

I thought about Darla's statement as I drove in to Bakerstown to pick up paint. Knowing the part-time reporter's nose for a good scandal, I wondered how someone would find out about the health of a privately held company.

"Not your monkey, not your circus," I muttered as I turned into Home Heaven's parking lot. I was pretty sure I could hear laughter coming from my conscience.

# CHAPTER 8

After unloading the paint and supplies, I left them in my laundry room and headed upstairs to start clearing out the boxes and crap that had taken over the room I now called Project Guest Room.

I'd almost gotten all the boxes sorted into three piles: trash, give away, and attic. Glancing at the piles, I wondered if my attic pile was too large. I still had boxes from high school and from when I'd cleaned out my mother's house after her death seven years ago. I still hadn't heard from Greg, and it was beginning to worry me. Even on big cases, he tended to check in either by stopping by the house or by a quick text.

Instead of dealing with the pile, I sat on a step stool and pulled out my phone. I dialed Greg's cell, and it rang three times, then went to voice mail. "Hey, if you want to eat dinner together tonight, text me and I'll either grill something or drop something off at the station. I miss you."

I put away the phone and concentrated on hauling the trash boxes down to the kitchen and out the back door to the garage. Typically, my garbage can was pretty empty most weeks, but I estimated I had enough trash and recycling to fill both of the ultra-large receptacles for a month or more. I set aside a few copies of the more recent magazines so I could drop them off at the police station. Last time I had to sit and wait for Greg, I'd read a copy of *Guns & Ammo* that was over ten years old. At least this way, some of the magazines wouldn't go to recycling unread.

My phone buzzed in my pocket and I read the text aloud. "Fire up the grill, I'll be there around six." Emma looked up at me from her kitchen bed and thumped her tail on the floor. "Yep, girl, we're having company tonight."

I dug through the freezer for some sort of meat—anything—but I came up short. I glanced at the contents of the fridge for a side. I'd forgotten to stop at the grocery store in Bakerstown, and since I hadn't bought much last week, expecting to be off on our cruise, the pickings were sparse. I still had enough for a quick pasta salad, though. I set a pan on the stove to boil the pasta and another for boiled eggs and went back upstairs to bring down a load of giveaway boxes.

These I set on the other side of the garage. I'd drop them off at the Youth Ranch thrift store sometime next week. Halfway through that project, I started the eggs and took a break to fix a quick lunch. Opening a can of tuna, I heard a knock on the door. Emma ran to the door and sat at attention. I wiped my hands off and went to let my aunt in.

"What are you doing here? I figured you'd be visiting Josh." I kissed my aunt on the cheek as she buzzed past me, bags in hand. The smell of fresh baked bread filled the room.

"They let him out." Aunt Jackie unpacked the bags that were filled with groceries. Fresh vegetables were piled on the counter along with the bread and what looked like fresh seafood from the local fishmonger. There was also a packet that appeared to be New York strips. I bet she'd hit three to four different stores on the way home from Bakerstown.

"Uh-oh," I started putting away the food, eyeing the wrapped package labeled *scallops* and then my opened can of tuna. "What happened that has you all shopping therapy crazed?"

Aunt Jackie took a can of seltzer water out of the fridge and settled into one of the kitchen chairs. She set her purse on the table and seemed to collapse into herself. Opening the can, she took a drink.

"You don't want a glass for that?" I'd never seen my aunt drink out of a can before, not even when we'd taken a lunch to the beach last week.

She stared at the can like it had just appeared in her hand. "I'm fine. I just can't believe they let Josh go home already."

"He's been released?" I grabbed the celery and green onions out of the fridge and started chopping. "Can I make you a sandwich?"

She nodded. "I haven't eaten today. Put it on that seven-grain bread and slice a few peaches to go along."

Should have known she'd have a menu planned around my offer.

"So, tell me about Josh. When we visited, I thought they were trying to get his diabetes under control."

"He doesn't have diabetes. He's just fine." Aunt Jackie sighed. "Well, as fine as a massively obese man in his seventies can be."

"Then why did they keep him?" I stirred mayonnaise and sour cream into the bowl with the tuna and chopped veggies. I grabbed a few thyme stems off one of my herb plants that lined the kitchen window and rinsed them, then pulled the leaves off and chopped them. Finally, I added a bit of salt and pepper and the salad was done.

"He kept telling them he felt weak. They did all kinds of tests, and when the results finally came back, he's healthy as a horse. Except for his weight." Aunt Jackie reached down and stroked Emma's head. "I was so worried about him, and he was just being Josh."

I finished up the plates and set them on the table. "So, why did he collapse on Saturday?"

Aunt Jackie stood and let Emma out the back door, then washed her hands in the sink. "The doctor said he probably was dehydrated. All of this and he just needed to drink the water the volunteers had been offering the entire walk."

"Well, it's good that he's okay." I took a bite of my sandwich and watched my aunt cut her sandwich into bite-size portions. "But that doesn't explain the shopping frenzy."

Aunt Jackie leaned back into her chair. "I guess I was so worried about him that knowing he's okay, well, I just kept thinking about what could have happened."

"You're upset that he's not sick?" I took another bite. "I bet he took that well."

She took a bite of the sandwich and then wiped her mouth with a napkin. "He doesn't know I'm upset. I dropped him off at his apartment, then went driving."

"Sasha said you were visiting a doctor. What's going on with you?" I decided to push the issue, not sure if I really wanted the answer. "Is this about you?"

"Sasha should keep her mouth shut." She focused on the sandwich. Finally, she pushed the half-eaten lunch aside. "Maybe I am a little worried about my own mortality."

"Aunt Jackie, what's wrong?" My heart felt like it was beating out of my chest.

She held up a hand. "Calm down, dear. I've got a touch of arthritis. I'm just feeling my age I guess."

"And Josh made you worry about the future." I pushed her plate toward her. "Finish your lunch."

"I'm too upset to eat." My aunt looked around the room. "Why do you have boxes all over?"

"I'm redoing the guest room upstairs." I put my hand on my aunt's. "Are you sure you're okay? There's not something you want to tell me?"

My aunt tossed most of her uneaten meal and then put her plate in the sink. "Thank you for lunch, dear. I'm perfectly fine. Thank you for listening to an old lady's worries."

"We aren't done talking about this, you know."

"Yes, dear, we are." My aunt kissed me and disappeared to the front door. "Make sure you replace the curtains in that room, as well. They're hideous."

I followed her to the door and watched as she drove away. She was such a strong woman, I worried she was hiding something more from me. But until she wanted to tell me, there wasn't anything I could do except worry.

I went back to clearing out the upstairs room. By three, I'd stripped the room bare, including getting rid of curtains that I had thought were kind of quaint. I looked around, happy with my progress for the day. Tomorrow I'd start the transformation.

Now I needed to get ready for date night. Greg would be here at six, and I wanted dinner ready to go in case he only had a short break. I could do this supportive-girlfriend thing. And I wouldn't even react to the cancelled vacation. On the outside.

When Greg showed up, he handed me a small bag as he came through the front door. He leaned down to wrestle with Emma, and I closed the door. "What's this?"

"Open it and find out." Greg had Emma plastered against his chest and was rubbing her belly. He gave her a kiss on the head. "Who's a good girl?"

Emma barked and melted further into the belly rub. My dog was predictable and could be bought for very little attention. At least from her favorite guy, Greg. I went to the couch with my bag and sat. I could feel Greg's gaze on me as I pulled out the little blue box. My gut gripped, and for a second, fear slowed my movements. It was too soon for this, too soon for *that* question. Taking a deep breath, I flipped open the box and found a pair of dolphin earrings with what appeared to be diamonds in the middle. I felt my lips curve into a smile, and all of a sudden Greg was by my side.

"Do you like them?" He touched one of the silver earrings with a finger. "I had planned on giving them to you on board, you know, for that dress-up night?"

"They are beautiful." I set the bag down and took out the earrings, putting them on and making sure the backs were securely fastened before I turned toward him. I held my hair away from my face and turned my head back and forth. "How do they look?"

"They would be better with that black dress you have with the slit up the leg." He grinned. "Sorry about cancelling the cruise."

"Your job is part of the package, big guy." I leaned into him, smelling his cologne mixed with the scent I'd come to define as Greg. Irish Spring soap, a no-name shampoo, and, right now, a little bit of Emma slobber. "I knew things might come up. Like a murder."

"Yeah, but seriously? Five days later, and we would have been gone and Bakerstown's sheriff would have taken lead. Sometimes I think my luck is nothing but bad." He leaned against the back of the couch, bringing me with him.

"So, Sandra was murdered? You're sure?" I ran my hand over his button-down shirt, loving the feel of the pressed cotton over what I knew were rock-hard abs.

Greg chuckled. "I'm not that easy, you know." He took my hand in his and held it still over his heart. "But you'll probably be reading about the whole thing in this week's paper if I know Darla, so yeah, Sandra was murdered. Doc Ames says she was hit by a vehicle, then her body dumped on the greenbelt. Thing is, I'm not sure the killer really wanted to hide her."

I tipped my head upward, looking at his expression. "You think they wanted the body found?"

Greg nodded. "Of course that's only a theory, and right now, I'm the only one going down that path. The DA thinks her husband is just a bad planner. He'd have to be totally stupid to kill his wife then put her where he knew, what, a thousand people would be the next day?"

"We had six hundred sign up for the race, so with friends and family, about that."

"Doesn't make any sense at all." Greg rolled his shoulders, then looked at Emma. "Want to play ball for a while?"

"How much time do you have?" I sat up and Greg pulled me to my feet.

He put his arm around me, and we walked to the kitchen. "About two hours before I need to be back and going through all the security tape we have from Main Street. Of course, the mayor bought the cheaper system, so I have to look at each site one at a time. And it's not motion-activated, so it just films every minute of the day. I have ten files left, which means I'll be watching nothing else until Wednesday."

I took out the scallops and the steaks. I seasoned the meat and put everything on a tray. "You go play with Emma, I've got dinner."

"Looks good." He kissed my neck. "You must have gone shopping."

"Actually Aunt Jackie brought some stuff over after she took Josh home from the hospital. She's upset about his prognosis." I waited for the water to boil, then added the pasta.

"Wait, is something really wrong with Josh?" Greg picked up the tray and held open the back door for me.

Following him out onto the deck, a pair of tongs in my hand, I opened the grill. "No. He's fine. She was just scared, and when she's scared, she shops." I told him about my conversation with my aunt that afternoon as I let the grill heat.

Greg threw the ball for Emma, then stood watching her run. "Sometimes I just don't get women."

I put my arms around him and squeezed. "You're not supposed to get us, just hold on for the ride."

As I finished cooking dinner, I told him about my meeting with Darla and the Mission Society. "Apparently Michael is blaming the lack of communication on Sandra, and the society is supporting him. Honestly, I was surprised he was even at the meeting. I mean, there has to be stuff you need to do when your wife dies."

"He's been at the station for interviews several times. Jack wants me to arrest him, but I know there's not enough evidence, not yet, at least." Greg had stopped playing ball with Emma and now stood at the sink washing his hands. "I don't like rushing, and I've told him that."

"Sasha says Michael was drinking shots at the winery Friday

night after Sandra left. Do you have a time of death? That could exclude him if he was still sitting at the bar then." I mixed the pasta with chopped vegetables, a little olive oil, and some balsamic vinegar, tossing the mixture together into a warm salad.

Greg tasted the dish, then sprinkled some salt and pepper over the mix and stirred. He tasted again before he answered. "Thanks for the tip. I mean, as a trained investigator I would never have thought of checking time of death against the murder suspect's alibi."

"Fine, I get the point. Not my monkey." I took the bowl and set it on the table and gave him a platter and tongs. "Go get the steak and let's get this dinner started. I'm starving."

He kissed me on the forehead and headed outside. I finished setting the table as I thought about the way Sandra had died. And what the discovery site really said about the murderer. I was sure Greg was right. The killer had wanted Sandra to be found. And not only that, he or she had wanted Sandra found during the race.

As we sat down to eat, Greg's phone buzzed. I watched as he checked out the text message, typed out a quick response, and slipped the phone back into his pocket.

"Do you need to leave? Is it about the murder?" I could pack up his dinner into Tupperware containers and send it with him.

Greg shook his head. "Toby was just at The Train Station. Someone broke in last night and tore up one of the display models. He's trying to handle it, but Harrold wants me on site to do the investigation."

"So, you're going to finish eating?" I took a bite of the grilled scallop—fresh, buttery, and just done. Exactly like I liked them.

"I'm not leaving a New York strip to cool while I deal with a vandalism charge. I do have priorities, you know." He grinned. "I told Toby I'd be there in thirty minutes. Which gives me time to eat and help you with the dishes before I have to be there."

"Glad to know I'm one of your priorities." I paused and pointed my fork toward his steak. "Along with the meal, I mean."

As we finished our dinner, the conversation turned to the race and how the event, minus the whole dead body thing, had gone. From a law enforcement perspective, it had been almost flawless. No angry losers, no fights on the beach, just a huge group of people and cars to deal with as they left the area after the race. "I don't know, this type of event might just be worth having again." Greg took a slice of the seven-grain bread and covered it with butter. "How'd business go at the coffee shack?"

I shrugged. I hadn't even thought about the cash box sitting in my office waiting for me to do the paperwork for the deposit. "I'll find out tomorrow morning. I kind of forgot about the bookkeeping."

Greg took his plate to the sink and filled up one side with hot, soapy water. "That's the mark of a true business professional. Do you even know where the cash box is?"

"Yes." I grabbed my own plate and glass and set it on the counter. I paused, certain my answer was going to get me a lecture on the safety of keeping money around the house. He waited, so I caved. "Okay, it's in my office. But I've got it locked in my file cabinet. And no one knows it's here."

"Except Toby, Jackie, Sasha, and probably Sadie and Nick. And now me. Oh, and anyone else in town who knows you." He washed and rinsed the glassware. "Someday you're going to have an issue, you know that, right? Especially with The Train Station messed with now twice in a week. I'm worried about you."

"I promise I'll do the deposit tomorrow. Aunt Jackie will be on my case if I don't anyway." I finished clearing the table, put away the leftovers in the fridge, and picked up a drying towel. As I dried and put away what Greg washed, I thought about the problems at The Train Station. "Doesn't what's happening to Harrold seem personal? I mean, he wasn't robbed or anything."

Greg took the dishrag and wiped down the table and counter before he responded. "That's got me bothered, too. But seriously, who would have a problem with Harrold? He's got to be the nicest guy in town. Didn't he play Santa a few years ago?"

I thought about the rumor about Lille's expansion plans. Could she be mean enough to torture the guy into selling? I decided that in addition to stopping by the bank tomorrow, I'd also make a stop at The Train Station. Just to see if I could help out in any way. I was the chamber liaison, after all. It was my duty.

Even the angel on my shoulder laughed at that logic.

# CHAPTER 9

After getting the deposit ready, I slung a tote bag over my shoulder and headed into town. First stop, The Train Station. I'd purposely timed my visit for after ten so the shop would be open, in theory. After last night's events, I wasn't sure Harrold would have normal hours today, or even this week.

The door to the shop creaked open, and I stepped into the showroom. Harrold had made a miniature display of South Cove, with one important change. Running along Main Street, up to the winery, was a train trolley. The train even wound up a mini-mountain to include The Castle in the trip. The display was so well loved, I'd had customers ask when the real trolley was being built. Walking up to the miniature, I noticed The Train Station had been demolished. Not just the building removed—it looked like a real miniature bomb had taken out the station. Pieces of wood lay around the display and the trolley was on its side, the wheels crushed. No way was this random vandalism. Someone was sending a message to Harrold.

"A little creepy, don't you think?" Harrold came out of the back room, a broom and empty box in his hands. "The little jerk purposely destroyed the station. Looks like someone doesn't like me too much."

I stepped away to let the elderly man step closer to the display. "This is crazy. Who would do such a thing?" I put my hand on his shoulder. "Are you okay? Were you here?"

"That's the thing. I was back in the living quarters watching television. I can't believe I didn't hear the commotion, but I guess I keep the volume pretty loud." He tapped the front of his ears. "My hearing's not as sharp as it used to be. Too bad Tiny isn't here anymore. That boy could hear a pin drop out in the middle of Main Street. Used to drive me crazy."

Until last year, Tiny had been a mascot for the shop. The little Maltese had been Harrold's wife's dog until she passed. Then Tiny became Harrold's protector. The dog had died in his sleep last winter. "Maybe you should think of getting another dog. I don't know what I'd do without Emma."

"That's what Christopher's been saying for the last few months. Honestly, I'm sure if I don't get a dog soon, he'll be dropping off a pit bull puppy for my safekeeping." Harrold chuckled. "Like a dog is going to keep me safe."

"I know I feel better with Emma, especially since I live alone. Bakerstown has a shelter. Maybe you should go check out what they have available. Or do you want another Maltese?"

Harrold snorted. "Tiny was Agnes's dog. I've always been partial to German shepherds myself." He picked up the biggest part of what was left of the station and put it in the box. "Maybe I will take a drive later. I was planning on rebuilding The Station today, but I probably need some materials anyway."

"Sounds like a plan." I glanced around the shop, thankful the damage had only been to the miniature South Cove. I touched the replica of Coffee, Books, and More, and smiled at the little tables and chairs Harrold had put on the street outside the shop, just like in real life. "You've done a great job with this. You should be proud."

"I would be if people would just leave it alone." Harrold stopped picking up the broken pieces and looked at me. He leaned on his broom and appraised me thoughtfully. "Hey, maybe you can help."

"I'd be glad to, but I'm all thumbs when it comes to craft things." I motioned with my hand around the tiny village. "No way would I be able to make something like this. Just ask my aunt. She'll tell you I don't have a creative bone in my body."

"I wasn't thinking about the miniatures." He motioned to the chairs near a woodstove that I'd never seen lit. A small table with a chessboard sat between the chairs. "Come sit with me a minute. I've got a favor to ask."

I followed him, wondering what type of favor he could want and hoping it had nothing to do with my relationship with Greg. Sometimes people thought I had more influence with Greg's professional side than I actually did. We had an agreement. He didn't tell me how to make a mocha latte supreme, and I didn't tell him how to run his investigations.

Or at least I tried not to tell him. It wasn't my fault that people liked to talk to me and that I was amazing at putting pieces of puzzles together. Snoopy, my boyfriend would say, but even he'd have to admit I did have skill.

I didn't say anything to Harrold, just glanced around at the surroundings and waited for him to ask his favor. I didn't have to wait long.

"You're good at this investigating stuff." He sat in the chair across from me, leaning forward with his forearms on his thighs. "Right?"

I shrugged, not sure I liked this turn of conversation at all. At least if he wanted me to ask Greg for something, it was one and done. Ferreting out a vandal, though, that would be a whole 'nother project. "I guess so."

"No, you are. Darla says you should be some kind of PI or FBI gal, you're that good."

I felt my face heat. "I think Darla just likes telling good stories. She can overstate things sometimes."

"Whatever." He studied the chessboard and moved a knight into position. Then he returned his focus to me. "Can you find out who's doing this crap to my shop? I don't think your boyfriend has time to deal with real crime and find a two-bit vandal."

"Greg's very good at his job." I paused. Harrold was right, even though he didn't know why. Greg didn't have the time or energy to treat Harrold's issue as urgently as solving a murder. The investigation would have to take a secondary place in his schedule, that was just the way life went. I thought about Greg's latest warning to stay out of his investigations. At least this way, I wouldn't be helping him solve Sandra's murder. He couldn't be mad at me for looking out for a fellow shopkeeper. Besides, I mused, this kind of fell under the umbrella of the chamber liaison position if you thought about it.

I'd convinced myself. I pulled out my trusty purple notebook and opened to a clean page. "Tell me everything about the two events."

An hour later, I had made the bank deposit and dropped the receipt off at the shop. Sasha was taking my shifts, and she cornered me about her book club order so I finished that, as well. As I was walking home, I let my mind wander to what Harrold had told me about the vandalism, and I stopped in front of Diamond Lille's.

Maybe it was that simple.

I entered the restaurant and headed to my favorite booth. Since it was before noon, the place wasn't jammed, and as I sat, I noticed Lille at the counter talking to a man in leathers. His vest told me he was part of the gang who had been rumored to be dealing drugs in the area last year. Of course, they'd lawyered up, thrown a few guilty soldiers under the bus, and had claimed their mission was more of a social club than the dangerous street gang law enforcement suspected.

Carrie stopped at my table, her hands filled with menus and her order book from the table next to me. She held out a menu. "You know what you want or do you need one of these?"

I took the menu, nodding toward the counter. "Who's that with Lille?"

Carrie took a quick peek, then leaned closer to me. "Mick Evans, Ray's replacement. I don't know what draws her to the bad boys. You would have thought she'd learn after Ray went off to prison last year, but no. Same club even."

"They're dating?" I took in the broad shoulders and long, dark hair that he'd pulled back into a ponytail. The guy looked good in a motorcycle, bad-boy kind of way. He even had tattoos on each shoulder, which I could see since under the leather vest, Mick must have either worn a muscle shirt, or he'd cut the sleeves off the T-shirt underneath. Or maybe he was shirtless . . . My inner girl sighed. I could see the attraction—if he wasn't also part of a group that didn't think there should be any law but their own rules of life.

"I think dating is a little tame for what they're doing, but yeah, you could say that." Carrie shrugged. "He's in here most mornings, and I see him pick her up when she leaves the diner at night. I'm pretty sure she's staying with him. I'll be back for your order in a couple of minutes."

I opened the menu and noticed the flyer in the middle. A new salad, just for this week. Southern California mahimahi grilled and served over a mix of fresh greens, tomatoes, and peppers with a honey-mustard dressing. Lille's cook was going all out for this summer salad challenge. With the lunch choice done, I pulled out my notebook and started making notes about Lille and her new beau. Could he be the one who was messing with Harrold? Wanting to help Lille get Harrold to sell?

Darn it, I'd forgotten to ask Harrold what he'd fought with Lille about. I put that on a list of questions I needed answered. When Carrie came back, I closed the notebook. No use broadcasting my new project. While I waited for my food, I watched Lille walk Mick out to his bike, which was parked—illegally—on the sidewalk. The window in my booth was positioned perfectly for me to watch the couple say their good-byes without them noticing my attention. Which was good since the kiss was more heated than you'd usually see on the streets of South Cove.

They broke apart as a group of teenagers in a pickup went by the couple, hooting and honking. I was pretty sure I heard one boy yell, "Get a room." I didn't hear Lille's yelled response, but I heard Mick's deep laughter at her words. He slapped her on the butt, then started up his Harley. And then he was gone, making a U-turn on Main and roaring out toward the highway.

My food came, and I got lost reading while I enjoyed the salad. A thin man in jeans and a Coastal Museum T-shirt paused at my table. When I looked up, he grinned. "Sorry. I've been thinking about reading that book. How do you like it?"

I closed the book to show the cover, holding my fingers inside to save my place. "I love his work. I've read everything he's published, but this is over the top." I dug a business card out of my tote. "If you're really interested, stop by Coffee, Books, and More and give them this."

He took the card and turned it over. "Owner's discount—twenty percent off your first book purchase." He turned the card back over. "So you're Jill Gardner? You look too young to own a bookstore."

"Flattery will get you nowhere, buddy, I already gave you a discount." I grinned and reopened the book, but the man didn't leave the table. I closed the book again. "Something else?"

"Just wondering about the food here. I guess as a native, you must eat here a lot." He nodded at my salad bowl, which was almost empty. "What do you recommend?"

Wow, this guy didn't make a move without a recommendation. I guess he was the type of person the travel guides were made for—giving out specific instructions on how to be a good tourist. Eat here. Visit this site. Don't forget your camera. I decided to throw Lille a bone and hope she did the same when my shop's name came up in conversations. "I love everything. Well, not the chili, but that's because I don't eat beans. But I have friends who love that, too. So you can't go wrong with whatever you order."

The man nodded and turned. "Thanks for your honesty. I can be a pretty picky eater at times."

He walked away, and Carrie appeared with my check and a pitcher of iced tea. As she filled up my glass, she watched the man sit in a booth a few feet away. "You know that guy?"

I shook my head. "I thought he was a tourist. He asked about the book I'm reading. Why?"

Carrie pursed her lips and shook her head. "No reason. I've seen him around here a few times the last week or so. Maybe he's working on one of the construction projects down the highway."

"He doesn't look like a builder." I snuck a glance at the clean jeans and upscale tennis shoes. "Maybe he's a software geek from up north on a retreat. He really likes recommendations."

She turned toward his booth and whispered before she left. "Whoever he is, he's a good tipper, so I guess I'll let him stay."

When I got home, I had planned on starting the painting in the upstairs bedroom. Emma convinced me that a run was more important, so I didn't get upstairs to start painting until after two. I'd just laid out the painter's cloths to protect the floor when my phone rang.

"Hey, beautiful." Greg's voice filled the room as I put him on speaker. "What are you doing today?"

"Painting. Want to come help?"

Greg's laugh made me smile. "Sorry, I have to work. Just checking in to see if you'd heard from Rachel about the refund for the cruise. Maybe they can give us a credit for a future trip if we can't get the money back."

"She said she was working on it, but I'll stop by tomorrow and give her the option about the credit. That might make her job a little easier." I stopped rolling the paint on the wall. "Do you think we will be able to plan another trip?"

"Honey, murders don't happen every week. All I need is a clear day or two on the calendar, then anything that comes up is out of my control." Greg paused, lowering his voice. "We'll sneak out one night if we have to and call from the ship."

"You're so funny." I filled the roller with more of the peach color that was mellowing me out just with the little bit I'd painted so far. The room would be lovely when I was done. Two more rooms to remodel, then I needed to update both bathrooms, and my house would be all modern and reflect me, and not Miss Emily, the former owner.

Well, two rooms, the bathrooms, the basement, and the attic. I thought about turning the attic into a library.

I heard rustling on the other side of the line and Greg came back. "Sorry, I've got to go. I'll call you tomorrow. Maybe we can do lunch or something."

"Or something," I said into the dead phone. For having a boyfriend, I sure was eating a lot of meals alone. Not like Lille, I mused as I slathered paint on the walls.

By the time I'd finished painting the room, I was ready for a quiet evening on the porch finishing the book I'd started at lunch. My mind went back to the mystery tourist, and I wondered if he'd redeemed my coupon. I didn't give out many of the cards. Aunt Jackie gave out more, but for the ones I did hand over, more of my cards were redeemed than hers. A fact that made me smile every month as we compared marketing ideas.

I ignored the notebook with Harrold's problem and possible solutions that sat on the kitchen table as I walked through to grab a glass of wine and a piece of cheesecake. Tonight I was taking time off from all problems, both mine and those of South Cove.

A few hours later, when the car pulled up in the driveway, I waited for the door to slam and then called out to my aunt, "Come around the back."

The sun was setting, activating the solar-powered butterflies I'd put around the back fence between the yard and the driveway in the butterfly bushes. During the day, real butterflies visited the area, spinning around on their colorful wings. At night, the stationary insects glowed with one color then another. The best of both worlds.

My aunt opened the gate and shooed Emma back. She handed me a chilled bottle of white zinfandel. "Pour me a glass, won't you?"

"Are we drinking?" I glanced at my aunt's face. "If so, give me your keys."

She handed them over without a fuss. "I'm not sure yet, but I'll play by your rules."

I took the keys and the bottle into the kitchen, and when I returned I handed her a glass filled to the rim. "Tell me what's going on."

My aunt seemed to sink into herself. She took a sip of the wine, then another. Then she looked up at me and with tears in her eyes, she confessed.

# CHAPTER 10

"I'm old," my aunt said, her lips trembling in the soft light. "Somehow, somewhere, I became this." She waved a free hand over her body. "When did I turn old?"

"You are not old." I patted her hand, but she swatted me.

She took another sip. "I'm over seventy. In some cases, that's considered late admission to the nursing home set."

"You are active. You still hold a job. You love entertaining and going out to the theater and dinner." I rubbed my shoulder, which was throbbing from all the painting I'd done earlier. "I wish I could do as much as you can do in a day."

My aunt sniffed. "You could, if you stopped reading so much."

Great, now I was getting advice I didn't really want. "Look, you just need a project, something to get your mind off things. Are you and Josh still walking?"

"He says he's too tired from all of the excitement lately. I told him we were going Friday, no excuses."

I hid my smile. That was my aunt. You got one, maybe two days for your pity party, then it was back to life as normal. The fact she wasn't letting Josh get away with anything was a good sign. "Well, you have extra responsibilities this week anyway since I'm on vacation." I held my arms out like I was basking in the sun that had set a few minutes ago.

"Yet you still did the deposit. Late, but you went to the bank. I saw the receipt on the desk." Aunt Jackie took a sip of her wine. "I don't know, maybe I should sign up for a class. Bakerstown College has one on investing that might be interesting. And that way, I would know when I was being bamboozled out of my money."

"You were cheated. I don't think knowing more would have stopped that guy." Or maybe it would have. For a long time, all my aunt had lived for was traveling. Now, without most of the nest egg my uncle had left, she was stuck back at a full-time job in a small town that only changed for the seasons and the tourists. "On the other hand, taking a class might be just the boost you need right now."

"Of course, I'll be the oldest person there." My aunt sighed. "Maybe I should reconsider this plan. It's making me feel ancient already."

"You could totally hit on some hot forty-something who is looking for a cougar to complete his life," I teased, curling my feet up under me on the swing and throwing my lap quilt over my legs. The ocean breeze was starting to cool the air now that the sun's heat had left. As we watched the moon rise over the trees in the back, I thought about businesses and relationships. "Hey, is there any way to see if a business is doing well? I mean, without getting into their books? If someone was considering buying our shop, where would they go to see if it was profitable?"

My aunt didn't answer for a bit. "Are you thinking about selling the coffee shop?"

"What?" I choked on the swallow of wine I'd just taken. "No. I love the shop. Why would I sell?"

"Then what are you talking about?" My aunt refilled her glass from the wine bottle I'd left out on the porch so we wouldn't have to keep going into the kitchen.

"You can't tell Greg," I muttered, knowing I was wading into deep water.

Aunt Jackie groaned. "This is about Promote Your Event and Sandra's murder, right?"

"Maybe." I sat up straighter. "I was just wondering if there was a way to see if the business was as stable as they made it seem. I mean, they totally screwed up the Mission Run event, at least in the eyes of their client. Maybe they weren't doing a great job on other accounts."

My aunt considered the idea. "Well, I think they would have to file annual reports with the Bakerstown chamber. Kind of what we do for South Cove."

"We file annual reports?" I'd run the business for five years before my aunt arrived and I hadn't filed a report during that entire time.

"Well, we do now. I had to catch up all the late reporting when I got here last year. You were lucky Amy was ignoring your lack of submitting. I swear, you don't know half of what you need to know as a business owner. I've made a desk manual for you in case something happens to me or I just take off for Fiji."

"Don't talk like that." I thought about the work my aunt had done with the business side of the shop. At first, all I wanted was for her to babysit the shop for a week or two and then leave. Now I couldn't imagine running Coffee, Books, and More without her or the newly acquired staff we'd taken on. "I admit, I probably let too many things slide before you joined the team."

"Whatever, this isn't a dump-on-Jill session. I just said you didn't really understand the business side of things until I arrived. So, back to Promote Your Event. We could go to Bakerstown and see if they have filed their reports." My aunt patted my leg. "It's my understanding their business liaison is a paper Nazi about annual filings. We should find something."

"Would they put any problems they're having into a report?" I didn't want to drive to Bakerstown and find a crap load of nothing in the reports. "Isn't that just asking for trouble?"

"There will be clues. Like revenue for the reporting year versus estimated revenue for the upcoming year. You pay less in taxes if the revenue decreases and there's a valid reason. They may have been trying for a lower tax bracket." My aunt stood and grabbed the wine bottle. "Let's go inside and make a list of what we need to check out. I don't have to be at the shop until five. We should be done sleuthing by noon, and then you can buy me lunch at that little tapas place that went in next to the mall."

I followed my aunt into the house, calling Emma to come in, as well. Time to plan our attack. She'd already grabbed a new notebook from my office and was busy writing when I finally sat at the table, a plate of fruit in the middle and iced teas for both of us.

"So, we go to City Hall. Anywhere else?" I opened up my laptop in case we needed to do some virtual snooping.

Aunt Jackie tapped her pen. "What address do they list for the business? Their home, or do they actually have an office space?"

I searched the web to find the Promote Your Event website and came up with two. One in Bakerstown, and one in Orlando, Florida. I clicked on the link to the one in California. "Looks like they have a real office over near the courthouse." I read off the street address and she wrote it in the book.

"Now Google the street address and let's see what type of office building this is," Aunt Jackie directed.

When the picture of the building came up with a listing of several open luxury office opportunities, I frowned. "Most of the other clients are law firms or high-level accounting firms. How much work was Promote Your Event doing to afford digs like this?"

"The better question is, who were they doing it for?" My aunt wrote something down in her notebook. "This next search is going to take a while. I want you to look for any connections between Ashford and all the other companies in the building. So put Ashford, the plus sign, and then each of the other business names. One at a time."

I glanced at the clock. It was almost ten. "Fine, but I'll let you know right now I'm probably running out of steam in the next hour or so. I painted today."

"Poor baby." My aunt pointed at the iced tea. "Switch that out for coffee if you need to. I want to make sure we're not missing the obvious when we make our plan of attack for tomorrow."

I took a big sip of tea and grabbed my own notebook. My memory would be crap after a few of these searches, so I started writing down my search process, including the two Ashford links I'd found originally and the address search. No use starting at ground zero tomorrow just because I'd forgotten I'd already researched that idea.

A rap sounded on my bedroom door the next morning. Groaning, I turned over and looked, bleary-eyed, at my alarm. Six-oh-five. I was going to kill my aunt. I'd set her up in the third bedroom, where I had a bed made up for visitors. When I finished the real guest room, I planned on turning that room into a home gym. Greg had drawn out the plans for the equipment three different times already. He was pumped about the idea. But for now, it was my only guest room.

Aunt Jackie and I had called it a night minutes before two and she'd said we'd sleep in. I guess six o'clock was her idea of a lazy morning in bed.

"What? Is the house burning down?" I croaked when the rapping came again.

The door creaked open. My aunt called Emma to her side and sent her downstairs with a snap of her fingers. "I've got banana-peanut-butter muffins coming out of the oven in ten minutes. You have that long to shower and get ready. We've got a plan to develop."

Me and my big mouth. I had to get her involved in this investigation even though I'd promised myself I'd stay out of it. Greg was going to kill me. But what harm could we do in checking out Promote Your Event? It wasn't like the time we ran into the motorcycle gang at the storage center at the docks.

*Maybe it's exactly like that.* I shushed the logical part of my brain and stumbled to the bathroom.

Fifteen minutes later, I was buttering my second muffin and had consumed two cups of coffee. Four hours of sleep wasn't enough for anyone, yet my aunt looked chipper and alert. I hated her right now.

"So, first we'll stop by my apartment so I can change into jeans and a dark shirt." Aunt Jackie rattled off our schedule.

"We're not breaking in to the place. We're just looking for reports, right?" I glanced at the notebook I'd been working with last night. I'd gone through almost every renter in the business office building with no luck finding even a hint of a connection. I ripped off a page and put it on the center of the table. "We'll have to stop by these five places when we're there and see if there's some connection. They didn't have websites."

My aunt glanced at the list. "We'll have to think up a cover story." She stirred creamer into her coffee. "I know, we're thinking of hiring Promote Your Event for a media blitz and we're talking to people they've worked with. That should work, right?"

Honestly, that should be enough of a cover story to get us the reports we needed and explain why we were even in the building if anyone asked. "You're a genius."

My aunt sipped her coffee. "You think you got your smarts from your father's side?"

I fed Emma my last bite of muffin then stretched as I stood to take my dishes to the sink. "I'm going to need a nap later." I let Emma out the back door and filled up her water and food dishes. By the time I was finished, my aunt had her purse and stood at the front door.

"Let's go. By the time I've changed and we drive over, the records department at City Hall should be open. Then we'll go to the office building. Follow me in the Jeep. I'll leave my car at the apartment." Then she disappeared into her sedan.

I watched as she turned onto the street and headed to town. Locking up the house, I muttered, "Abandon hope, all ye who enter here. Or follow their crazy aunts."

We were still ten minutes early when we pulled up in front of Bakerstown City Hall. I dialed Amy and waited for her answer.

"South Cove City Hall, how may I direct your call?" Amy's too-perky voice hurt my eardrum.

"Hey, it's me." I glanced at my aunt, who was accessorizing her spy outfit with a black and white silk scarf tied around her neck. Yep, that would be inconspicuous. "What do you call the annual reports businesses file with South Cove?"

"Annual reports? I guess we call them 1062s because that's the form number." Amy paused. "Don't worry about filing; your aunt has done all of yours since you opened the business. You're not due for a new one until January."

"She told me." I put the phone against my other ear. "Actually, we're looking for the name that Bakerstown would call the report. Are they still 1062s?"

Amy laughed. "Of course not. Each town sets up their own form numbering system, silly. Seriously, did you pay attention in civics class at all?"

"I don't need a lecture." My head throbbed. "Do you know what they call them or not?"

My aunt pointed at the clock on the dash. Time for the office to open.

I held up one finger, motioning her to wait.

"Well, aren't you grumpy this morning? Of course I know what they are called. I've worked with their city planner for years trying to standardize the form. Bakerstown In-City Business Annual Report form. Boring bureaucratic form 101."

"Thanks, Amy. I'll call you later if I'm available for lunch."

My aunt raised her eyebrows. "You won't be back for lunch, you know that."

"I will be if this turns out to be nothing but a dead end," I muttered as I stepped out of the car. I waited for my aunt to meet me at the bottom of the stairs, then used the remote to lock the door. As the car beeped, we started up the marble steps to the front door, where a too-modern security system invited us to put our purses on the scanner along with any metal objects in our clothes.

"Pretty fancy system for a small county." Aunt Jackie turned to the security guard. "Who paid for this?"

He shrugged. "Homeland, I guess. All I know is you need to walk through that scanner."

She walked through, then glared at me. "Our tax dollars at work. No wonder our rates keep increasing. They have to scan every grannie who comes in to pay her water bill."

I kept my head down and didn't meet her eyes. No way was I going to play into her conspiracy notions, especially when the security guards had real guns strapped on their belts along with handcuffs and what I assumed was a Taser. One jolt with that and my aunt's heart might just stop beating.

"Be good," I whispered as soon as I was close to her. We were waiting for our purses to make it through the scanning process along with a man in a suit who tapped his foot constantly as he waited. Something about him seemed familiar, then I realized it was the other jerk from the California Mission Society. Oscar. I turned to face the man, catching him by surprise.

"Hello there. We just keep running into each other. Are you following me?" I smiled and turned it up a notch as he stared, then quickly shook his head.

He reached over in front of me and grabbed his wallet and keys, stuffing them into his pocket, then took the handle of his briefcase and tucked it under his arm. "Believe me, Miss Gardner, I have much more pressing business than to follow a shopkeeper from South Cove around all day."

I watched him stride away, aiming toward the bank of elevators.

"Friend of yours?" My aunt stood next to me, holding out my purse.

I slung the tote over my neck. "Member of the Mission Society. I don't think the man has a friendly bone in his body. He's been rude and snide every time I've met him."

We stepped toward the elevators, but by the time we checked the directory, the man was gone. As we waited for our ride to the fifth floor and the Business Records Department, my aunt watched the floor indicators on the various elevators. "Some people just don't know how to be nice." She nodded to the far elevator, which had stopped on the top floor. It was also the elevator that Oscar had taken. "Especially those who think they are above everyone else."

A woman with a cheery smile and a name tag that read *Madeline* greeted us as soon as the elevator doors opened on the fifth floor. Apparently the Business Records Department took up the entire floor. South Cove records were filed in a basement room with one light and a table. And what I assumed were mice, due to the traps Amy had to clear out once a week.

This looked like a modern doctor's office with a large waiting room and a receptionist who could schedule your next appointment and take your payment for your bill.

"Welcome to Bakersfield Records Department. What can I do for you this glorious day?" Madeline gave us her entire attention as we stepped off the elevator. As we approached, she held up one finger and answered a phone call using her headset with a built-in microphone. She routed the call and then refocused on us. "Sorry about that. Anita is supposed to be on the phones, but she hasn't shown up yet."

My aunt leaned close to the reception desk. "We need to review the business filings for a"—she pretended to stop and check her notes—"oh, there it is, Promote Your Event?"

Madeline handed her a clipboard with a pen. "Fill this out and provide the twenty-dollar copy fee and we'll have copies ready for you by two."

"That's it? A form and a fee?" I couldn't believe we were getting this lucky.

The receptionist took another call before she answered. "I'm going to kill that woman when she finally gets in. Seriously, who can't get to work by nine?" She shook her head. "Sorry, you don't want to hear about my problems. Anyway, if Anita was here, I could get them done as you wait, but a girl only has two hands."

We went to the lobby area to fill out the form. "I guess I'd better call Amy and change lunch to tomorrow."

Aunt Jackie didn't even look up from the magazine she was studying. "I told you so."

# CHAPTER 11

After leaving our request form and the mandatory copy fee with Madeline, we headed over to check out the building where Promote Your Event was housed. The Jeep was parked in the county parking lot, so we walked the two blocks to our next stop. The smell of flowers masked the traffic fumes even though Bakerstown had ten times as much car activity as South Cove. It almost felt like walking down Main Street at home—with a lot larger buildings and more people. South Cove businesses called Wednesdays the dead zone. Typically we only had those few vacationers who had booked an entire week at one of the bed-and-breakfasts in town wandering through. And most of those were heading to the beach to relax for the day.

"It's nice here." I dodged an oncoming pair of women in suits heading toward the courthouse. "In a formal business kind of way."

Aunt Jackie sniffed and made a face. "You can't smell the ocean here. It's just a nice little town with summer flowers lining the streets."

"Can you believe Josh wants to put air fresheners up on the street lamps? You'd think he'd just focus on buying dehumidifiers for his shop rather than say something that stupid." I laughed, but when I saw the look of anger on my aunt's face, I started walking faster.

"Can we not talk about that man?"

"Sure, sorry. I wasn't thinking." I paused at a restaurant that had their menu posted. The place was a bar and grill but seemed to turn that definition into something a lot more upscale than the dive places where Greg and I liked to eat that lined the coastal highway. I pointed to the menu. "This place looks good. Maybe we can stop here on our way back."

*Yes, it is all about the food for me.* My stomach grumbled at the thought of crab cakes and a lobster roll, topped off with a dark craft beer.

"Maybe. I'd rather have sushi if there's someplace close." My aunt looked at the wrought-iron fence enclosing the patio. "I guess they are afraid of walk offs."

I hurried to catch up with her. "A lot of places enclose their outdoor seating. There's a lot of good reasons to do it besides walk-off customers."

"Get the money up front, makes people honest." My aunt paused, touching the black grate fence. "Reminds me of a prison yard, not a place to relax."

Boy, I was striking out on acceptable conversation starters today. I scanned the area, but it took a few minutes before I found a new topic. A woman passed us carrying a small toy Maltese. I pointed at the dog. "I think Harrold's getting a replacement for Tiny, finally."

My aunt turned her head. "Harrold?"

I nodded. "The Train Station owner? Over by Diamond Lille's? Haven't you met him yet?"

She shook her head. "I don't believe so. When I moved here, he'd just lost his wife, so he wasn't attending any of the committee meetings. I think the last time I stopped by with a marketing basket from the shop, a young man was running the shop."

"That must be his grandson. I'm going to invite him to our next Business-to-Business meeting to talk about websites. I guess The Train Station is getting most of their orders online these days."

Aunt Jackie looked thoughtful. "It makes sense. People are too busy with their lives to visit a hobby store. Unless it's in the same place as the normal weekend errands, ordering online would be much more convenient."

We walked in silence for a while. I thought about the bookstore part of the shop. We could do announcements and book club meeting schedules on our website. Currently the page had a picture of the shop, a pickup order menu for the coffee selections, and our address and phone number. I'd seen better sites for estate attorney's offices when I was researching the building last night. "Do you think we should increase our web presence?"

My aunt nodded. "Let's see what he has to say and talk to Sasha about this. She's always on that tablet of hers. She could give us some practical advice."

One more thing for my to-do list, but at least this one I was starting to get excited about. I started listing off all the possible things we could add, when my aunt held up her hand.

"Stop. We're here." She pointed to the address in gold block letters on the side of the all-white building.

I held open the door and went to the directory posted by the elevator. I found the listing for the Ashfords' office. "Seventh floor, suite seven-fifteen."

When we arrived, the elevator doors opened onto a white hallway. As we stepped out, a glass-windowed sitting room dead-ended to our right, so we turned left. The hallway stretched out in front of us.

"Remind you of something?" My aunt took a step toward the end.

As we passed office after office, I tried to place my unease. "Crap, this setup is just like *The Shining*. If two little girls ask us to play, I'm throwing you in front of them so I can escape to the elevator."

She giggled, grabbing my arm like a vise grip. "You'll drag me with you. Either both of us are getting out, or neither."

"You're very selfish." I fake-winced under the grip. "But strong."

"I've started lifting weights with a video at home. You should try it." My aunt stopped me at a glass door. The lights were off, but *Promote Your Event* was written in black paint on the door. Along with *Sandra and Michael Ashford, Owners.* "Here we are, but I don't think it's open."

I jiggled the door. Locked. A handwritten sign had been taped on the inside of the door. *Closed due to a death in the family. Reopening soon. Leave a message on our phone machine and we'll get back to you.* I'd had to write one of those *closed because of death* notes before, but boy, this guy had even left the phone number on the bottom. "He sure didn't want to miss out on any business."

"It's a little odd, I'll grant you that, but it's amazing customer service." My aunt tapped the bottom of the door, where mail had been shoved through a slot. "From the looks of it, the place has been closed for days. Look at all that."

Sandra had been dead less than a week, and the office floor looked like there was at least two months' worth of bills piled up. I heard a door open behind me.

"Sorry, they're closed," a woman behind us said.

We turned to see the blonde dressed in a conservative dress with a blazer over the top. I put on my best *just wondering* smile and asked, "How long have they been out of the office?"

The woman locked her door, putting the keys in a bag that I was sure was a knock off. If she was one of the attorneys at that law firm, they weren't pulling in any money. "I can't be sure, but it's been a couple of weeks now. My husband and I went to Mexico for our anniversary at the first of the month, and when I got back, they were gone."

"I guess I'll just call and leave a message then. Thanks for your help." I wrote the number down in my notebook.

"No problem. I hope you reach them. That brunette's been here quite a few times this week and says Michael never calls her back." The woman waved and headed to the bank of elevators.

"Brunette?" Aunt Jackie glanced around the hallway, then pointed to an upper corner where a camera with a blinking light was situated. "Maybe your boyfriend should check out the security feeds for the building."

Sure, I'd get right on asking him to do that. And right after he gave me a lecture about staying out of his investigations, he'd probably just break up with me to solve all of these types of issues in the future. "I'm sure Greg's already on it. Let's go check out the other five businesses."

We split up the names and agreed to meet at the bar and grill we'd passed on our way at noon. "Just don't seat us outside in the cage. I've spent my time behind bars, I don't need a reminder," my aunt said.

"You were in there less than twenty-four hours, it's not like you did time," I reminded her. Aunt Jackie had stolen a secret account book from a guy who made his business setting up phony travel plans for gullible seniors. The guy had pressed charges, but changed his mind once the book was discovered and proved his shady business practices. My aunt had been telling tales of the big house ever since.

"Still traumatic." She claimed the first elevator that was going up for her two stops. I waited for another one that would take me down to the sixth floor.

"Still dramatic," I countered to myself as I stood looking out the window at the sunny day.

It took me less than an hour to talk to the three businesses on my list. None of them had even known Promote Your Event was housed in the same building. At my last stop, I did get an offer from the CPA in 502B to take over our accounting and tax filing. The guy handed me a folder with a couple of handouts including *Five Reasons You Need an Accountant* and *Top Ten Warning Signs Your Business Is Failing*. He also had his business card and a 10-percent discount coupon on our first month of services tucked in the promotional handout. I thanked him for his time and hurried out to meet Aunt Jackie for lunch.

I found her at a table near the window, an iced tea already waiting for me. "How'd Operation Ashford go?"

My aunt rolled her eyes. "Seriously? That's all you got? Operation Ashford? You'd never be a good spy. You might as well call it Operation Digging Up Dirt to Find Sandra's Killer."

I scanned the menu. Crab cake appetizer, check, but no lobster roll. I settled on a fish-and-chips basket to go with my crab cakes. I set the menu down and took out the folder, handing it over to Aunt Jackie. "Here, in case we want to hire an accountant."

She raised her eyebrows but took it. "Do you think I'm doing a bad job?"

I spit out the sip of tea I'd just taken. Grabbing a napkin, I mopped up the liquid. "No. One of the names on my list was a CPA, and in order to get what I wanted to know, I had to listen to his sales spiel." I tapped the folder. "And we get ten percent off his services."

"We don't have an accountant now, so that's a ninety percent increase in costs." She shook her head. "Honestly, until the shop starts making some real money, we're better off hiring and supporting our staff with a livable wage than adding on costs like this."

"You don't have to convince me. Like I said, I had to listen to a twenty-minute sales pitch just to find out the guy had never even known the Ashfords had an office in the building." I sipped my tea. "How did you do?"

"I talked to Amanda Forest, who runs an organizational design consulting company. She knew about the Ashfords and had talked to Sandra about doing some joint cold calls on local businesses. I guess she thought the two services worked well together, but from what Amanda said, Sandra wasn't interested in any partnership." Aunt Jackie leaned forward. "Amanda got the impression that Sandra was closing the business."

"That doesn't make any sense. When we met with the Mission

Society, Adam made it very clear that we would be working with Michael's company next year if we chose to host another run."

Our waitress came and took our orders just then. Me with my fried food delight. Aunt Jackie with a fresh salad with grilled tuna on top. As she walked away, I noticed the tourist guy from yesterday's lunch at Diamond Lille's. He was sitting at the bar, his lunch appearing to be almost finished. I waved, but he turned away, apparently not recognizing me from our short conversation yesterday.

"Who's that?" My aunt smoothed her napkin on her lap.

"I met him in town yesterday. We were talking about books and I gave him my special discount card. Let me know if he comes in and uses it during your shift, okay?"

My aunt stared at me. "Why?"

I glanced back at the man, who was now laying cash on the bar for his meal and leaving the restaurant. "I don't know. There's just something off about him."

"He's very attractive." She watched as he exited through the door farthest away from our table and turned down the street away from our window.

"I'm not interested in him that way. I just think it's odd he's here at lunch and he was at Lille's yesterday. Doesn't he have a job?" I pulled out my notebook and wrote down everything I could remember about the guy's appearance.

"You were in both places having lunch yourself. Is there something odd about you?"

"That's not the point." I started to explain, but then our waitress arrived with our food and my attention turned to eating. Especially after my stomach growled as the smell of French fries distracted me.

I'd already polished off the crab cakes when my aunt paused from her salad feast. "Did you get his name?"

"The tourist, no. But Carrie said she's seen him in the diner before." I started attacking my fish and chips. "It's probably nothing. Something about him just feels off, you know?"

She nodded. Pausing her fork midway to her mouth, her eyes widened. "I forgot to tell you about the second person on the list. It was a campaign office for a local county commissioner."

"They might have used a PR firm." I considered all the political ads that had just finished running for the primary elections last month. You couldn't turn on a local station without hearing about one or more candidates who were going to clean up the county or state or federal government. Match a name to the office, and you had the same commercial, over and over. *He's bad, I'm good. Vote for me.*

"Exactly." My aunt took the bite.

I waited for her to finish her thought, but when she didn't continue, I prompted, "So, did they hire the Ashfords?"

"Who?' She frowned as she considered my question. "Oh, the campaign office? I don't know. No one was there. I got the feeling they'd lost the campaign and moved out."

"Great, no lead there." I dunked a French fry into the restaurant's "special sauce," which appeared to be a mixture of ketchup and cocktail sauce.

Aunt Jackie pushed her salad away, half eaten. She took a round, flowered pillbox out of her purse and took one of the white pills with a big swallow of tea. "Actually, it does give us a clue. If the Ashfords did work for the candidate, they would have had to file a more detailed financial statement with the county. So, the records we get from Madeline"—she paused as she checked her watch—"in less than an hour, might just have a peek at the company's financial records."

My aunt was good at this investigation thing. I felt bad we were going behind Greg's back, but honestly, he and I hadn't really talked about the murder. And he hadn't told me to stay out of things specifically. At least, not this time. Besides, our research would probably turn up nothing and there wouldn't be anything for me to have to tell Greg.

And my aunt seemed happier than she'd been in days. That was worth any lecture I'd get from Greg, especially when I told him about her arthritis. She just wanted to feel useful again.

I finished my lunch as I listened to her talk about how she and Uncle Ted had been part of the campaign staff for Jerry Brown's first term as California's governor. I hadn't heard this story before, and the fact that they were so involved in the local politics made me smile. My aunt had lived a long and exciting life. And if she needed some investigatory play every once in a while, I guess she deserved it.

"Hey, Harrold wants me to find out who's been vandalizing his shop. Do you want to help me with that?"

She didn't answer but nodded her head toward the door. "Look who just showed up for lunch?"

I turned my head and saw Rachel Fleur enter. The travel agent was laughing at something her male companion had said. As I waited for him to come through the door, all I could see was a suit jacket. Then the hostess walked them toward us and to the back, and I got a good look at Rachel's companion.

Michael Ashford followed the hostess to a table, his arm wrapped around Rachel's waist.

"Looks like the grieving widower has a new playmate," my aunt observed as she motioned our waitress over to the table.

# CHAPTER 12

After picking up the envelope from Madeline at the records department, we headed back to South Cove. As I drove, Aunt Jackie read through some of the pages. A few minutes in, she stuffed everything back into the large manila envelope and set it on the seat in the back. She leaned back in her seat and closed her eyes. "You go through those tonight. My head is pounding, and I still have to work in a couple of hours."

"You okay, besides the headache?" I glanced over at my aunt, who looked a little pale and drawn.

"Stop fretting over me. I didn't get much sleep last night on that mattress of yours. You really need to upgrade when you set up your new guest room." She snapped the words, then sighed. "Seriously, I'm fine. Nothing that a long, hot bath and a good night's sleep won't fix."

I pulled the Jeep into our small private parking lot behind the shop and turned off the engine. "Here we are."

Pausing as she opened the door, she looked back at me. "Do not tell me you're going in to work now. Isn't this supposed to be your vacation?"

"Some vacation," I muttered. My aunt opened her mouth to say something else, but I held up my hand. "Don't start. I'm not working. I'm going to Josh's to see if I can find a bed frame for the guest room. I'd rather have an antique than go to the furniture store and buy something new."

"You'll have to buy a new mattress and box springs anyway." She left the Jeep, shutting the door and meeting me in front of the steps that led up to her apartment.

I shrugged. "I know, but I really want one of those old wrought-iron beds. Besides, he might also have a dresser and one of those full-sized mirrors. And I need to find a quilt shop and see if I can snag a proper quilt."

"You seem to have a vision." My aunt took the first few steps slowly up toward her apartment. "Call me if you find something you don't understand in the filings. I'll expect a full report tomorrow morning."

"Yes, sir!" I clicked my heels together and threw her a salute, which did no good since I was wearing flip-flops and her back was turned to me.

"Don't be a smart butt." As she opened her apartment door, she waved to me and then was gone. I stood there considering the location of my aunt's apartment and her condition and wondered what I was going to do if she couldn't handle stairs anymore. When we'd talked last night about her health, I'd been supportive, but dismissive of the changes that might be coming. Now, everywhere I looked, I thought about my aunt and her ability to stay independent. Remodeling a guest room on the second floor of the house might not have been the best idea.

I clicked the remote to lock the Jeep and went to wander through Josh's store. If I was lucky, his new employee, Kyle, would be working instead of the owner.

Unfortunately, when the bell rang over the door, Josh looked up from a chair behind his counter. He'd been reading something that he quickly tucked under the counter. "What do you want now, Miss Gardner?"

"Well, good afternoon to you, too. I'm surprised your store isn't packed with customers as warmly as you welcome people to your shop." I closed the door and started scanning the first room for anything that even resembled bedroom furniture. Just because I thought I knew what I wanted didn't mean that I couldn't be swayed toward the right surprise find.

"You aren't a customer," he said flatly. "You just run that meeting where we never really talk about the problems facing the shop owners of South Cove. What a complete waste of my time."

I squinted my eyes and stared at him. "Like the issue of removing the sea air from South Cove's streets?" I paused. "Important items like that?"

To his credit, he actually blushed. "I may have gone a bit far on that agenda item."

I took a breath and pushed away all the things I wanted to say. "We can agree on that. But today, I'm actually here as a customer." I went on to explain what I was looking for, and Josh pointed me toward the far back room.

"If I have anything like that bed you described, it will be back there. There isn't a lot of demand for pieces like that." He tapped a finger against his lips. "But let me look at my notebook. Maybe someone called with a consignment I haven't accepted yet."

I left him poring through a three-ring loose-leaf notebook with pages sticking out the sides. The book must have been three inches thick, but it was stuffed beyond full. Unless he had some organization system that wasn't apparent, he'd be flipping through pages for days.

I wandered through the rooms, reaching out to touch the polished wood on furniture that had been made and used years before I was even born. I imagined the scratches on the legs were from being moved from one house to another year after year. If these items could talk, what story would they tell of the people who owned them? I pulled out my cell and took a picture of a walnut full-length mirror I absolutely loved. The wood frame was carved in curls at the top and bottom of the mirror. I spied a quilt holder next to it and took a picture of that, too. The quilt on the rack was too faded and worn for actual usage, but it would fit in the corner of the room next to the window perfectly.

I pushed through to the next room. This was piled high with bedroom furniture. Wooden sleigh beds, dressers, and nightstands filled the room. I wandered through the area, taking pictures of some items I might consider, but when I reached the end of the room I'd run out of options for the bed frame.

Disappointed, I wandered back to the front and stopped at the counter. Josh was still leafing through the notebook.

"You find anything?" I leaned over the counter, trying to see the page.

He pulled the book away. "If I had, I would have said something." He put a book in between pages like a bookmark and closed the notebook." He looked at my empty hands. "I suppose you were unsuccessful, as well?"

"Kind of." I pulled out my phone and showed him the pictures of the items I'd found. "Can you write me up an estimate of these? And hold them until I make a decision?"

"Why don't I drag them over to your house so you can see how they look inside, too? That way, if you don't want them, I can just bring them back here."

I thought about the convenience, then saw the look on his face and realized he wasn't serious. "It won't hurt you to hold the items for a week or so. If you get an offer before I make up my mind, just call me."

Josh wrote down the descriptions of the three items on an order pad with the word *estimation* circled twice. "I suppose I can do that." He paused, his breathing heavy from the exertion of standing up, I guessed. "How is Jackie? I haven't seen her today."

"We went in to Bakerstown for a few things this morning. She'll be working in the shop this evening. You can ask her yourself." I headed to the door and put my hand on the knob. "Just be gentle with her. I haven't seen her this upset in forever."

As I left the antique store, I thought I heard Josh mumble, "This is all my fault."

By the time I arrived home, Emma was begging for a run. Since she'd been good and hadn't chewed up anything while I was gone, I thought I'd reward her. I ran upstairs, changed, and for a few minutes, forgot about the craziness surrounding my life.

When I returned home, a truck was parked in my driveway and Greg sat texting on my porch. Emma pulled on the leash to greet him, so I let her off as soon as I was inside the front yard fence. He didn't have time to put his phone away before being attacked by the Slobber Queen.

"What a good girl," he crooned, leaning in to Emma's fuzzy body. "Who's a good girl?"

My dog wiggled in pleasure, then barked a response. She loved Greg. She'd just had a run. Her life was heaven right now. I walked around the lovefest and unlocked the door. "Can you stay for dinner? I'm sure I have something I can make."

"Best offer I've had all day." Greg followed me into the house, and when we entered the kitchen, he let Emma out the back door, grabbing her water dish. He walked over to the sink. "I don't want to watch another minute of video. Do you know how boring it is to watch nothing happen for hours?"

"I can imagine." I decided bringing up the video feed for the Ash-fords' hall could wait for a better time. I opened the freezer. "Brats?"

Greg finished washing out the dish and filled it for Emma. He set it next to her half-full food dish and returned to the kitchen. "Perfect. Especially if you make that olive oil potato salad."

"Sounds like a plan." I took out the meat and put it in the microwave to defrost, then grabbed a pan and filled it with red potatoes from the vegetable stand I kept on a wooden cart in the corner of the kitchen. Taking the potatoes to the sink, I washed and prepped them, then started some eggs boiling, as well. Finally I joined Greg at the table. "You look tired."

He put his hand on mine and pulled it to his mouth, kissing the palm. "I am tired. And I just can't help thinking we'd be sitting deck side looking at icebergs and drinking some fruity drink that's served with an umbrella right now."

"Life happens." I guess I should have said "murder happens," but Greg knew what I meant. "I've been busy anyway. I got to spend some quality time with Aunt Jackie this morning, and I went shopping for furniture for the guest room."

"Any luck?" Greg leaned back in his chair and studied me. "Do I need to go pick something up in the truck?"

I shook my head. "Not yet. I'm going in to Bakerstown tomorrow to see if I can find something at the flea market over on Bloomer Street. If I run into something, I might just borrow your truck and run back to get it." I pushed my notebook to the other side of the table, hoping he would think I'd been making notes about planning the remodel and not about Sandra's murder. "Sorry the videos were a bust. You didn't see anything on them?"

Greg tapped the table with his fingers, then shrugged. "I've got a clear shot of Sandra walking through town and right past the bed-and-breakfast where they were staying. Then after Diamond Lille's, the feed ends. I guess the council didn't get the rest of the cameras installed to the end of Main yet."

"Too bad, you might have been able to find who's been messing with Harrold if they had."

"Poor guy. He doesn't need this kind of harassment." Greg ran his hand through his hair. "So, Sandra was heading out toward the highway, and that's the last she was seen until Josh found her the next morning."

"Maybe it was just a hit-and-run," I theorized.

"That's a rational theory, except"—he paused, looking at me—"we're just talking, right? No trying to solve the case on your own, promise?"

Darn, now I felt like a total heel. But I hadn't done anything to get myself in hot water yet. And Aunt Jackie had enjoyed our little trip. Tomorrow I'd tell Aunt Jackie we needed to focus on Harrold's request for help and ignore the stack of Promote Your Event filings sitting on the backseat of my Jeep. I held up my hand. "I promise."

Greg laughed. "Somehow I don't believe you, but this one point has me confused and I'd appreciate your input. You are good at these puzzles."

"Gee, thanks?" I leaned forward a little, my heartbeat speeding up to match my excitement. "Why can't this be a hit-and-run?"

"Because whoever ran over Sandra did it three times. Doc's found evidence of the initial hit, then two sets of tire tracks where the driver drove back over the body." He watched me as I thought about his words.

"A hit-and-run would have been a single strike. Unless there were three vehicles involved, and even then, one of the drivers would have felt a stab of conscience and reported the accident by now."

Greg nodded. "Exactly. So, whoever hit Sandra went back to make sure the job was done. Not to mention the fact they got out of the car and moved her body off the road to the trail."

His words triggered a memory, and I stood and opened the cupboard over the washer, retrieving the Baggie with the cup I'd found a few days ago. I put it on the table in front of him.

"What's this?" He turned the cup over and read the logo. "A cup for the winery? Am I running prints or DNA?"

"Stop teasing." I leaned against the kitchen wall. "I found that on my run on Sunday and thought you might be interested. It was on the road by where the dump site was located."

Greg sighed and put the cup aside. "Even if there is something, do you know how much trash we collected after the race? Someone could have thrown this out of their car weeks ago."

"Look, I know it's a long shot, but I didn't want to leave it there, just in case." I walked to the cabinet and grabbed the kettle-cooked potato chips and a jar of salsa from the fridge. I poured the chips into a large wooden bowl and the salsa into a container shaped like Texas that I'd gotten as a present years ago. I returned to the table with the treats and a handful of napkins. "Going back to the hit-and-run, there's one other reason they would run someone over more than once. Maybe the killer was too angry to stop. You know, that whole act of passion thing."

We munched on the snack, not talking for a few minutes. Then Greg glanced out at Emma, who stood at the screen door watching us eat, drool dripping from her chin. "One more thing, I saw several coyotes wandering through the streets. You may not want to keep Emma outside for very long. And definitely not when you're not home."

"Great, there go my new sofa pillows." I wiped the grease from my hands and glanced toward the living room. "You sure they're coyotes and not just wild dogs?"

Greg stood and let Emma inside. She went directly to her kitchen bed and curled up to sleep. "Either way, they could do a lot of damage, especially if they're running in a pack."

"Better tell Esmeralda, too. I'd hate to see something happen to Maggie." I turned off the eggs and checked on the potatoes. "I need about twenty minutes on this salad before we can start the brats."

"Then why don't we go sit outside and you can catch me up on what you and your aunt did today." Greg headed to the fridge. "You want a soda?"

What I wanted was to not talk about my day. "Sure, but can I show you what I got done on the guest room instead?" I took the soda can and leaned in to him. "I'd like your opinion on a few things."

He groaned but nodded, kissing the top of my head. "Let's go." As we took the stairs, he opened his cola. "Who's Maggie?"

It was still early by the time we'd finished cooking, eating, and cleaning up after dinner. Wiping down the counter, I put my hand on the coffeepot. "You want some dessert and coffee? Or popcorn and a movie?"

He came behind me and put his arms around me. "Sorry, I'm going to have to take option three and head back to the apartment. I'm beat. Can I buy you dinner Friday night?"

"Dress up or fast food?" I sank into his hug, feeling the warmth of his arms and body ease the tension in my own. I closed my eyes and swayed with him.

"How about somewhere in between? There's a new diner over in Bakerstown. Kind of American casual, or that's what the signs are saying." He kissed my neck, then turned me around for a proper kiss. My knees buckled as I fell into the softness of his lips.

When we came up for air, I smiled. "I guess I won't wear my LBD then."

Greg stared into my eyes. "I'll bite, what's an LBD?"

"Little black dress. I've got a new one that's backless that I was going to wear on the cruise for the Captain's Dinner." I started walking with him toward the front door.

"Maybe once this case is done, we can go up to Napa Valley and spend a night at that winery we like. You can wear the LBD then." He paused again at the door. "You know, you're pretty special. Most women would have gone on the cruise without me."

"What fun would that be?" I touched the curve of his face and felt the stubble from his beard breaking through. "I would have had to find my own dance partners for each evening."

He touched my hair, then tapped me on the nose. "Honey, you wouldn't have to look far."

I stood in the doorway as he walked to his truck, the plastic Baggie in hand. When he saw me he waved me inside with a hand gesture that said, *Lock the door, now.* I gave him one last wave and retreated into my house.

When I knew he was gone, I unlocked the door and headed to the car.

# CHAPTER 13

By two that morning, all I'd found in my reading of the Promote Your Event filing reports was that the couple was often late on reporting and fairly incomplete with their accounting. And the reports were always filed by Sandra, according to the signatures on the receipts. "A hundred pages down, twice that to go." I stood and walked the pile into my office, placing them on the top of my desk. I shut the door after me and grabbed a bottle of water to take with me upstairs to bed. Time to crash.

I'd turned off my alarm for the week since I didn't have to be anywhere anytime, but my phone rang promptly at seven. I didn't check the caller ID before answering. "Yes?"

"Is this Jill?" A man's voice that seemed familiar brought me out of my sleep daze. I guessed five hours' sleep would have to do today.

"You're talking to her. Who is this?" I swung my feet over the side of the bed, waiting for an answer.

"Harrold, down at The Train Station? They hit again last night. You have to come see this." He swore a few choice words that I didn't realize he knew and then came back on the line. "Sorry, but it's bad. Can you come down?"

"I'll be right there." So much for sleeping in. I grabbed some clothes and headed to the bathroom to freshen up, which mostly meant washing my face, brushing my teeth, and pulling my hair back into a ponytail. Getting dressed took another three minutes, so even with the five-minute walk, I was at The Train Station in less than ten.

This time the damage was more severe. Instead of the windows being painted, the front window had been smashed. The park bench that typically sat on the edge of the sidewalk to provide seating for holiday parades now tilted awkwardly on the edge of the windowsill. Harrold was talking to Toby when I arrived.

As I walked up to the pair, Harrold turned toward me. "See? I can't take all of this. I thought you were going to find out who was doing this and stop it!"

"Sir, we are looking for the guy." Toby looked at me with a shrug and took Harrold's arm. "Now, if we can just finish your statement."

Harrold pulled his arm away from Toby. "Not you. You and your boss are worthless. I asked Jill to solve this problem. But all that seems to be happening is that it's getting worse."

I pulled Harrold to one side. "Look, I'm working on it, but you need to talk to Toby right now and we'll talk later." I waited for Harrold's nod, then I waved Toby over. "He's ready."

Toby looked at me. "Greg's not going to be happy when I tell him about this."

"Then don't tell him." I put my hand on his chest. "Seriously, don't say anything. If I find something that implicates someone in this problem, I'll tell you. I'm not going to run out and get myself hurt. I'm just doing some of the legwork since you guys are all involved in solving Sandra's murder."

We stood frozen for a second while Toby considered his options. He shuffled back and forth on his feet, and with that one movement, I knew I'd won the argument.

"Fine, but if you find out anything, you tell me so I can check it out. You don't need to be talking to whatever nut job could have done this." He frowned down at me. "Promise me?"

I nodded. "Paper chasing only." I held my hand up. "Scout's honor."

"From what your aunt's told me, you were never a scout." A smile creased his face.

"Details don't matter. I'm sure I would have been an excellent Girl Scout."

"Don't make me regret this."

I nodded to the matching park bench still on the sidewalk in front of Diamond Lille's. "I'll wait over there for you to finish your report."

I took my notebook out of my tote and started writing notes about

Harrold's misfortunes. My thoughts kept going back to Carrie's comment about Lille and why Harrold didn't visit the diner anymore.

Before I could finish the thought, a black Harley pulled up next to the diner and Lille got off. She kissed the man driving, and as he turned back around to leave South Cove, she watched until we could no longer see the bike. As she turned, the wide smile that had been gracing her face fell as she saw me sitting on the bench.

"What are you doing here?" She put her hands on her hips. "Trying to steal my breakfast customers with your little cookie stand?"

"Coffee, Books, and More isn't a cookie stand," I countered. Taking a deep breath, I pushed past Lille's barb. "I'm waiting on Harrold. We're coming in for breakfast right after he deals with the latest attack on his shop."

Lille turned and gasped when she saw the bench through the window. Her shock seemed real to me. "Oh my God. Poor Harrold. First the paint, then the display being trashed, and now this?" She turned and frowned. "What's your boyfriend doing about this? You know, any one of our businesses could be the next target. We have to find this guy."

I went with my standard line. "Greg and I don't discuss open investigations with each other. You really think that the other businesses are in danger?"

Lille turned toward me and held out her arms. "Diamond Lille's is right next door. You know the little creep will get tired of harassing an old man. Then where's he going to attack? Not the winery on the other side of town. My place, that's where." She pointed to the camera attached to the street lamp. "Why did we pay for a system that's not keeping us safe? You take that to the city council and tell them to get the rest of those cameras activated right now."

As she started to stomp away, I called out, "Who dropped you off?"

She spun around and glared at me. "Why do you want to know? Want someone else to pay attention to you so you can make your man jealous?"

"I've told you before, I don't need to make Greg jealous. I was just wondering who you were dating now. I've seen the two of you around a few times. Is he a local?" I turned in the bench so I could see her face.

"He is, but of course, you knew that from his club leathers." Her gaze moved to the road where the guy and his motorcycle had disappeared. "Let's just say he's someone I'm hanging out with, and if and when I think you need to know more, I'll call Darla and have her publish it in that little newspaper of hers."

I watched as Lille finished her trek into the diner. Her prior good mood had all but dissipated into a rage. And rage was caused by fear. So if Lille was afraid of the vandal attacking her diner, it stood to reason she wasn't the one who'd hired the guy to scare off Harrold. Which took my one and only theory regarding the case down the tubes.

I wrote a note in my list of to-dos. I needed to talk to Mayor Baylor and see what it would take to get the rest of the cameras online. That was the only way Greg would be able to catch whoever was doing this. As I closed the notebook, Harrold came and sat beside me. His body almost crumpled into the bench as he heaved out a sigh.

"This is getting hard to deal with," he muttered. "Who would hate me this much to damage my store?" His head turned to the side, and he focused on the diner.

"You think Lille had something to do with this?" I needed to know what the argument was between the two.

He rubbed his hands together. "I don't think even she's this conniving. But a month ago, she came to talk to me about selling The Train Station. She said she was looking at expanding the diner."

"What did you say?"

He laughed a short bark. "I told her that I would keep The Station open until they dragged my dead body out of the building. Why would I want to sell? I get great walk-in traffic during the weekends, and now with the online business, I'm selling twice the number of model trains I did two years ago."

"So you told her no, and the vandalism started." I said what both of us had been thinking.

He shook his head. "I know Lille. She's prickly and hard to like, but she has a good heart. She and my Agnes were best friends for years. In fact, Agnes developed Diamond Lille's first menu and taught Lille how to cook the dishes. There's no way she'd turn on me, not like this."

"Then we'll find out who is doing this." I put my hand on Harrold's blue button-down shirt, which made him look like he was going to work in an office, not a model train store. "I promise."

Harrold glanced over at the damaged shop window. "I hope so."

I stood and nodded toward the diner. "You want some breakfast? I'm buying."

"I can't. Christopher is on his way in from Bakerstown along with a fellow from one of the glass shops to do the repair. But I appreciate the offer." He stood and shook my hand. "You just go do your snooping around and figure out who's responsible. I'd appreciate that more than a free meal. And I'm sorry about the outburst earlier."

I walked him back to his shop and then decided to head home. After my run-in with Lille, I didn't want to eat breakfast at the diner. You had to let the woman calm down or she had a habit of erupting like a volcano. I'd probably be okay to resume visiting the diner in a few days. One thing about Lille was that she didn't hold a grudge for long. Too many other people to be angry at, I guess.

When I got home, I sat for a minute and then made a new to-do list. My vacation days were disappearing faster than I wanted, so I needed to make a plan about what I had to get done before I went back to work next Tuesday. I wandered upstairs to peek at the paint in Project Guest Room. It needed one more coat and then I could put up wainscoting around the ceiling. Which I still needed to buy and paint. I wrote down these items on my list and thought about the pieces I'd found at Antiques by Thomas. As long as I could find the right bed frame, each one of the other items would be a perfect match. I drew out a rough look on what I would put where and then took measurements of the room.

As I was considering the window treatment, my cell rang. Glancing at the caller ID, I punched the button to answer. "Hey, Aunt Jackie. What's on your plate today?"

"Good morning to you, too." She paused. "I was calling to see if you got through the filings. I didn't hear from you last night."

"Come with me to Bakerstown and I'll give you what I've gone through and we can talk on the drive." I paused, knowing there was one thing I could say that would make her say yes. I decided to push that button. "Unless you're not feeling well enough?"

"To drive to Bakerstown? I'm not dead, you know," she grumbled. "Give me twenty minutes to get ready. I haven't even showered yet."

"No problem. Let's make it an hour and that way I can take Emma for a quick run." I looked around the room.

"You're going to owe me lunch, you know." And with that, my aunt hung up. I guess she didn't think her statement needed an answer. I was going to owe her lunch, but spending time with her this week wasn't going to be a problem. I wanted to. I found the camera app on my phone and took several pictures at different angles of the guest room so we could compare furniture as we shopped.

Then I changed into my running clothes and Emma and I took off for thirty minutes of joyful not talking, thinking, or doing anything but running. Well, Emma found a dead fish, but I convinced her to leave it for the gulls and thankfully she didn't decide to roll in it today.

As I got ready for the trip to Bakerstown, I stashed my couch pillows in my study and grabbed the part of the Ashford filings I'd read through last night. I still had a pile to get through tonight, but Greg wasn't coming over for dinner, so I should have lots of quality time to read.

I just wished it was a novel I was reading rather than the boring accounting that had made my eyes cross last night a few pages into the pile.

With Emma safely in the house and my pillows safely in another room where she couldn't use them for chew toys, I started up the Jeep and headed into town. When I passed by The Train Station, the bench was already back in its place on the street and the broken glass had all been cleaned up. By the time I returned to town, the window would be replaced and the shop back to normal. Three attacks in three days. No wonder Harrold looked like he'd been up for days. The guy probably wasn't sleeping, listening for problems.

I passed Coffee, Books, and More, then did a U-turn at the next block, parking on the same side of the street as the shop. This time I entered through the front, where Sasha was finishing an order for a local customer.

"Hey, boss. Coming in to check up on me?" Sasha put a sleeve on the cup and handed it to the customer. She focused on the woman and added a quick, "Thanks for visiting."

As the customer went out the front door, I glanced around the empty shop. "Thursday mornings, got to love them."

Sasha laughed, throwing a clean bar towel over her shoulder. "I have to admit, you do have the easy shift. Once the commuters are caffeinated and on their way to work, it's kind of dead around here until Toby arrives in at noon."

"Exactly why I love this shift." I grabbed the phone and dialed my aunt's number. "Hey, I'm downstairs talking to Sasha, so whenever you're ready . . ."

My aunt mumbled something about distracting the help and hung up on me again.

"So, you and Jackie taking off again? Didn't you road-trip yesterday?" Sasha sipped on a glass of water she had behind the counter.

"We did. And today we're going to a flea market to find a bed frame. I hope that we're successful so I can also buy a new mattress while we're there. I like shopping, but I don't want to spend all of my vacation in stores." I nodded to the coffee. "Pour me a large black hazelnut to go, will you?"

"No problem." Sasha grabbed a cup and filled it with the coffee. "I heard you're redoing the guest room. What colors are you using?"

I took out my phone and showed her the almost painted room, pointing out the placement of furniture I'd planned for the room. As we were talking, Aunt Jackie came in through the back of the shop dressed in a white pantsuit with a coral-colored shirt underneath. The perfect outfit to go hunting through dusty, dirty rooms in antique shops and flea markets. I guess I should have been more specific.

"You know we're going antique shopping, right?" I pointed at her outfit. "You're going to look like you're wearing brown by the time we return. I know you own jeans, you wore them yesterday."

"You need to learn to wear something besides jeans." Aunt Jackie looked down at her outfit. "Besides, I wore low-heeled sandals. I'll be fine. I know how to act like a lady and not get grubby."

Sasha laughed. "Besides, I don't think a speck of dirt would dare land on you."

My aunt shook her finger at the girl. "Don't be smart. And pour me a large black to go, as well, since my niece forgot to order one for me."

"I was just showing Sasha the floor plan. I want to start at the flea market, then move to the shops on antique row, and end up either at Home Heaven or the mattress store, or maybe both." I listed off my agenda.

My aunt handed me an envelope. "Josh brought this by last night for you. It's an estimate for the pieces you wanted. He said he'd throw in delivery for free."

"Since it's less than a mile, I would hope so." I put the envelope in my tote with my notebook. I'd open it if I found a piece to replace the ones I'd found at Antiques by Thomas. Even though the man was dating my aunt, I was pretty sure I wouldn't get a family discount.

We said our good-byes to Sasha, Aunt Jackie leaving a new list of to-dos for her to complete since the customer traffic was so low. As we settled in to the Jeep, I strapped on my seat belt. "You know you don't have to leave her a list of things to do every time you see her. She knows her job now."

My aunt clicked her own belt and shrugged, looking back into the shop. "It's good for her to learn exactly what it takes to run the shop. I think she'd be a great manager someday, if you don't let her get lazy and read books all the time when she's supposed to be working."

I pulled the Jeep onto Main, heading to the highway. "Part of her job is to run the kids' book club. If she's not reading the books, how is she supposed to lead the discussions? Besides, reading isn't just a requirement for the job, it's the best part."

"Let's just say we have a different opinion on the priority of tasks we assign our staff." My aunt grabbed the papers from the backseat. "Is this what you've read through?"

Nodding, I turned the Jeep onto the highway, passing by the beach parking lot, which was completely empty this morning. "That's it. And I didn't see anything that would lead us to Sandra's killer."

"Don't give up on my method quite yet." She went to the first page, where I'd put a colored sticker. "What's this?"

"I marked places where she talked about her client list and the number each year. I also marked places where I didn't understand what they were talking about." I shrugged. "Well, not all the places. I would have had a sticker on every page that way."

"You really need to learn more about the business of running a business." My aunt set the pages down. "Tell me what you didn't understand and I'll walk you through the process."

It was going to be a long drive. I took a deep breath and started listing off the parts of the reporting process I didn't understand.

By the time we reached Bakerstown, I knew more about reporting requirements than I ever wanted to know or cared to admit. As a family lawyer, I knew there were tons of laws and regulations I should understand about the store, but business law had always bored me to the core.

Today's drive had reminded me not only of why I hadn't chosen corporate law for my career, but also why I counted so much on my aunt to help me with the business side of the shop. Heaven help me if I ever lost her.

# CHAPTER 14

"What about this one?" Aunt Jackie held up a quilt. The patterns and colors screamed modern and didn't even match my vision of what I was looking for.

I shook my head. We'd been to almost all of the booths with no luck for the bed frame or a quilt to cover the bed or one to hang on the quilt frame sitting in Josh's back room. "It's not what I'm looking for. I want something that looks old, maybe a scrap quilt or even a log cabin pattern."

"I don't know why you don't just buy something new. There's a linen store just up the street," my aunt grumbled and headed to the next booth. "This one looks promising. At least it has some furniture."

I followed her into the room and ran straight into a woman with a walker. The metal walker tipped, but the woman stayed standing. "Oh, I am so sorry. I didn't see you." I looked into the face of Rachel's neighbor, Cathy Addy.

"No harm done, dear. They don't make the aisles here very old-lady friendly." She peered into my face. "You're Rachel's friend, aren't you?"

"Yes, well, I mean, she's my travel agent." I wouldn't have called the two of us friends. "I stopped by a few days ago."

"I remember. I was watering the plants. Good thing, too, since that girl still hasn't shown up at the office. I put up a sign on the door saying she'd reopen next week. At least that way, people aren't coming over and bothering me about her hours." Cathy ran her hand over a pillow that pronounced that *Coastal California Is for Lovers* in hand-done cross-stitch. "Although her shop does bring in stragglers to the yarn store."

"I run the coffee shop and bookstore in South Cove, so I get a lot of drop-ins from the other businesses on Main Street." I didn't think yarn had much to do with travel, though, and I figured the traffic went more from Cathy's store over to Rachel's. I thought about seeing Rachel and Michael meeting for lunch. If she wasn't running the agency, where was she? "Have you heard from her?"

"Honestly, no, and I'm beginning to worry a bit. You don't think something's happened to her and she's hurt in the house somewhere?" Cathy shrugged. "I looked through all the windows yesterday, but I couldn't see anything out of place. The girl keeps a clean house, that's for sure."

I could just see Cathy positioning her walker up to the first-floor windows and peering inside. On an instinct, I asked another question. "You don't remember seeing a man around, do you? Was Rachel dating?"

Cathy shook her head. "I tried to set her up with my grandson. He's a plumber and makes an excellent income, but she said she wasn't in the market for a man. I assumed there was a heartbreak somewhere in her past. Of course, she had clients coming in and out during the day, but I never saw her leave with anyone. It's too bad."

"What's too bad?" I had been scanning the booth for my aunt and hadn't heard past the failed matchmaking comment.

Cathy pushed her walker past me and toward a pile of Beanie Babies. "I just meant if she had been involved, I'd know she was safe. A woman needs a man to take care of her."

Like a fish needs a bicycle. I pointed toward the other side of the booth. "Oh, there's my aunt. I'd better catch up with her. Nice to see you again."

As I wandered through the tables to meet up with Aunt Jackie, I wondered if the reason Rachel had turned down the blind date was because she was already involved with Michael. I took my aunt's arm and led her out of the booth. "Time to check out the antique shops."

An hour later I'd found the perfect wrought-iron bed frame. Or what would be perfect after I scraped off the flaking paint and repainted it shiny black. The frame was in good shape, too, and would hold a queen-size mattress, which I ordered after a quick stop at the mattress store. Delivery would be on Monday.

"I'm hungry, you know." Aunt Jackie pointed toward a local fast-food drive-in. "Stop there and I'll buy us burgers for the drive home.

I need to get back and get ready for work. Some of us aren't on vacation."

I glanced in the rearview mirror, where I could see the frame. We'd had to put the back seats down, but luckily it had fit in the back of the Jeep. After spending way too much money at the mattress store, I'd popped into Home Heaven and bought the wainscoting, paint, and sandpaper. If everything went well, I'd have the bed cleaned, prepped, painted, and set up upstairs before the mattress delivery occurred next Monday. I was feeling pretty good about my progress.

We ordered, and as we waited for the food, Aunt Jackie pointed to a name on one of the filing reports. "Did you see this?"

I leaned forward and read the line she had her finger resting on. "Diamond Lille's was a client of the Ashfords?"

My aunt flipped backward through the report. "At least they were a couple of years ago."

The window opened and the bag with our food appeared. I drove over to a parking spot and distributed the food. The place was known for the best tater tots in town. I could smell the pounds attaching to my hips as I pulled out the paper container. "What would Promote Your Event do for a small diner?"

My aunt unwrapped her bacon cheeseburger and shrugged. "A lot of shops do a marketing campaign to see if they can bring in more business."

I thought about Lille's plan to buy out Harrold. "Or maybe they need to pave the way for an expansion?"

My aunt took a bite of her burger, then waved it at me. "Don't even think that way. There's no evidence that Ashford was involved in what happened to The Train Station. Besides, Sandra was already dead before the first vandalism happened. I don't think Michael is in any condition to harass an old man. He seems like he's barely hanging on."

I thought about his lunch with Rachel. Didn't seem like he was a grieving widower that day. But Jackie was right, it was leaping to conclusions to blame Ashford for Harrold's trouble until I saw a pattern. But at least I knew what to look for in the pile of reports I still had to review tonight. And if Diamond Lille's was an ongoing client, that might give me enough to talk to Greg about my suspicions. I dug into my mushroom Swiss burger with an enthusiasm I hadn't felt for a long time. The pieces were all falling into place.

Finally.

By ten that night, I was feeling less optimistic. The paint on the bed frame wasn't coming off, and an Internet search of the problem told me I needed to return to Home Heaven, again, to pick up the chemicals to strip the paint from the frame. Sanding the stuff would take me a few months, if even then. I kicked myself for not talking to one of the yellow-vested experts running around the store. Greg laughed at me when he called to check in and I explained my problem. He also gave me a list of the type of paint stripper and tools I'd need to pick up. So eventually, I kind of forgave him for laughing. Especially when he reminded me of the earrings he'd given me earlier in the week.

My shoulders and arms ached from the wasted effort trying to sand off the frame, so I stood in the shower until the hot water began to cool. After that, I dressed in my favorite camisole and pajama pants, then went downstairs to heat up a can of soup. I took the pile of unread pages out of my office along with the sofa pillows and set the papers on the coffee table. When I had my bowl of soup and a peanut butter sandwich ready, I added a soda and took the food out to the living room on a tray. Emma sniffed the air, but I told her to lie down. "You have dog food in the kitchen if you're hungry."

She huffed and turned a few circles before she lay next to the coffee table within smelling distance of my cream of mushroom soup. Ignoring her pleading eyes, I dug into the soup as I turned on the television. The local news was just finishing, and there was a story on the Bakerstown Business Council. Watching the interview of their liaison, I thought about both the Ashfords and Rachel's business. Maybe they attended the business council meetings? I knew things about the people who attended South Cove's Business-to-Business meeting. Maybe I should call up my peer and see if she had any gossip for me. I wrote down the name of the liaison along with the name of her shop, Bakerstown Floral. Looked like I'd be making two stops tomorrow.

Finished with dinner, I gave Emma the crust off the bread and pulled the pile of papers onto my lap. Two hours later, I'd gone through the rest of the papers, and not found a single mention of Diamond Lille's in the paperwork. So Promote Your Event wasn't working with Lille. Or at least, they weren't putting it down on paper. I pushed off the idea. There was something going on with the diner and Harrold's.

I didn't think Lille had actually done the window painting or smashing, but that boyfriend of hers was a definite possibility.

I took my tray into the kitchen and started turning out lights. Tomorrow would be soon enough to worry about what I didn't know.

First stop in the morning was to Aunt Jackie's to drop off the rest of the Ashford records. Since my initial review had gotten me nowhere, I hoped my aunt had a magic touch. Besides, I wanted the papers out of my house to keep Greg from seeing them. I didn't mind keeping some secrets from him, but explaining our digging into the Ashfords would be hard. And he'd probably ask for the earrings back or something.

As I drove past Diamond Lille's, I saw Lille outside talking to someone who looked familiar. I slowed the Jeep and realized she was talking to Homer Bell. Homer, who owned the food truck. He got in his car and drove away as I pulled into the parking slot on the street he'd just cleared.

I quickly stepped out of the Jeep and called over the top of the roof, "Why are you talking to Homer?"

Lille paused and frowned. "Why do you care?"

I walked around the Jeep and stood in front of her. "Are you trying to buy the food truck? He said there was another party interested."

She laughed. "I should have known it was you. Homer's playing both of us. Now he says there's a third party interested."

"Great." I shook my head. "I'm not sure I can deal with a price war. Why do you want the food truck anyway?"

"Like it's any of your business?" Lille leaned against the diner wall and lit up a cigarette. She took two long drags, then put it out again, using the side of the building. She smirked at me. "Don't judge. I know I'm not supposed to smoke in front of the shop."

I held up my hands. "No judging here. But aren't you expanding the shop?"

Her head jerked up, and she stared at me. "Where did you hear that?" She held up her hand. "Don't tell me. Carrie's been gossiping again."

"I, well, Harrold told me you were looking at buying his place." I tried to duck the fact that Lille's best waitress was the original source of the rumor. No use getting her in trouble. I liked Carrie.

"And he also told you he told me no." She tucked the cigarette back into her pack and put it into her apron pocket. "I've been thinking about expanding into the food festivals. That way I can increase my business and keep the diner here the same." She glanced toward The Train Station. "At least for the next few years. Who knows how long Harrold will want to keep the place going? Eventually I might get lucky."

"That's what I was going to do with the truck." I leaned on the Jeep. "Well, I guess good luck with the deal. I hope one of us gets the van."

Lille snorted. "I'm sure you really mean that." She spun around on her heel and went into the diner.

I climbed back into the Jeep and headed into town. When Aunt Jackie answered her door, I held out the pile of papers for her to take. "I know who our competition is for the food truck."

"Let me guess, Diamond Lille's?" She took the papers and turned to let me in the door. "Do you want some breakfast?"

The smell of fried ham and fresh baked bread filled the small apartment. "I could be convinced." I went over and poured myself a glass of orange juice from the decanter she had sitting on her table. "How'd you know?"

She filled a second plate with ham, eggs, and a slice of fresh-from-the-oven bread. "Just did the numbers. Homer doesn't know that many people, and he doesn't like going in to Bakerstown because he sees it as the big city."

"So, if he was working a buyer, it would have to be someone here." I slathered butter on the bread and took a bite, thinking about the sale from Homer's perspective. "But that doesn't make sense. He's got a third buyer and there's just the two of us in town who could use a food truck."

My aunt held up her fork. "Three."

I turned my head and watched her eat the piece of ham. "I don't know a third."

My aunt smiled. "Of course you do. We're one of their best customers." She waited, but when I didn't catch on, she said, "Pies on the Fly."

I shook my head. "Sadie doesn't want a full-time job. Just something to keep her busy."

"The food truck wouldn't have to be full-time. She could take it to festivals on the weekends, like we were planning." My aunt focused on her breakfast for a few minutes, then added, "Look, I know she's your friend, but friends don't tell each other everything."

"Maybe not, but if Sadie was looking at something this big, she would have told me." I finished my orange juice and refilled the glass.

Aunt Jackie shrugged. "If you say so. But I know Homer. He didn't reach out past South Cove's borders for his buyers. I guess they might have come looking for him if someone knew he was thinking about selling. Have you decided on our maximum bid level? We need to have a firm figure before we start negotiating. If we don't get this one, another truck will come available someday."

"I'll do some number crunching tonight. I was hoping it wouldn't be much. Since we put Sasha on full-time, the profit margin has been a little tight." I finished eating and took my plate to the sink to rinse.

"You do have the Miss Emily fund," my aunt reminded me. My friend had left me a sizeable inheritance as well as the house I was continually remodeling last year when she died. Well, when she was murdered. So far, I'd spent some of the money for remodels and set up a couple of college funds for some very distant relatives of my friend.

I finished off the rest of my orange juice. "I'm considering that money my rainy day fund."

"It might be time to think about the rain." My aunt shrugged. "I just think if we're going to jump into this season, we may want to buy soon so we aren't late to the party. If they already have a coffee/treat vendor, we won't get invited to the festivals."

I thought about my aunt's warning as I drove into Bakerstown for the third day in a row. This time it was just me, and I turned the stereo up to full-blast level, singing along with my favorite songs, trying to get the food truck out of my mind.

Maybe we needed more information. Like a field trip to a festival to see if they did already have a coffee truck. No use getting worked up about something that might never happen. I made a mental note to check out local festivals on Sunday. Maybe Amy would want to come along and we could make a girls' day out of the errand.

One decision done, I turned in to the parking lot of Home Heaven and grabbed the list of items I'd need to strip the metal bed frame. After that, I drove to Bakerstown Floral. Allison Delaine was working on a floral arrangement in the front of the shop when I entered.

"Good morning, how can I help you?" she called out, her Southern accent softening her words.

I handed her a card that listed off my position as liaison for the South Cove City Council. "I'm Jill Gardner, and I run the Business-to-Business committee for South Cove. I saw you on the news last night and realized we'd never met, so here I am, meeting and greeting."

She broke into a wide smile. "I can't believe they finally ran that interview. We recorded it almost three months ago. I guess yesterday was finally a slow news day."

"Well, any publicity is good, right?" I took in the shop. The smell of cold, fragrant flowers was overwhelming. "I'd love to chat about your committee and how you run things. I've been liaison with South Cove now for over five years, and it feels like it's time to mix it up."

Allison tucked the last red rose into the bouquet and turned it from side to side to check its balance. The final piece was stunning. "I'm sure you'd find our little meeting boring. I barely can get anyone to come unless they want to complain about something. Last month I invited a guest speaker on shop safety and had three regular members show up. It was embarrassing."

"But those three members got good advice, right?" I played with a dangling ribbon that had come unrolled while Allison was working. "Believe me, I'm fighting with the same problems. Maybe we can brainstorm some solutions."

She took out her planner. "I could do coffee next week, if that will work. I've got an employee to cover the early shift on Wednesday. How about I come by your place at ten?"

I took one of her cards off the counter and wrote the day and time on the back. "Perfect. I'm looking forward to chatting."

"I am, too. I had talked to a PR company about doing some pro bono work for the committee last month, but she turned me down." Allison put the calendar back under her counter and then put the completed bouquet into the refrigerator behind her. "One down, six more to do today before my delivery guy gets here."

Clearly, that was my clue to exit stage right. "I'll be out of here then." I tapped the card on the counter, curious whether the PR company she'd referred to was Promote Your Event. "The agency must have been doing really well for her to turn down your offer. I'm sure they would have gotten a lot of business from the committee members just by doing a little free work."

She took a purple vase off a nearby ledge and pulled a pile of different-colored lilies from a box on the bottom refrigerator shelf. She shook her head. "Actually, no. Sandra, she's the owner, said she was selling the business. That's why she didn't agree to take on our work. I got the impression the deal was already in the works."

# CHAPTER 15

Returning to South Cove, I drove through town on my way back to my house. Sadie Michaels's purple PT Cruiser sat in front of Coffee, Books, and More. I parked the Jeep behind it and went into the shop. Toby looked up from checking off the delivery list. "Hey, boss, what are you doing here?"

"Stopped to see Sadie. Is she in the back?" I walked around the counter and headed to the back office door.

"Yep. They're finishing the last load of the order." He pointed to the clipboard. "We've been killing it with the Sweet Summer Lemon Surprise this week."

"Sadie and her specials." I paused, remembering that tonight was date night. I needed to hurry if I was going to get anything done before Greg showed up. The cheesecake would be perfect with coffee after our dinner. Or maybe iced tea. I'd put a jar of sun tea on the porch as soon as I got home. "Pack one up for me, will you?"

"It's a lot of calories. You sure you don't want just a slice?" Toby set the clipboard down and leaned on the counter. "You know you can't resist temptation."

"Jerk. Greg's taking me out tonight, and I thought I'd serve dessert on the back porch." I studied my midday barista. "If it's any of your business."

Grinning, he saluted me. "Your wish, yada, yada, yada. Greg didn't mention he'd be off-duty tonight. I guess I'd better think twice before calling and interrupting your date. I'd hate to lose both of my jobs at once."

"Whatever." I pushed through the swinging door separating my back office and storeroom from the front of the building. Sadie was standing by the walk-in wrapped in the arms of Dustin Austin, her new boyfriend. She must have heard my entrance because her face turned beet red and she pushed away from Austin.

"Jill. I didn't expect to see you today." She ran her hands down her hair to make sure it was straight and snuck a peek at Austin as she did. She reached over to straighten his T-shirt. I had to admit, the guy made sixties grunge look good on a middle-aged man.

"Apparently not. Hey, Austin, how are things in the bike rental business?" I looked around the crowded storeroom. At least they'd put away the delicate desserts before falling into each other's arms for a steamy kiss.

"Actually, better than I expected. I was concerned when that walk was scheduled for last weekend. You know, Saturday is my highest rental day of the week, but apparently, the participants are fitness nuts. I got more rentals Sunday than I have all season. And I'm expecting a tour group this weekend that's renting over the three days." He checked his watch and kissed Sadie on the forehead. "Sorry, sweetie, but I've got to go open the shop. I'll call you tonight."

I watched as he walked out to the front of the shop, then I turned back to my friend. "So, things are going good?"

She slapped my arm. "Stop teasing. I wish you hadn't seen that."

"Believe me, I've seen two people kissing before." I pointedly looked at the storeroom. "Although I think this is the first for this location."

"Austin was helping me with my deliveries this morning. We don't get a lot of time together on the weekends." Sadie smiled and grabbed hold of the handcart. "I bet you and Greg have the same issue right now."

"If tonight's date goes as planned, this will be the second time I've seen him since the walk." I held the door open for her as she maneuvered the empty cart. "I started remodeling my guest room to keep myself busy."

Toby snorted. "And took on the task of finding Harrold's vandal."

"Jill, you didn't." Sadie stood the cart next to the counter. "You could be in danger. What if the person finds out you're looking for him or her? They could go after you or your shop."

"Where devils fear to tread, Jill jumps in," Toby deadpanned.

I sat on one of the stools. "Look, I'm not doing anything dangerous. I'm just trying to help out a fellow business owner."

"I hope you're having more luck than the official investigation is.

Whoever's been doing this is hiding their tracks well. And they knew that the city hasn't turned on the cameras after the corner where Diamond Lille's is set." Toby sighed. "Either they are extremely smart about their actions or just plain lucky."

"I hate to see Harrold have to go through this." Sadie leaned against the counter. "I can't stand it when I see bad things happening to good people."

"I know. Harrold's gone through a lot in the last few years." I felt strands of guilt with my words. I hadn't been focusing on The Train Station vandalism. I'd been off on some wild-goose chase with Aunt Jackie, trying to solve Sandra's murder. Which I had no business doing. And if Toby or Greg found out, I'd be in a bunch of trouble.

Sadie's face brightened. "I know, I'll drop off one of my Sweet Summer Lemon Surprise Cheesecakes to the shop right now. I've got one last one in the truck that I was going to give to Austin, but I think Harrold needs cheering up more." She shrugged. "Besides, Austin just seems to devour everything I give him. I swear, he'll consume a full cheesecake in a day."

"The best way to a man's heart is through his stomach." I quoted the old saying. "But it looks like you've already caught that guy, hook, line, and sinker."

She blushed and pushed the cart to the door. "I'm off to see Harrold, then home. Nick has the afternoon off, and we're going shopping for his dorm room today. He's so excited."

Nick Michaels, all-around good kid and Sadie's pride and joy, had scored a full-ride scholarship to Stanford. In Sadie's world, that was the best of all possible options. The kid was in a great school, but close enough to come home on the weekends. I didn't want to burst my friend's bubble, but I thought the chances of him coming home most weekends was as slim as if he'd been accepted to Harvard. Nick loved being involved in school projects, so I assumed by the end of his first semester, he'd be a member of, if not running, several school clubs. The kid just liked people.

"Tell him hi for me." I watched through the window as Sadie put the cart in the back of her car and then sped away to the other side of Main Street. I turned to Toby, who had been watching her, too. "She's just too nice."

He nodded, then pushed the box holding the cheesecake toward me. "I'm afraid she's going to get hurt."

I put my hands on the box but didn't lift it. "You mean by dating Austin?"

Toby nodded. "He's too smooth. There's something off about the guy."

I started to ask Toby more, but then Aunt Jackie burst through the back door dressed in her bright pink walking outfit, complete with a pink sun visor and oversized sunglasses. She took two bottles of water out of the front cooler and put them into a mini backpack. Then she noticed me. "What are you doing here?"

I held up my hands. "Just picking up dessert for tonight. Greg's taking me out for dinner."

She eyed me suspiciously. "They serve dessert at most restaurants, you know."

"What can I say? I like to be prepared." I shrugged and picked up the box. "Besides, Sadie was here and I wanted to say hi."

"Well, I'm glad you stopped in, actually." She looked at Toby, then dropped her voice. "The files we picked up from the courthouse aren't complete. I've called Madeline and she has another stack for us. Can you go pick them up?"

"Today? I've already been to Bakerstown this morning." My hopes of getting the bed frame stripped were decreasing by the minute.

She nodded. "If you don't go today, we won't be able to get them before Monday. The courthouse isn't open on the weekends."

"You could have called me."

Aunt Jackie shrugged. "I just realized there were years missing about an hour ago. When I called Madeline, she told me she had the second file on her desk and had forgotten to give it to us. What part of this is my fault?"

I held up my hand. "Fine, I'll go. But I swear, this is my last trip into Bakerstown this week."

My aunt started to say something, but then the bell over the door rang and Josh entered the shop, dressed in his knock-off tracksuit. Aunt Jackie went around the counter and handed him the backpack. "Well, we're off. If I don't show up for my shift, we're somewhere on the Mission Trail, probably dead from exhaustion."

"Not funny," Josh muttered.

I looked at Toby. He grinned and responded, "I thought it was a little funny."

The two disappeared out the front door, and I watched as they started walking toward the beach and the entrance to the Mission Trail.

"I still don't see those two together as a couple," Toby muttered, then when the bell over the door rang, he smiled at the group of women who piled through the opening. "Looks like I've got work to do."

"I'll talk to you later." I picked up my box and wound my way through the chatting women. Toby knew how to draw in the customers; his personality and good looks had women driving miles just to get his coffee and a smile. He was my best marketing ploy, one that my aunt had hired without my permission. I set the cheesecake on the driver's seat and glanced at the car clock. If I hurried, I could pick up the additional records and be back at the house in just over an hour. I threw my jacket over the cheesecake to keep it cool and out of the sun. Pulling out of the parking spot, I turned on the air-conditioning.

When I arrived at the courthouse, I found a rock-star-front-row parking spot on my first spin around the lot. And then Madeline was at her desk and held out the papers as soon as the elevator doors opened. I parked the Jeep next to the garage and then, using the backyard gate, ran the box to the house. The day's temperatures had even worked in my favor. Instead of the ninety-degree heat we were forecast for the weekend, today had been cloudy and fair, the breeze keeping the temperatures in the seventies.

I slipped the cheesecake box onto the bottom shelf of my fridge and grabbed a bottle of water. Fifteen till two by the kitchen clock. Greg would pick me up at six. So that gave me four hours to strip the old paint off the bed frame. I let Emma out to the backyard and grabbed the Home Heaven bag out of my car. I sat on a small bench I'd installed outside the garage and started reading the directions. The stuff had to set for fifteen minutes, and the warnings said to keep it off your skin. I prepped the area in the garage, laying down newspaper, went inside and got a flannel shirt and my gardening gloves, then started brushing away.

The fumes were making me dizzy by the time I'd finished the back railing, but as I stepped away, I could already see the paint dripping away. If this worked, tomorrow I could paint and Monday I'd set up the bed in the morning in time for a new mattress to be delivered that afternoon.

Except, as I thought through my plan, I realized I'd forgotten one thing. I'd already stripped the wood floor, but I needed to varnish it and find a large rug to go under the bed. And I didn't want to have to set up the bed myself. I reevaluated my weekend. Okay, if the bed frame was ready to paint tomorrow, after I got that done, I'd varnish the floors. Then Sunday, I'd drive back into town to find a rug.

But Sunday I was planning to hit a few festivals to check out the food truck option. I could do both. Why not? Maybe some of the flea markets in the area would sell a rug and I could find a quilt, too. I could do it all.

Feeling proud of my ability to time-manage all my tasks into the weekend, I started clearing off the old paint. An hour later, I'd only finished the first pass on the back side. I'd have to reapply the stripper and work harder. As I used the putty knife, I suddenly realized the one flaw in my carefully planned-out weekend. I didn't have wood varnish to finish the floors. I'd have to drive into Bakerstown *again* sometime on Saturday and buy some from Home Heaven.

I was still sure I could do it all by the time my cell rang. I put the phone on speaker so I didn't have to pick it up, as my hands were still in gloves and covered in old paint and stripper. "Hey."

"Hey, yourself. Where are you? You sound like you're in a tunnel." Greg's voice boomed through the speaker and I heard Emma's excited whine from the backyard.

"Working in the garage stripping this bed frame I found." I reached my arm up and pushed my hair back out of my eyes with my forearm. "I'm considering the wisdom of purchasing new right at this juncture."

He chuckled. "You like doing things the hard way. And it usually works out for you. I'm on my way over. Do you need anything?"

I looked down in horror at my worn and stained clothes. I'd been hoping for an hour to shower and change. "You're leaving the station now?"

"Actually I'm in Bakerstown. I was with Doc Ames this afternoon." Which meant he'd been looking over the autopsy records and talking about the cause of death, but we both skipped that part of the sentence.

"Hey, can you stop at Home Heaven and get five gallons of wood floor sealer? I need the clear stuff. Ask Joe, if he's working. He knows what I've been using on the house." My weekend just got a little less complicated, and I'd have time to get ready for date night. I started putting away my tools from today's activities. At least I'd gotten one thing done and I'd learned a better way to finish the other end first thing in the morning.

"I was thinking something simple like picking up your dry cleaning or a bottle of wine." Greg sighed. "But yeah, I can stop."

"I'll see you in thirty to forty minutes?" I pulled off the gloves and took off the oversized man's button-down shirt to reveal a soaked tank below. I really needed a shower. I picked up my phone and turned it off speaker.

"You're going to owe me," Greg said.

I let myself into the backyard. "You offered," I countered. "That doesn't count as a favor. Now, if you're available to actually help seal the floor tomorrow, then I'd owe you."

"Sorry, kid. I'm tied up with the case. Otherwise, I'd be there first thing."

I entered the cool kitchen and grabbed a cold bottle of water from the fridge. "Somehow I doubt that. See you in a few." I headed upstairs to turn myself from Frank the Furniture Restorer into something at least a little sexy and feminine.

He chuckled before he signed off with his normal, "Love you."

I thought about those two words as I got ready for date night. He'd been closing out our phone conversations that way for the last couple of months. *Love you.* Two little words that could mean so much. Or so little, I reminded myself. My ex-husband had said it for months even though he'd been seeing someone else during that time. Did Greg's sign-off mean *I adore you, I want you in my life forever, marry me now*? Or *I'm glad you're here and I want to see if there's a future for us*?

Words. So many ways to misunderstand and misconstrue. I finished drying off and decided to banish the heavy thinking for another time. Tonight we were going to have a fun evening out. I might even take a stab at karaoke if we ended our night at the independent brewery and pub nestled above Highway One a few miles away. I sang a mean Mary Chapin Carpenter if you asked me. I took a blue sundress out of the closet with the flowered flip-flops Amy had dared me to buy on our last girls' shopping day and finished getting ready for the evening.

Digging through the refrigerator, I found a few items for a fruit tray to have as an appetizer, but since Greg was more of a meat and potato fan, I thought he'd probably ignore the offering. Considering an opened half-gone bag of pepperoni, I was digging through my pickle jars to see if I had any pepperoncini peppers when I heard a knock on the door. "Come on in. I'm in the kitchen," I called out.

When the knock sounded again, I closed the fridge door and strolled to the living room. "Sorry, I thought I'd unlocked," I said, but when my hand went to the doorknob, I realized I had unlocked the door earlier. I slowly opened the door, knowing now it wasn't Greg.

Adam Truman stood there, his hands folded together. "Miss Gardner? I apologize for the late visit."

I leaned against the doorframe, leaving the screen door closed between us. My finger itched to reach up and lock the screen, but even I knew the tiny lock was only a delaying tactic if the guy was really up to no good. I folded my arms in front of me. "Adam. This is a surprise. Is there something I can do for you?"

"I was wondering if Sandra left a package with you." He tensed as he asked the question. "She had said, well, I mean . . ."

"You're talking about Sandra Ashford? Why would she leave a package with me? If it was about the Mission Run, she probably gave it to Darla." I turned my head and considered the suited man in front of me. Why hadn't he brought this package up during our meeting at the winery? Something was off. Bells and whistles were going off in my head, but I couldn't put the pieces together. "Did you ask her?"

"Look, I know you've been snooping around Sandra's death, and if it's because of what she gave you, you have to understand. I didn't do what she said." He reached his hand toward the door handle. "Just give me the package and I'll be on my way."

I reached the screen lock faster than he could open the door. I saw anger flash in his eyes. "Go away. I don't know anything about a package."

He considered the cheap metal frame that stood between us. "I don't believe you. Why else would you pull up the records from the courthouse? I have my sources there, too."

"Obviously, there is something more to Sandra's death than just a hit-and-run." I saw Greg's truck slow down on the road in front of the house. I decided to push the issue since the cavalry was pulling into the driveway. "Did you kill her?"

Confusion filled Adam's face. "What? No. I didn't kill Sandra." He turned to see Greg step out of his truck. "Look, I just want the package back. Then I'll leave you alone."

He turned away from the door and went down the steps, greeting Greg as he passed. I unlocked the screen and stepped out on the porch to watch him drive away.

Greg watched him from beside his truck. I knew he probably had a hand on his service revolver in the bed of the cab, just in case. When Adam's car disappeared toward the highway, Greg shut the truck door and walked up to greet me on the porch. "Do I want to know what that was about?"

I leaned into his arms and melted, the fear from the visit overwhelming me for a moment. "Honestly, I'm not sure. He said he's looking for something Sandra had. Something he thought she gave me."

Greg tilted my chin toward him. "Did she give you something?"

I shook my head. "I only saw her that one time at the shop. Well, and on the trail, dead. Darla was the one working closely with the marketing and promotion for the run. Why would Sandra give me anything?"

Greg turned his head to scan toward the highway. He couldn't see the car anymore, but I knew he was thinking about Adam's reasoning. "Now, that's not the only question. What did Sandra have that he wants back so bad and why?"

I groaned as I watched him go into cop mode and consider the questions. "I suppose this means we aren't going to dinner."

Greg squeezed me and laughed. "Actually, it means I need to pay closer attention to you. Obviously I missed something in this case. And like most problems, the roads all lead to you."

I pulled away. "That's not fair. I haven't done anything..." My words trailed off as I thought about snooping with Aunt Jackie a few days ago. Adam had said someone had seen me at the courthouse. Me and my aunt. "Maybe we need to talk."

Greg nodded to the door. "Go get your purse and take care of Emma. I'm starving and you can tell me what you've been up to over a steak dinner."

# CHAPTER 16

A s we drove to the restaurant, I used my cell to call my aunt at the shop.

"Coffee, Books, and More, how can I help you?" my aunt's voice greeted me, and my shoulders dropped a few inches.

"Hey, it's Jill. Has Adam Truman been in the store?" Greg glanced at me as he pulled the truck to a stop at the junction of Main Street and the highway. I saw him glance in his rearview mirror, then just wait for me to finish the call.

"Okay, that's weird. Yes. He just stopped in about a half hour ago and asked where you were." Aunt Jackie called out a good-bye to a customer. "I told him you were at the house. Is this about next year's Mission Run? Did we lose the event?"

"No. I mean, I'm not sure. But I don't think so." The clock in the truck said it was six. "Are you busy?"

"The usual. Our mystery book club is starting at about six thirty, and Sasha's already here to help out." She paused and I could imagine her counting out the potential customers in the shop. "We have a good group of about thirty here."

"Fine. Do me a favor? Don't be alone in the shop. When the group ends, close up and go upstairs to the apartment. Don't let anyone in, especially Adam."

"What's going on?"

I shrugged. "I'm not sure, but Greg and I will pick you up later tonight and you can stay with me until we figure it out."

To my amazement, she didn't argue. "I'll have a bag packed and ready. And I'll have Josh come over so he can walk Sasha to her car and stay with me until you get here."

"Great." There was a pause on the line as I waited for her to ask more questions.

Instead, she broke the silence. "Look, I'd better go get ready for the book club. I'll see you soon."

When I hung up, Greg put the truck in gear and headed to the restaurant. No karaoke tonight for me. He put an arm up on the bench seat, then focused on me. "Maybe you'd better tell me what's going on now."

I filled him in on our visit to the courthouse and the business filings. Then I told him about going to the building where the Ashfords' office was located. He didn't say anything until I mentioned the woman who had talked to us in the hall.

"Did you get her name?" He opened the glove compartment and pulled out a notebook. "Write it down on this and I'll talk to her tomorrow. If they're in the office."

I dug in my purse and found a pen. I wrote down the names on the office door and her description, but I couldn't remember if she'd even said what her name was. I paused as I thought about the piles of mail on the floor of the office. "You know, no one's been in the Promote Your Event office for what looks like weeks. Why wouldn't they at least go in and pick up their mail?"

Greg turned into the already-crowded parking lot and scored the last end slot big enough for the truck to fit. He took the notebook, closed it, and threw it into the glove box. "Good question. I'll ask Michael tomorrow. Tonight we're just eating. Like a normal couple."

I put away my pen and cell while I waited for Greg to walk around and open my door. I might be wearing flowered flip-flops, but he always made me feel like a princess in glass slippers when we went out.

I stopped in front of him and looked up into his face. "You're not mad at me?"

He leaned down and kissed me. When he came up for air, he smiled. "Oh, I'm mad at you, but mostly I'm frustrated that I didn't realize you were sleuthing. Typically, I know where you've been before you come clean and rat yourself out. Tonight was a bit of a surprise for me."

"I just wanted Aunt Jackie to feel better." My lip trembled a bit. I hated it when Greg was upset, but disappointing him was so much worse.

He put his hand on my back. "Oh, you are so going to have to explain that reasoning." We walked into the restaurant, the night air cooling my arms as I pulled close the wrap I'd put on over the sundress.

As we walked through the crowded dining room to our table, I bumped into a man's shoulder. When I leaned down to excuse myself, I saw a glaring Lille staring at me from the other side of the table. "Sorry about the bump." I nodded toward the woman. "Hey, Lille. Seems like we had the same idea for date night."

The man I'd run into laughed. He grabbed Lille's hand and squeezed. "That's what they call this now? Date night? I thought it was eating dinner."

"Shut up, Mick." Lille pulled her hand out from under his grip and stared at me. "Look, you got noticed, just go away now."

Greg put his hand on my arm and led me away to our table, where he pulled out my chair for me. As he sat, unrolling the cloth napkin and putting it on his lap, he looked up at me. "Why do you always have to poke the lion?"

"I didn't. I ran into the guy, and wanted to apologize. I didn't know it was Lille and her latest loser." I leaned closer. "He's in the same gang where Ray was a member. Is he a criminal, too?"

Greg looked at me like I had three heads. "Are you really this naïve, or do you just like to play dumb?"

Stunned, I leaned back in my chair and stared at the menu. This was not what I'd expected for date night. All the warm-fuzzy feelings I'd come into the night with had disappeared quickly. First with my concern about my aunt, now with Greg's sharp words.

I felt his hand on mine, and I looked at him over the menu. "Sorry. I'm just a bit jumpy right now. Seems like I've had to save you from yourself twice tonight."

"You didn't have to save me." I laid the menu down. "Well, at least not from Lille. She's always nagging at me for something. I swear, I could say good morning and she'd think I was commenting on her lateness or the fact she'd made the world turn too fast."

Greg chuckled. "The two of you are oil and water." He reached over and lifted my chin to meet his eyes. "But I really am sorry for biting your head off. I swear, I'll be extra nice all evening."

"Until another shoe drops." I shook my head. "Seriously, I know we aren't a normal couple, especially with you being South Cove's lead detective. But sometimes, I'd just like to go out and not think about the latest murder."

"Or vandalism?" Greg asked, his eyebrows raised.

I focused back on the menu. "So sue me, I told a friend I'd help him out."

"By getting yourself knee-deep into another investigation? You just can't help yourself, can you?" Greg's lecture was cut off by the arrival of our waitress. I ordered a frozen strawberry margarita and he ordered a soda. When I looked at him, he shrugged. "One, I'm driving. And two, I'm thinking after dinner, I might head back to the station and check out this Adam guy. I want to know if you're really in danger or if he's just a blowhard."

"Happy Date Night to me," I muttered as I straightened my silverware.

Greg leaned back in the booth. "Would you rather I just ignore the fact that my girlfriend was being threatened?"

"No." I stuck my bottom lip out. "But I even brought home one of Sadie's new desserts, just in case you wanted to watch a movie or maybe just cuddle?"

"You're killing me here," Greg groaned. "I suppose it was one of her Chocolate Dream Cheesecakes?"

"Nope. Summer Lemon Surprise. She's trying out a new recipe." I pulled out a tube of lip gloss and ran it over my lips. The action reminded me of what I'd witnessed earlier. "Guess who I found kissing in the back room at the coffee shop?"

"Please don't tell me it was your aunt. Man, I don't want that visual in my head." He took a sip of his ice water.

I shuddered. "Ewww. No. Sadie and Dustin Austin. He was helping her with her deliveries. I bet by the time Nick goes off to college in the fall, they'll be an official item."

Greg took my hand in his. "You just can't stop hoping for the best for everyone, can you?"

"Sadie's good people. I want her to be happy." I squeezed his hand. "Especially if this new cheesecake is as good as I think it's going to be. Happy bakers make the best treats."

"Maybe I should take Toby a slice when I go down to the station." Greg lifted his eyebrows.

"And a slice for you, too?"

He grinned. "I can't let the boy eat alone. It would be rude."

"I'll set you up with a to-go bag when we get home." I folded the menu, knowing what I'd be ordering. "And I've got a box of old magazines for the waiting room. You can take that, too."

"How much stuff did you throw away out of that room?" Greg asked, then held up a hand. "Hold that thought."

We gave our orders to the waitress, including a full sampler plate appetizer filled with all kinds of fried goodies. He smiled at me as she took the order back to the kitchen. "What, you thought this would be a diet date night? No such thing."

"You know my weakness." I sipped on the frozen drink the waitress had dropped off before taking our order. "Anyway, the recycle container's full of old papers, magazines, junk mail, you name it. Miss Emily even kept every shopping bag she ever had."

"You're exaggerating." He took the margarita from my hand and took a small sip. "Good."

"And mine." I slapped his hand as he returned it. "And I'm not exaggerating. I found bags filled with newspapers that were from the Bakerstown Food King. That place closed ten years ago."

"Maybe she thought they'd be worth something someday." Greg chuckled. "The old gal was a collector, that's for sure."

"I'm beginning to think my friend had a tad of a hoarder in her. I'm not looking forward to starting to clean the attic." I took a bigger sip, okay, a gulp of the drink, which promptly gave me brain freeze. "Oh, ouch." I put my hands over my mouth and breathed in warm air trying to ease the pain.

"Serves you right. You shouldn't speak ill of the dead," Greg teased.

The pain gone, I shook my head. "I'm sure she's up there laughing at me right now."

The waitress brought our appetizer, and Greg filled a small plate with one of each of the treats, then set it in front of me. "Eat. You're kind of grumpy."

I bit into a mozzarella stick and nodded. "That paint stripper gave me fits today. And I've got to finish up tomorrow along with sealing that floor. If you can't reach me on my cell tomorrow, call nine-one-one because I'll probably be too high on fumes to answer the phone."

"I could probably help on Sunday if we started early." He put an entire jalapeño popper in his mouth. My body shivered from the thought of the spice hitting his taste buds. "If you want help."

"You're busy with the case. I can handle remodeling a guest room on my own. I haven't even been working at the shop. I should do something with my time." I dipped a fried green bean into the peppered ranch sauce. Now this was the way to eat veggies.

"Just remember I offered." He held out the last popper. "You want this one?"

Greg pulled the truck into my driveway and walked me to the door. He kissed me on the porch, then leaned on the side of the house and with his finger outlined the curve of my cheek, making me weak at the knees. "Thanks for a lovely dinner."

"You're welcome." I held up my hair, turning my head from side to side. "You didn't even mention how pretty the earrings were."

"I didn't see them. You were shining too brightly for me to see any baubles." He ran his hand down my arm.

I laughed and pulled out my keys. "Man, you're good. Too bad you have to go back to work." I unlocked the door and handed him my keys.

"What are these for?" He frowned at the teddy bear key chain with the Napa Valley medallion in the bear's tummy.

"Take my Jeep to pick up Aunt Jackie. She doesn't like your truck. It's too tall for her to climb into the seat and you don't have side rails yet. I'll give her a call and let her know you're on the way." I kissed him lightly on the lips. "And I'll box up the cheesecake slices for you."

He watched me walk into the house and made a turning motion with his hand when I looked out the window and saw he was still there. "Lock the door, I get it."

I turned on lights as I wandered to the back of the house, let Emma out the back door, and started a pot of coffee. I probably wouldn't sleep for a while after a cup, but Aunt Jackie would be expecting coffee to go with her dessert. I didn't know how the woman slept at all considering the amount of caffeine she consumed during the day.

As I waited for Greg to return, I pulled open my notebook and turned to the page marked *Sandra*. So far all I had listed were questions. Like the financial status of the business? And the emotional status of the marriage? Under that heading, I wrote *Rachel and Michael* with another question mark. Just because we'd seen them having lunch together didn't mean they were having an affair. On the other hand, Rachel had mentioned she was seeing someone during one of our conversations. Then I added the newest question: What package did Sandra have that Adam was looking for? I listed off the obvious answer—something to do with the Mission Run, or at least Adam's spot on the California Mission Society. I drummed the pen on the notebook. Heck, it could have been pictures of Adam and someone together. I tried to remember if I'd seen a wedding ring on his hand. Maybe Michael wasn't the one having an affair? Maybe Sandra and Adam had had a torrid weekend and she'd taken pictures to blackmail him.

And maybe pigs flew. I wasn't getting anywhere. There were more questions here than answers. So I turned pages until I found my notes on Harrold and The Train Station. I wrote down my notes on Lille's conversation. She'd seemed shocked about the damage on Wednesday. And she'd even admitted she had talked to him about selling, but now that she had the food truck in her sights, it seemed like her plans of expansion had changed.

So if it wasn't Lille, who could be behind Harrold's troubles? My memory flashed to the scene at the restaurant earlier that night. Could her new boy toy be trying to help and hadn't got the memo on the change-of-business plans? I shook my head. That seemed unlikely since every time I saw Lille outside of the diner, he was at her side. You would think they'd talked about Lille's plans for the diner and the food truck at some time or other.

I heard a knock at the front door and quickly closed the notebook. No need to get Greg worked up about my snooping. Checking through the window, I saw my aunt standing on the porch with Greg holding her overnight case and the envelope from Madeline at the county courthouse. One glance at his face told me that I couldn't be so lucky that when he found the packet in the car he hadn't seen what was inside. So much for my promise to stop sleuthing.

I opened the door to face the music.

# CHAPTER 17

"You seriously need to stop disrupting my life." Aunt Jackie pushed past me and into the living room, where she turned on the television. "I'm in the middle of watching *The Hero Next Door*."

I turned back toward Greg, who had set the overnight case on the floor and was holding out the envelope for me to take.

I put on a very big smile. "Thanks for bringing those in." I reached out to take them, but he didn't let go. "I'll trade you these for the cheesecake," I offered.

"You are in so much trouble," he whispered, finally releasing the papers. I took them and then put the envelope on my desk.

"Let's talk in the kitchen so we don't interrupt the show."

As we left the room, my aunt called out, "Is the coffee ready yet?"

I looked at the pot just finishing and lied, "Not quite. I'll bring you a cup when it's done brewing."

Greg leaned against the doorway. "So, why are you still looking at the business filings for the dead woman's company?"

I grabbed the cheesecake out of the fridge and cut two big slices for him and Toby. I found a plastic Tupperware container big enough for the treat, then sealed it up and handed the box to Greg. "I told you Aunt Jackie and I were looking at these. She needed something to do to take her mind off things."

"I thought you were done. No wonder Adam thinks you know something. Why are you always involved in things that you should stay out of?" He took the cheesecake container.

"Look, I didn't plan to do anything. I was just trying to answer some questions I had about Sandra and Michael's business." I shrugged. "Besides, I figured you'd have the killer in chains by now. Do you really think this is about the business?"

Greg shrugged. "Honestly, I don't know. It feels more personal than that. But you need to stay out of things while I figure this out." He nodded to the living room. "And keep that one close. She likes pretending she's a private investigator. Remember what happened when she tried to help out Mary a few months ago?"

I totally remembered, and just thinking about the situation made my heart race. My aunt had broken into an office, been arrested, and stolen a ledger that proved the travel agent was a fraud. Of course, then he'd broken into her apartment, looking for the book. The woman was lucky she wasn't in jail. Or dead.

"I really thought it would be a dead end." I sank down into one of the kitchen chairs, my legs unable to hold me up.

Greg's face softened. "I know. Just try to stay out of things until I find whoever did this to Sandra, okay? I'd hate to think of something happening to you."

I followed him out to the front door.

"Lock up," he said, then disappeared out the door.

I closed the door and turned the locks like he asked. As I did, I heard Aunt Jackie stir behind me.

"That boy is in a snit tonight." She lowered the volume on the television. "I suppose those papers are the ones you picked up from Madeline this afternoon? Can I take a look?"

I walked into the office and took the envelope off the desk. Returning to the living room, I dropped the packet onto the table. "Knock yourself out. I'm getting Emma then heading up to bed. It's been a long week."

My aunt opened the folder and scanned the front page. "Can you bring me a cup of coffee and whatever sweet you sent Grumpy off with?"

I returned to the kitchen and let Emma in, locking the back door, as well. Then I poured my aunt a cup, plated a slice of cheesecake, and put both on a tray. I carried the treat into the living room and set it on the coffee table. "I'll see you in the morning. I can drive you back into the apartment before your shift or whenever Greg tells us that Adam isn't a threat."

"I don't know that Greg is going to be able to clear him off the suspect list that quickly," my aunt observed. "Haven't you noticed the steady increase in money from the Mission Society to the public relations business for the last five years?"

I shook my head. "I didn't even compare the numbers," I admitted. She smiled. "And that's why you have me helping to run the coffee shop. Face it, dear, you're impossible when it comes to the business side of the store."

As I climbed up the stairs, I realized she was right. If anything, digging into the financial records of the Ashfords' business had taught me I needed to learn more about running a business. And not just researching what books to order and taste-testing new coffees and dessert treats. I promised myself I'd look into the local business schools. Maybe there was an online MBA that I could work on from the house. As long as Aunt Jackie was around to help me with my homework, it might not be so bad.

I woke Saturday morning to my aunt banging on my door. I really needed to get her back to her own apartment sooner than later. "I'm up," I lied through the door.

"Good, because Sasha needs our help for the teen book club meeting today. She tried to reach you on your phone, but all she got was voice mail." She opened the door and peeked inside. "You aren't even out of bed. Come on now, time's a wasting."

I waited for Aunt Jackie to close the door, then threw myself back on the bed. I'd totally forgotten about Sasha's group. When the cruise got cancelled, I'd opened my mouth and volunteered to help. Now I had to finish the bed, seal the floor, and help manage twenty or more teenagers who might or might not want to talk about a book I hadn't even read. My day couldn't get any more complicated.

I pulled on my running clothes, determined to take just a quick break for myself before the crazy hit. Emma was already downstairs, sitting in the middle of the kitchen and staring adoringly at Aunt Jackie, who was telling the dog our plans for the day. She jerked and shut her mouth when she saw me in the kitchen doorway. I reached down and patted Emma's head as I passed and got a slurpy kiss on my hand for my effort. I grabbed a bottle of water and drank down half of it, looking longingly at the coffeepot and the chocolate brew my aunt had started.

"Do you really think you have time to run?" Aunt Jackie looked at the clock. "The group starts at eleven."

"And Sasha has everything ready for them. All she needs is for us to man the front and deal with any issues." I glanced at my watch, calculating the morning schedule. "Emma and I will run for thirty minutes. I'll go finish the bed frame, which will probably take me until ten. Then I'll shower and we'll drive in to the store, arriving at ten thirty, which gives us plenty of time."

My aunt took a sip of her coffee. "If you say so. I've always thought it better to be early than just on time."

"We are going to be early." I held up my hand. "Let's not argue. Keep the doors locked while I'm gone, don't let anyone in, and we'll talk about what you found in the stack of papers while I'm working on the bed frame."

Honestly, I hoped the frame wouldn't take as long as the first one had and I'd be able to fit in the first coat of sealing the bedroom floor, too. But I wasn't going to tell my aunt that or she would probably explode in front of me.

I clicked Emma's leash on her collar and stepped onto the porch. I pulled the door closed behind me and checked the doorknob to make sure the lock had engaged. My aunt made a shooing motion with her hand.

I laughed and headed to the road toward the beach. Running helped clear my head, and with a jam-packed day like this Saturday was developing into, I needed some downtime right up front.

Returning to the house after the run, I finished off the rest of the water and grabbed a banana from the fruit bowl. My aunt was settled on the couch reading a Princess Diana biography. I poked my head into the living room. "Come get me at ten if I'm not back in by then."

"Ten," she repeated and went back to her reading.

An hour later, Greg found me covered with old paint, stripper, and sweat in the garage. I heard his truck in the driveway, and when I looked up, I jammed the putty knife into my finger. "Crap." I shook it off, checked it for blood or a cut, then shook the hand again, hoping to stop the pain.

"Hey, sunshine." Greg leaned against the garage door watching me. He looked all sharp in clean jeans and a pressed shirt. He'd probably also had a shower, something I was looking forward to, too, as soon as I finished the last six inches of the bed frame. Six inches that might as well have been six miles.

"What time is it?" I sat back on a stool that I kept in the garage and surveyed the project.

"Ten to ten. Why, you have a hot date? I thought you were focusing on projects at the house today."

I rolled my shoulders back and forth trying to loosen the knots. Ten minutes? There was no way I could do six inches of paint stripping in ten minutes. I started putting my tools on the bench and closing lids on jars and cans. "I told Sasha I'd help with the bookstore today. I'd forgotten, but she got ahold of Aunt Jackie, so we're due there at eleven."

"Tough break. Another hour or so and you might have finished this." He squatted down to the still-painted section of the frame. "You really had a mess here. This must be ten different types of paint."

"Tell me about it. The only thing I've accomplished is running Emma. This will have to wait until we get back from the store." I looked at him, hope filling my veins. "Tell me you found out Adam isn't a killer so Aunt Jackie can return to the apartment tonight."

"Sorry, can't say that."

I stopped mid-stretch and straightened to look at him. "Adam is a killer?"

Greg shrugged. "Can't say that, either. The only thing I can say about Adam Truman is that before five years ago, he didn't exist."

"Whoa. That's not what I was expecting to hear." I took off the shirt I'd been working in and hung it on a rack. I could see the sweat beads on my arms.

"Exactly. Now you know why I want to keep you out of investigations like this." Greg looked at his phone as a text came in. "Toby just found where the guy lives and he's heading there now. I'll let you know what we find out as soon as we're done."

"You'll share the information?" My smile got a little wider. "Great, I've got a lot of questions about—"

Greg held up his hand. "Easy, hon. I'll let you know if I think it's safe for Jackie to go home. That's all I meant. You need to keep your pretty little nose out of this thing."

"I'll try." At least that was a promise I could keep. Somehow I always got dragged in, and most of the time, it wasn't because I wanted to be there.

"That's all I can ask for." He stepped closer and kissed me quickly on the cheek. "You going to shower before you go?"

"No, Greg. I thought I'd go to my place of business smelling like paint stripper and sweat. I'm not an idiot."

He held his hands up, warding me off, and took a couple of steps backward. "Forget I even said anything." He walked back to his truck and paused in the doorway. "My offer to help tomorrow morning still stands."

I waved him off. "I'll call you if I need rescuing." I swear I could hear his laugh above the roar of the truck's engine when he turned the ignition.

As I promised, we pulled into the parking lot behind the shop at exactly ten thirty. I'd had to drag myself out of the shower long before I'd started to feel human again. But at least I smelled like my floral shampoo and conditioner mix rather than the horror I had a few minutes earlier. We walked in the back door without talking.

A buzz of sound echoed in the back room, and when we entered the counter area, my jaw dropped. There must have been thirty people, well, teenagers, milling around the area, joking and laughing. Some carried the book we'd ordered; some had library copies. Sasha turned and squealed when she saw us.

"Thank God you're here. I didn't expect this many to show up, especially on a summer Saturday." She looked at the line in front of the cash register. "Can you start taking orders and I'll get caught up on the drinks?"

I nodded and stepped up to the counter while my aunt stepped behind me to wash her hands and put on an apron. We worked side by side, and with ten minutes to spare, had all the drinks and eats served. The number of books sold was twice that of a normal Saturday. And that was just in the last thirty minutes. I nodded to Sasha. "You're on. Go knock 'em dead."

My aunt watched as Sasha took off her apron, smoothed her hair, and grabbed the book she'd tucked under the counter. She'd set up a podium at the children's side of the bookstore and had lined up chairs and floor pillows. From what I could see, every chair was taken, and there had been several tables moved over to the area from the dining room.

I looked at the almost-empty display case and nodded to Aunt Jackie. "I'll handle this if you want to watch the front."

She nodded and leaned against the counter, sipping on a bottle of water.

I pulled out three new cheesecakes and a box of cookies from the refrigerator section in the back. Then I replaced those items with frozen ones so that if we needed to restock again, we wouldn't be waiting for the treats to thaw.

As I brought the last cheesecake out to cut, I noticed the guy I'd seen in Lille's heading out the door. "Hey, he showed up."

My aunt closed out the register, then looked at me. "Who showed up?"

"The guy I gave my business card to for the discount. What did he buy?" I slipped the slices onto plates and put them on the last rack of the display case.

"A travel book about the area and a large coffee." My aunt looked at me. "Why are you so interested in the guy?"

"I don't know. He's just around a lot, and I haven't been able to find out why." I glanced at the register. "Tell me he paid with a credit card."

My aunt shook her head. "Cash. Have you thought that maybe he's a tourist? That's what we mainly have in town, tourists."

Something niggled at the back of my mind. Had I seen him somewhere before? I started restocking the cups and supplies for the front. Sasha had turned the podium over to kids who wanted to talk about their favorite section of the book. And surprisingly, several of the readers were lined up to take their turn. She glanced over at me and gave me two thumbs up. She'd hooked them with these books. Now it was time to keep the momentum going. I made a note to do some research on possible topics for future meetings.

The bell rang over the door, and Sadie and Austin wandered into the shop. Sadie hesitated, looking at the bookstore side, but she smiled when she saw me at the register.

"What's going on?" she whispered when they got close.

"Teen book club day. Isn't it great?" I lowered my voice. "When Sasha said she wanted to start this, I assumed we'd have the five girls who almost run the school library now. But no, she got a crowd."

"If you expect the best, you get it." Sadie looked at Austin. "We've come in for a couple of large iced teas to go, then we're going to wander down to the beach and have a picnic lunch."

"On a Saturday? Who's watching your bike rental place?" I looked over at Austin, who blushed.

"I hired someone to help me out on weekends. I'll be back at the shop in an hour." He took Sadie's hand in his. "You have to wake up and smell the roses sometimes. No one said work was the only important thing in life."

I swear my friend almost swooned to the floor. I was a bit more skeptical of Austin's reasons. The man had been known to shut down in the middle of tourist season so he could spend a week backpacking in Colorado. To say he was dedicated to his shop was a bit of an overstatement. I handed over the teas that Aunt Jackie had made while we talked. "Sounds like an excellent date. That will be four dollars and fifty cents."

Austin handed me a five and then gave one of the cups to Sadie.

I tried to give him his change, but he waved it off. "Do you want sugar or sweetener?"

He shook his head. "I've got all the sugar I need right here." He touched Sadie's face and she laughed. I fought the temptation to roll my eyes.

"Well, you two have fun." But I was talking to myself, as they had already started walking toward the door, their gazes locked together. I dropped the quarters into the tip jar and turned toward my aunt. "Man, they've got it bad."

Aunt Jackie watched them leave the shop and sighed before she spoke. "I remember when I first met your uncle. We were inseparable just like that."

I shook my head. "You don't think it's a little too clingy?"

"Jill Gardner, when did you become a love scrooge?" My aunt swatted me with a bar towel. "There is nothing wrong with a little public display of emotion and young love. Well, young-to-them love."

"If you say so. I just hope he's as devoted as he appears. If he hurts my friend, I'm going to have to kill him." I nodded toward the meeting. "Get ready, it looks like Sasha's closing up. We might get another run on drinks."

It was almost four before the shop died down enough for me to even consider returning to the house. Aunt Jackie stayed on to run her evening shift, and Sasha called in some favors to stay for a couple more hours. I'd come back to get my aunt at closing. Aunt Jackie made a call to have Josh come and be with her when Sasha left.

"This really isn't necessary," Aunt Jackie fussed as I was leaving. "I know how to protect myself."

"Humor me. Until Greg locates Adam and finds out what he's looking for from Sandra, I'd rather not have you staying alone." I grabbed my keys and headed to the back parking lot.

My aunt's voice called after me, "What about you?"

"I've got Emma." I didn't stop walking as I answered. No need to give her a reason to keep me at the shop longer. I would get that bed frame done today.

# CHAPTER 18

A man grabbed my arm and pulled me into the walkway between Coffee, Books, and More and Antiques by Thomas. I squeaked out a protest but before I could go into full-blown scream, his hand covered my mouth. "Just be quiet. When I get what I need, I'll let you go."

The voice sounded familiar, but I wasn't taking any chances on exactly what it was this man needed from me. I stomped on his foot, then, as he released his grip, I spun around, digging in my tote for my pepper spray. I'd started carrying it when I worked in the city and had considered putting it in the kitchen drawer now that I lived in a small safe tourist town. Now I was glad my paranoia had prevailed. My fingers wrapped around the cylinder as I recognized my attacker. Adam Truman. He stepped toward me, and I pointed the canister at him.

"Stop right there." My voice was calm. A lot calmer than I felt.

He stepped back, limping a bit on the foot I'd injured. "Look, all I need is the packet that Sandra gave you. Then I'll be out of this town and you'll never hear from me again."

"Which you is leaving?" I dug into my tote for my phone, not moving the pepper spray or looking away from the crazed man. "The one who just started existing five years ago? Or the person your mother named when you were born?"

He seemed to crumple as I watched. I dug deeper for my phone.

"So you read the papers Sandra gave you." He shook his head. "I should have known that even though I followed through on her instructions, she was never going to let me get away."

"I'm not sure what you're talking about, Adam Truman." I spoke loudly so anyone walking out on the street could hear the conversation. "I never got a packet of papers from Sandra Ashford."

"Right. Then how did you know I changed my name?" He rubbed his hands through his hair. "Look, I did all three things on the list. Even after Sandra died. She said you'd be handing over the documents after I destroyed the window. I held up my end of the bargain, now it's your turn."

"Are you crazy? Why would Sandra give me anything? I barely knew her." I took a chance and glanced down at my purse. But then Adam's words sank in. "Wait, you're saying you were the one vandalizing The Train Station? Why?"

"Are you deaf or just not listening? Sandra said if I did what she asked, she'd stop blackmailing me. Now you're telling me you're not her partner?"

"No, I'm not." I abandoned my search for the cell phone and started yelling, still holding the pepper spray focused on Adam's face. "Help, someone help me!"

I heard rocks crunch under running feet and looked up to see Greg and Toby flying through the opening between the buildings. How they got there so fast, I didn't know, but right then I didn't care. I'd never been so happy to see anyone in my life. I swallowed away tears as Greg stood in front of Adam.

"Put your hands behind your back and turn around, slowly." He slapped on a pair of handcuffs and handed Adam off to Toby. "Jill, do me a favor and put the pepper spray down."

I looked at my outstretched hand, now shaking violently, and then dropped my arm, putting the spray back into my tote. Then I sank into Greg's arms. "Thanks."

"It's my job. Although your antics make it an ongoing task on my to-do list. Maybe you should just stay put sometimes when things are crazy." He squeezed me, then looked at Adam. "Toby, read this guy his rights."

As Toby walked Adam through the walkway and out to the street where I assumed a South Cove police car was waiting, I looked up at Greg. "So, what are you going to charge him with? Sandra's murder?"

"First, your attack. And don't tell me you're not going to press charges because he's such a wounded soul." He stepped back and looked me over. "He didn't hurt you, did he?"

I rubbed my arm where he'd originally grabbed me, and shook my head. "Scared the crap out of me. When I stomped on his foot and he let me go, well, I didn't know what he wanted. All I knew was I wasn't going to let him take me."

"Smart girl." Greg put his arm around me and we walked to the street. Toby already had Adam in the cruiser. Aunt Jackie ran toward me as soon as we cleared the building.

"You're safe. I was so worried. I saw you disappear and so I ran in to call Greg. Good thing the station is so close." She kissed me on the forehead. "I could have lost you."

Gratitude overwhelmed me as I realized, not for the first time, I was truly not alone in the world. I had my over-the-top nosy aunt, and because of her watchful eye, I'd been saved by my equally as overbearing boyfriend. Well, overbearing at times. I hugged her back and then looked at Adam in the back of the car. "I don't know what he thought I had, but it had to do with his identity change five years ago. When I asked him about it, he lost his fight."

Greg kissed me. "Stop investigating. I'll take it from here." He nodded to my aunt. "Thanks for giving me a call."

My aunt took my arm and led me back into the coffee shop, where the rest of the teenagers who had still been at book club had surrounded the front door. "Move out of the way, nothing to see here. Go do something productive with your lives."

By the time we got into the café, my legs were shaking. "I need to sit down." I pointed to the couch. "Can someone bring me a glass of water or something?"

Sasha put a glass into my hand. "My goodness. That was quite a scare. Are you sure he didn't hurt you?"

I drank down the entire glass before I answered. "No. No, I'm not hurt." I smiled at Sasha and Aunt Jackie, who were staring down at me like I'd been murdered or something. "Back off, guys, you're freaking me out here. I'm just glad Greg showed up when he did. I still don't understand how he got from the station to the shop that quick."

My aunt sat next to me and patted my leg. "It's not a miracle. I called him earlier because I saw that awful man looking in the window during Sasha's book club."

"You what?" I set the empty glass on the coffee table. "Why didn't you tell me you saw Adam?"

"Well, I meant to, but then we got busy and Greg said he and Toby would take care of it, so I kind of forgot about it." My aunt smoothed the fabric on her pants. "I was going to call the station and see if they'd found him before you came back for me this evening."

I leaned back against the couch, turning my face to heaven and closing my eyes. I wondered if this was how Greg felt sometimes talking to me. I took a deep breath and gazed at my aunt. "So, why didn't you tell me before I started for home? It might have helped."

"You weren't walking home. How did I know he was lying in wait for you? The man's insane. How am I supposed to predict crazy?" The bell over the door rang and she stood. "I'll handle this. Apparently, that's all an old woman is good for around here. Serving drinks."

"Aunt Jackie," I called after her, but her back was metal-rod straight. I'd upset her. I started to stand, but Sasha put her hand on my arm.

"Let her be. You don't realize how scared she was. If something had happened to you, she would have blamed herself. No need for you to poke at her with that stick." Sasha's cell rang in her pocket. She glanced at the caller ID and stood. "Got to take this. My granny has Olivia today and I'm sure she's tired of the girl tearing up her picture-perfect house."

I waved her away and thought about the last fifteen minutes. Well, one good thing had come from Adam's attack. We knew who had vandalized The Train Station. And probably why. I needed to talk to Lille and see if she'd hired Sandra for the work. She'd seemed upset about what had happened to Harrold, but that could have all been an act. Honestly, I didn't know Lille all that well. Probably due to the fact that she hated me.

Sasha came back to the couch and flopped down next to me. "I guess I'd better head home. I'm glad you're safe."

I gave her a hug. "Sorry to ruin your book club with all this. I thought you did an excellent job."

"It went really nice. I was proud of the kids. They asked great questions and really opened up to each other. I told them to e-mail me with suggestions for next month's read and we'd put up an online poll. Most votes wins." Sasha looked around the room. "Who knows what they're going to choose. I'm a little nervous."

"It will be fine. And if it's totally inappropriate, you have veto power." I grinned at Sasha's surprised face. "You're in charge. You can do whatever you want."

"I hadn't thought of it that way."

"Being the grown-up has to have some advantages." I leaned forward and grabbed the glass. "Well, at least now Greg has a suspect for Sandra's murder, as well. I'm sure he'll have the case all tied up before Monday."

Sasha glanced out the window where the police car had sat. "You mean, you think Adam killed Sandra? That's not possible."

"I don't understand. The guy admitted vandalizing Harrold's business. Why do you think he can't be a murderer, too?" Standing I rested a knee on the couch, waiting for Sasha's answer.

Sasha took off her apron. "Because the guy Toby put in the cruiser was drinking with Michael at the winery the night Sandra was run over. They closed down the place, and Darla had Matt drop them off at the bed-and-breakfast where they were staying."

This time when I left the shop, I actually arrived at the Jeep parked behind the building. Instead of leaving through the front door, I took the back door that opened out right into the parking lot. My aunt stood behind me and watched until I got in the car and waved. Then she slammed the door and probably locked it behind her. I was going to have to do some fast talking to get out of the doghouse with her.

When I got home, I grabbed a bottle of beer and Emma and we went out to the garage to finish the bed frame. Having a sixty-pound dog lying on the cool cement floor in between me and any intruder eased my nerves a little. The beer helped a little more. And when I got focused on the project, I'd pushed aside my fear. The sun was just setting when I'd finished stripping the last of the paint off the frame. I leaned back on my workbench and appraised my almost-final project. All I needed to do tomorrow was apply a couple coats of paint and let the frame dry. Monday morning, I'd have the bed all assembled and ready for the mattress delivery.

If I could get the floor sealed tomorrow. I knew it was all up to me. No way would Greg be available to help. I pushed off the worry and put a happy thought in my head. Like the little engine that could, I would be ready for the delivery truck Monday morning. "I can do this, right, girl?" I squatted down and petted the sleeping Emma.

She turned and looked at me, barking a short "woof" to answer my question. Or probably more likely to ask her own, like, *When are you going to feed me? I'm starving.*

I cleaned up the garage, sealing the cans, and put my special work shirt on the bench. I think I agreed with Emma, it was way past dinnertime and I heard the siren call of frozen tater tots from my freezer.

I'd set my alarm for six even though it was Sunday. As I swung my legs over the side of the bed, I groaned. My shoulders were on fire. Jerking steps took me to the shower, where I stood under the hot water until it cooled. Seriously, I needed to start adding some weight training to my fitness routine. Running with Emma wasn't doing a thing to build up my arm strength.

As I dressed, Emma whined at the door. "Sorry, girl, I'm moving a little slow today." I pulled on an old tank and cut-off shorts and followed Emma down to the kitchen, where I let her out. Pouring myself a cup of coffee, I spied the leftover cheesecake and cut myself a large slice. Breakfast of champions. Besides, I'd probably burned that many calories between yesterday's scare and stripping the bed frame. And today I had another calorie scorcher of a day planned. Heck, I might have a second piece of cheesecake for lunch.

I sat at the table and raised the fork to my lips. A knock sounded at the front door. Considering the fact I'd already done the hard part, I shoved the bite of cheesecake in my mouth, then went to answer. As I swung the door open, Greg stood in front of me, dressed in a ratty I Climbed Out of the Grand Canyon T-shirt and green cargo shorts. The man looked California beach fine. I swallowed the cheesecake, and quite possibly my tongue, and blurted, "What are you doing here?"

He laughed as he wiped the corner of my mouth with a finger. Looking at the crumb, he sighed. He kissed me on the cheek and looked toward the kitchen. "Please tell me you have some of this left? Sadie outdid herself with this recipe."

"You're here to work?" I held my arm out to block his forward movement.

He pulled me into his arms and power-drove me to the couch, where he held my arms above my head and kissed me more thoroughly this time. He pulled away from me, stared into my eyes, and murmured, "I'm your willing slave."

My stomach felt like I'd swallowed a bucket of butterflies. I bit my bottom lip so hard, I reached up to make sure it wasn't bleeding. And that was the moment Greg jumped over the couch and went into the kitchen. I stood up and followed. He had my plate of cheesecake in his hand as he looked in the fridge. Then he handed the plate back to me. "You're in luck. There's a slice or two left for me."

I took the plate and went back to the table, where I took another bite. I watched him cut an extra-large slice and put it on a plate. Then he poured coffee and joined me at the table. I pointed my fork at his plate. "That was going to be my lunch."

He didn't even pause. "You can take me for an early dinner in Bakerstown and we'll skip lunch."

"You think I have time to go out to eat?" I pointed to the list with *Sunday* written on top. "Look at that list. I'll be lucky if I can pause for a glass of water."

"I told you I was here to help." He considered the list. "We should be done by three thirty, four at the latest. We can get there in time for early bird pricing."

"The way I'm moving, we might qualify for the senior rate." I rubbed my left shoulder. "Who knew vacation could be so hard on a body?"

Greg set his fork down and came around the table. He put his hands on my shoulders and started to rub. "Not quite the cruise we'd planned, huh?"

I dropped my head, letting his fingers work out the knots in my muscles. "I'm not complaining. I'm getting another room done and earning bonus points with you as the understanding girlfriend. By the time we actually go somewhere, you'll owe me big-time."

Greg chuckled as he worked on a spot on my neck. I almost wanted to cry his massage felt so good. "I did save you from the crazed attacker yesterday. Doesn't that wipe out some of your understanding points so we're even?"

"Not even close, buddy." I rolled my head and sighed. Then I opened my eyes and put my hands up to still his hands. "Why aren't you working on the case?"

"Adam's a jerk. He's going to be charged with the vandalism and your attack, but when we ran his prints, the city called. Apparently he is wanted for skipping out on a court appearance, leaving his elderly mother holding the bond. She was weeks away from losing her home." Greg picked up my cup. "More coffee?"

I nodded. "I can't believe he would do that to his mother."

Greg filled both of our cups, then walked back and sat. "I know. Son of the year material, right?" He took a sip. "Anyway, the DA says we can't do anything until those charges are dealt with."

"What about Sandra's murder?" I wondered if Greg already knew what Sasha had told me yesterday.

"No dice there. Unless he hired it out. He and Michael were drinking together at the winery after the big celebrity party. Darla's already confirmed that." He took another bite of the cheesecake. "Besides, I don't see what he would have to gain from it, especially since he thought Sandra had already passed the blackmail material on."

"To me." I held up my hands to the heavens. "How on earth did I get involved?"

He laughed. "Honey, just face it. You're always involved." He held up a hand, stopping my tirade. "I know, you didn't do this. I'm beginning to think he misunderstood or had just guessed wrong."

"Whatever. I'm tired of getting dragged into these things." I stood up and took my plate and cup to the sink. "What do you want? Paint the frame, install wainscoting, or seal the wood floor?"

Greg followed me to the sink and wrapped his arms around me. "Remember that feeling next time you decide to go clue hunting with your aunt." He kissed my neck. "Give me the sealer and you take Emma with you to the garage. Just in case someone else comes to visit you."

Greg had been spot-on with his estimate of our arrival time at the restaurant. By four thirty, we were already eating our dinner salads. And that had included a quick shower and our drive time. I felt like I hadn't eaten real food for a week, even though we'd gone out just that Friday.

He took a swig off his beer and smiled at me. "You hungry?"

"Starving."

"What did you eat last night?" I thought about the pile of tater tots I'd scarfed down in front of the television last night. No use lying, he was a paid investigator.

"A huge bowl of tater tots and special sauce. And, before you ask, I had a banana split for dessert."

"Balanced dinner." He waved his fork at me. "I'm surprised your arteries aren't clogged from all the fried food you eat."

"What can I say, I'm blessed." A man walked past our table and I looked up into his face. It was the tourist guy. Now this was just getting weird. Either he was stalking me, or we just happened to eat at all the same places. I set my fork down. "Excuse me, I'll be right back."

I followed the man into the lobby, then caught up with him, turning him by grabbing hold of his arm. "Hey, I thought that was you."

"Do I know you?" He looked down at me, a smile crossing his lips.

I nodded, feeling my head bounce like a puppy dog. "I own the bookstore and coffee shop in South Cove. I gave you a discount card. So, did you enjoy it?"

He shook his head, looking back into the dining room. "I'm sorry. Did I enjoy what, my meal?"

"Sure, but I was talking about the book. Did you enjoy the travel book you bought?"

He studied me. "You have a strange way of doing customer satisfaction surveys."

I shrugged. "What can I say? I'm devoted to the shop and the happiness of my customers."

"Okay, then. Actually, I haven't read the book. I bought it for my girlfriend as a gift." He held his hands palms up. "Anything else you want to ask?"

I felt Greg come up behind me. "Is everything okay?"

I put my arm through his. "Just checking in on a customer. I hope your girlfriend enjoys the book."

I let Greg lead me back to the table. Our dinners had arrived while I had been talking to the tourist guy. I cut a piece of fish off with my fork and stabbed it.

Greg watched me attack the cod. "You going to tell me what that was all about? The guy looked scared. Don't tell me he has a secret, too."

# CHAPTER 19

Greg came inside after we finished dinner and the floors had dried hard enough to set up the bed frame. I frowned at the bare floor underneath the bed and put washcloths under each foot. "I was going to go flea market shopping with Amy today. But no, Adam had to ruin my planning."

"I'll help you put a rug under the bed later." Greg pulled me close. "I think it looks amazing."

"The room's not even halfway done. I need mattresses."

He nodded. "Which are coming tomorrow."

"And I don't have the rest of the furniture or a rug or even a quilt." My gaze drifted toward the ceiling. "Or wainscoting. We forgot the wainscoting."

He turned me around and tilted my head toward his so I could see his eyes. "Stop being a glass-half-empty girl. You're better than that."

I forced my shoulders down and sank into his chest. "You're good at this, you know?"

"What? Calming you down?" He chuckled. "Lots of experience with overwrought women in my life. You're easy. Your stress comes from the too-high expectations you put on yourself."

"I like setting and meeting goals, so sue me." I peeked around Greg to look one more time at the room. It *was* very pretty already.

Greg laughed as he guided me out of the incomplete room and closed the door. "Goals are one thing. You set up a timetable a Greek god couldn't meet."

We walked arm in arm down the narrow staircase, Emma following. "You want to stay for coffee?"

"We still have cheesecake?" Greg aimed us toward the kitchen. "If so, I'm all in for a cup and a slice."

We talked for an hour. When Greg stood to leave, I didn't object. My eyelids kept closing, and I was craving climbing in between the sheets of my bed and letting sleep overtake me.

He held me close for a minute. "Go to bed. You're almost ready to drop."

"Thanks for helping today. I could have done it..." A yawn stopped me from finishing the sentence.

"All by yourself, I know." He stepped out on the porch. "Lock up after me."

I nodded and followed his instructions. Three minutes later, I was snuggled in bed.

I was a load into laundry the next morning when my cell rang. "Hello."

"Where are you?" my aunt demanded.

"I'm home waiting for the mattress delivery, remember?" I sorted the rest of the clothes into whites and not whites. "You were there when I made the plans."

"I'll be right over. You need to see this." The line went dead and I put the phone in the pocket of my cut-offs. I glanced down at Emma, who was ignoring the laundry on the floor next to her.

"Your crazy Aunt Jackie is coming over."

Emma sat at attention at the mention of the name. I closed the door to the laundry room and went to the kitchen to make a fresh pot of coffee.

I heard her car pull up so I met her at the door. She was dressed in typical Aunt Jackie casual: silk shirt, a floating diamond necklace, and slim dress pants. She made a nod to the warmer weather with flat sandals. She kissed me lightly on the cheek and then looked at my tank and ratty shorts. "I guess you weren't expecting company?"

"You're here, aren't you?" I closed the door and flipped the locks. A habit Greg had forced on me with his multiple lectures about living right off a major highway alone. I'd never really had a problem, but the more I heard from him about break-ins up and down the coastline, the more comfortable I felt with keeping the house locked.

My aunt headed to the kitchen, pausing at the laundry door. "Oh, I didn't realize you were out of decent clothes to wear. You really should do laundry more often."

I watched her beeline to the coffeepot and pour a cup. Then she pulled out a bag of cookies from her oversized tote and arranged them on one of my good plates. She walked both back to the table.

"I like my outfit. I'm not out of clean clothes, but I've got a lot of work to do today." I eyed a cookie but went to fill my own cup instead. I went to the table, grabbed what looked like an oatmeal-raisin cookie, and pointed it at her. "So, now that you're done insulting me, what did I need to see?"

She pulled out a newspaper and opened it to the middle. She folded the paper so I could see the article. "This."

The headline read, *Out-of-the-Way Diner Evokes Classic Memories*. Underneath the headline was a small picture of the tourist guy. "No way. Evan McCurdy, food critic." I grinned. "I saw him yesterday at dinner with Greg and asked him if he liked the book he bought."

"You stopped by his table?" My aunt looked surprised.

Now I could feel the heat rise in my face. "No. Actually, I chased him down in the lobby as he was leaving. I think he thought I knew he was doing an undercover diner visit. When I asked him about the book, he seemed relieved."

"He probably thought you were going to out him." My aunt took a sip of her coffee. "What did Greg say when you ran off?"

"Actually, he followed me." Now I really felt like a fool. "I think he thought something was wrong. Then he caught me talking to this guy. I don't know what Greg imagined."

"I suppose he's used to you and your need to know everything right now." My aunt pointed at the article. "That's not all I wanted you to see. Read the review."

I started reading. This must have been the competition Carrie had mentioned that Lille thought was going to blast the diner into popularity. The tourist guy—Evan—I corrected myself, mentioned the contest and that even though Diamond Lille's had been a strong contender, there was just a lot of competition in the area. He ended the piece with a nice overview of South Cove's offering as a Sunday getaway or a staycation destination. I pointed to the last paragraph. "He mentions how cute and customer-friendly Coffee, Books, and More, the local bookstore–slash–coffee shop is."

"I wonder if he wrote that before or after you ran him down yesterday at that diner?" My aunt dug in her purse. "Anyway, when I went down to the shop to grab these cookies, this was on the fax machine."

I took the pages and saw on the cover, it had the county court-house number. "What is this?"

My aunt took a cookie and broke it in half before taking a bite. "I think that is called a clue. Read the attachment Madeline sent."

I read over the cover where she apologized for missing the attachment on my last visit to the records department. Then I read the rest. By the time I was done, my thoughts were racing.

"Interesting, right?" My aunt watched me over the top of her cup.

"This changes everything. I think this might just lead us to who killed Sandra." I thumbed through the pages. "It says here Bakerstown Public Relations had an exclusive option to purchase Promote Your Brand for thirty days. And as of last Friday, they were exercising the option."

"If I were Greg, I'd want to talk to that husband again. Maybe he was trying to sell the business and run away with Rachel."

I shook my head. "Michael has an alibi. He was drinking with Adam at the winery. And seeing him at the meeting with the California Mission Society, I don't think he could do it. He seemed heart-broken to lose her."

"Except when he was taking the other woman to lunch, remember?" My aunt shook her finger at me. "Don't let his puppy dog eyes fool you. The man offed his wife to be with his mistress. Oldest story ever told."

"If Michael was selling this place, all we have to do is give the owner"—I scanned down the papers to the named parties—"Thomas Brown, a call to see who he was dealing with on the sale."

"Then we turn it over to Greg?"

I nodded. "Then we turn it over to Greg."

I grabbed my laptop and searched for Bakerstown Public Relations. You would think there wouldn't be enough business for two PR firms in town. Maybe that was why this guy wanted to buy out Sandra and Michael. Except from what I knew, Promote Your Event mostly worked with agencies on onetime events and annual conventions. I guess they'd carved out a niche for themselves. A very profitable niche, from their annual reports.

I found the website and wrote down the number. When I dialed it on my cell, I got a recorded message telling me that the office would be open at ten. I hung up the phone and looked at the clock. "We've got just under three hours before the place opens."

"Should we drive in to talk to him?" My aunt grabbed for her purse.

I scanned the website for a physical address. "We can't until the mattress arrives. The delivery is scheduled between eight and noon." When I found the address, I wrote it in my notebook. "Interesting. This office is in the same building and on the same floor as Promote Your Event."

"Maybe that's how they approached Michael to sell." My aunt set her purse down again. "So what am I going to do until after ten, when we can call this guy?"

"You could work on the books for the shop." Last year when my aunt had taken over the bookkeeping for Coffee, Books, and More, she'd also networked my computer with both hers and the one at the shop. That way, we could work at home or in the shop on the accounting and supply ordering. I had a dedicated desktop that I only used for shop business in my office. Well, plus a little pinning of pictures of coffee drinks, books, and dessert treats to the shop's Pinterest board. Okay, a lot of pinning.

"I do hope you've dusted lately in your office." My aunt took her cup to the pot and refilled. "You know I'm allergic."

"Knock yourself out. You know where the cleaning supplies are. I'm heading upstairs to make sure there's a path to the guest room for the mattress guys." I loved my aunt, truly, but sometimes, she knew just the right thing to say that would jerk my chain. Besides, who had time to dust anymore? Probably the same people who ironed. I wasn't even sure where my iron was or whether I still owned one.

The truck with the mattress arrived at nine thirty. By the time the guys had wrestled the mattress through the living room and up the stairs, where it promptly got stuck in the hallway, it was after ten. We had to back it down the stairs, get one of the guys in the bedroom, and then retry the move. This time it worked, and we knew how to get the box springs in the room. I was beginning to rethink my plans for the third bedroom. I'd wanted to set up a home gym, but how would we get the equipment up the narrow stairs? I had a shed out on the property, maybe I should think of using that area.

"Lady, I know I shouldn't say this, but I hope you take your next mattress purchase elsewhere." The young man wiped the sweat from his forehead.

The other guy, older, shook his head, slapping the other guy on his arm. "Jake's just lazy. You don't worry about it. We can get anything you purchase up these stairs, no problem."

The younger guy grinned. "Whatever, man. I'm not the one who looks like he's going to have a heart attack."

"Would you like a bottle of water?" I agreed with Jake. The older man looked pale and drawn.

He nodded. "That would be nice. I'll have Superman here drive us to the next stop."

I grabbed a couple of bottles of water out of the fridge and bagged up two cookies from the plate on the table. I met the guys on the front porch as they gathered up their tools. "Here you are. Cookies are from Coffee, Books, and More in town. I own the shop and would love to treat the two of you to a coffee someday."

"My girlfriend loves that place. She's always making me take her there on Saturdays." Jake grinned. "I don't mind though. We tend to hang out on the beach afterward and man, she looks good in her bikini."

"You are a dog." The older man chuckled. He turned to me. "You are very kind. Maybe my wife and I will come visit someday."

As I watched the truck drive away, my aunt came up behind me. "I swear, you build the customer base one person at a time. How did you know that they would even be interested in visiting the shop?"

I closed the door and turned toward her. "Are you kidding? He wore a wedding ring so there was a chance his wife might enjoy a visit. And the kid? Well, South Cove is for lovers. It's our new log line. What do you think?"

"I hate it." My aunt handed me my cell, excitement pouring out of her body like a kid on Christmas Eve. "Call the PR guy."

I hit redial and when the answering machine picked up, it was the same message. But this time, I listened all the way through. "Closed for lunch at one." I glanced at the clock. We'd just missed him. I set my phone on the coffee table and nodded upstairs. "I'll get sheets on that bed and then come down and make soup and salad for lunch. What do you think?"

My aunt twisted her head to stretch her neck. "I think I'll go back to working on the accounts. Call me when it's ready."

I switched out a load of laundry and let Emma into the house before I went upstairs. She bounded around, looking for the men whom she'd known were in *her* house. "Too late, baby." I rubbed under her chin. "The delivery guys have already left."

She ignored my information and ran upstairs in front of me to keep me safe. When she saw the mattress settled on the bed frame, she sniffed the length of the bed, looking for any sign that the interlopers were still around. I got the sheets out of the linen closet and covered the new mattress. I threw on an old comforter I'd had in the closet, as well. I had to admit, the room was starting to look good. But by the time I was done, it would be as amazing as one of the theme rooms over at South Cove Bed-and-Breakfast.

As the soup thawed in the microwave, I made a final list of what I needed to buy for the new room. I didn't have a lot of sleepover guests, besides my aunt, but when I did, I'd be ready for them.

By the time we'd finished our green salad with grilled chicken slices and a tomato bisque soup, the clock showed two-oh-five. I grabbed the phone and hit redial. "Third time's a charm," I whispered as the phone rang. But I'd spoken too soon. I got the answering machine again. This time I left a message, leaving both my name and the store name. At least he might think it was a call on a possible job, which could get our phone call returned faster. My aunt sank into the chair.

"I'm beat. I'm heading back to the apartment and soaking in a tub filled with hot water and bubbles. I might even open a bottle of wine and have cheese and crackers for dinner." She kissed me on the cheek. "Are you going to spend the last few hours of your vacation relaxing? Or do you have another project?"

"I'm done. Well, except for laundry. I think I'm going to curl up on the couch and read until my stomach growls. Thanks for coming by today." I walked her toward the door.

"You sound like you really mean that." My aunt smiled softly and patted my hair. "I like spending time with you."

As she walked out the door, my phone rang.

# CHAPTER 20

Amy's voice boomed through the speaker. "Girl, where are you? I thought we were meeting at Lille's for a late lunch."

I squeezed my eyes together. My aunt waved and walked out to her car. "I guess you won't be relaxing after all."

"Hey, I totally forgot. I'll be there in ten." I looked down at my dirty shorts and shirt. I'd have to change and I really should shower. "Make it fifteen."

"Fine, but hurry up. I've already snagged us a booth, but the place is hopping and Carrie keeps asking if I'd rather sit at the counter."

"I'll hurry." I closed the door and ran upstairs, discarding clothes as I ran. I pulled my hair back with a clip and jumped in the shower to lather up and rinse off. My hair would have to be okay the way it was. When I toweled off, I glanced through what was clean and left in my dresser. I had a choice between a Halloween bad witch costume and a pair of old capris and a Heart tank I'd gotten at a concert too many years ago to remember.

I hurried Emma out to the yard, hoping coyotes didn't really hang out during the day, and had to stop and fill her water and food dishes before I left. I slipped on a pair of walking shoes and locked up the house. I glanced at my phone. Amy had called eight minutes ago. If I walked fast, I might even make the fifteen I'd promised.

It was twenty, and when I walked in, the diner was buzzing. Every table was crowded, mostly with people I didn't know. The counter even had most of the stools taken. I glanced around the crowd and saw Amy waving toward me. Lille was standing in front of the booth. When she turned around to see who Amy was waving at, her face hardened.

"I should have known she was waiting for you. Do you realize the faster I can turn a table here, the more people I can serve? Or did that nugget of information never make it into your fancy law degree?" Lille snarled.

"Sorry. My fault. I didn't remember about our date." I quickly looked at the menu. Since I'd just eaten, most of this meal would be put into a to-go box for dinner. "How about the fried chicken dinner?"

"Do I look like your server? I'll let Carrie know you're ready, finally." Lille turned toward the kitchen, then spun back around. "And tell your boyfriend to leave Mick alone. Just because he rides a bike doesn't make him a criminal."

"Greg interviewed your boyfriend?" I set the menu down and rapid-fired my questions. "Do you know why? Was it about Sandra's murder?"

"Like I'm going to tell you anything?" Lille sneered. "But no, Miss Have-to-Know-It-All, it wasn't about the murder. Of course, you'd love that. You're always trying to send my guys to jail, aren't you?"

"Only if they deserve it." The words were out of my mouth before I could stop them, and as I slapped my hand over my mouth, Lille stepped closer, fire in her eyes. "I'm sorry, I didn't mean that."

"Of course you did. I'm watching you. Everyone might think you're sweet and innocent, but I know better." This time she did leave the table.

"Boy, that was risky. You know she's kicked people out of here for life just because she got mad at them, right?" Amy's eyes were wide and she looked a little scared.

"Then we'd just have to eat up the highway at Mel's," I muttered, looking through the menu to see what I wanted for dinner. Not that I wouldn't end up ordering the chicken, I just wanted to check out my options now that I had a little time.

Amy's nose curled. "I hate that place. It smells like cigarette smoke."

"No one's smoked in there in years." Mel's used to be a biker hangout on the coastal highway, but when the old man Mel had died, his daughter had reopened as a sandwich shop. The bikers, used to heavier food at cheaper prices, had moved down the highway to a new bar and grill.

Amy pushed a lock of hair back behind her ears. "I don't care, it still reeks."

Carrie stopped by our table, her grin wide. "You two know how to cheat death, that's all I got to say."

"She still mad?" I asked, already knowing the answer.

"Honey, she's going to be spitting nails every time your name is mentioned for months now." Carrie positioned her pen to the order pad. "So, what can I get you for your last meal?"

Amy raised her eyebrows in an *I told you so* gesture.

"Oh man, don't tell me we got banned." I peeked around Carrie at the hostess station where Lille stood, glaring our way.

Carrie chuckled. "Nah, I'm just messing with you. What can I get started before she really does ban you for taking too much of my time." A bell sounded in the kitchen. "I've got food up."

We gave her our orders and then settled back into the booth. "You were almost on my bad list for the year." Amy pulled out her phone. "Along with the mayor, who's been riding my butt about some report we have to get done for the council meeting. Now, mind you, they don't meet for almost three weeks, but Marvin wants this report compiled and on his desk by Friday. The man is impossible."

"Maybe it will take him that long to understand what you said in the report."

Amy giggled. "You're probably spot-on there. So, how has your vacation been? I thought I might hear from you yesterday."

I explained the remodeling fiasco, along with Adam's kind of kidnapping or attack I'd suffered on Saturday. I finished the week's report with one additional line: "And then Aunt Jackie's in a mood, so we've kind of been investigating Sandra's murder."

Amy shook her head. "Seriously? You were attacked and you're complaining about stripping a bed frame? Did he hurt you? What did he want?"

"Beats me. For some reason, he thought Sandra had given me something that would prove who he really was. I tried to tell him I'd only met the chick once." I sipped on my iced tea. "Besides, stripping that bed frame was a real pain."

"You are something else. No wonder Greg worries about you." Amy read a text on her phone and then texted a short answer back. "I wonder if Sandra called you something else, instead of using your name. Like my friend from South Cove. Maybe that's why he thought it was you."

I nodded to the phone. "You need to go?" I didn't want her to get in trouble with her boss. My mind drifted to her words. *My friend from South Cove.*

"No way. I had to take a late lunch anyway, Marvin can just cool his jets." Amy picked up her milk shake. "Besides, this is the first shake I've had in two weeks. I'm not letting a report get in the way of enjoying one of Lille's shakes. I swear, she makes the best shakes in fifty miles."

I stared at Amy. Could it be that easy?

She cocked an eyebrow at me. "You don't agree? Whose shakes are better?"

I turned and looked at Lille still at the hostess stand talking to a waiting couple. "No, I mean, yes, I agree with the shake thing. But Amy, what if Lille was the friend?"

"I don't think Lille has any friends," Amy quipped. "Wait, what are we talking about?"

"Adam. Maybe Sandra said something to make him think that I had the proof because of the coffee shop, but really, it was Lille at the diner? We're the only two places in town that serve food. I'm sure Sandra didn't mean to say anything that would lead him to Lille, so maybe just a funny clue, one she thought he'd never figure out." My mind was racing now. "Aunt Jackie and I already found a connection between Promote Your Event and Diamond Lille's. Maybe the real connection isn't between the two businesses, but the two owners."

"Which is why he'd be asked to vandalize Harrold's shop." Amy tapped her lips with one finger. "So, how do we know if Lille and Sandra were friends?"

"We could wait for the funeral and see if Lille shows up, but who knows when the body will be released to the family?" I looked at the food in front of Amy that had just been delivered. "Or . . ."

Amy looked horror-stricken. "She's already mad at us. Now you want to ask her if she was friends with someone who may have ordered The Train Station's vandalism?"

I considered her words. "It does sound bad, worded like that." I took a bite of my clam fettuccini. "But, yeah, that's what I'm planning."

"Well, at least let me enjoy my last Diamond Lille's Monster Burger before you torpedo our ability to eat here."

We finished our meal in silence. I picked at my pasta, running the idea through my head. If Lille was Sandra's friend, she would have known about the plan to attack Harrold. But she'd seemed as upset for the man as a good neighbor should have been the day we talked. Unless Sandra was acting on her own. Which would keep Lille out of the problem if Sandra had been found out.

I still wasn't sure exactly how I was going to get the information out of Lille by the time we'd finished the meal and I had my to-go box all packed.

"Maybe she won't be mad at me if I'm not around when you ask." Amy scooted out in front of me, hugging me quickly.

"Chicken," I called after her as she wove her way through the tables. I left a tip for Carrie on the table and headed straight to Lille.

When I arrived at the front, she looked up and then returned to staring at the waitress station board. "What do you want now?"

"I wanted to ask you if you knew Sandra Ashford?" When Lille didn't respond or look up, I continued, "She ran Promote Your Event with her husband, Michael?"

"Michael didn't do anything at that business except for show up every day. And he only did that because Sandra drove the car." Lille studied me. "I don't know that it's any of your business, but Sandra and I went to school together. We've been friends for twenty years."

I didn't move, I didn't even breathe. This was the connection. I tried to think of a way to ask about the Ashfords' marriage when Lille spoke again, this time her words a little softer.

"Sandra was amazing. She grew that business from nothing to what it is today. She'd signed papers to sell it for over a million dollars. Not that she lived to see any of that money." The look in Lille's eyes was distant. "She could have made a whole new start."

"Was she leaving Michael?"

Now Lille stared at me like I was a complete idiot. "Why would she take that cheater along with her? He'd just find another floozy in the next town. She was finally going to be rid of that loser."

*Which again pointed the finger to Michael as the killer.* My thoughts raced as I wondered if Greg knew about the affair. I could guess who had been in Michael's sights last: Rachel Fleur, our travel agent. A voice interrupted my thoughts.

"Two of my favorite restaurant owners standing in front of me. Don't tell me you're working in cahoots to try to get me to change my mind." Homer Bell stood next to me, holding up his hands in a defensive move. "Don't kill me, but I've already signed the contract with the other buyer. In fact, that's why I'm here. I read the write-up in yesterday's paper and thought this would be a great place for me to celebrate."

"You sold the truck?" Lille and I both spoke at once.

Homer had the good sense to back up a few steps. "I would have called you later. I didn't actually expect to run into both of you so quickly." He adjusted his T-shirt, which was riding up and showing a bit of his belly over the jeans he wore. "I couldn't pass up the deal. Cash offer and a lot more than either one of you were offering."

"You said I had time to research the market." I didn't want to be the one to tell my aunt we had lost the option of buying the truck. Maybe I could find another one to purchase before she found out.

He shrugged. "I guess I forgot about saying that."

Lille poked him in the chest. "You told me you'd let me rebid if someone offered more. If I had known, I would have purchased it the day we talked."

"Ladies, it's water under the bridge now." He nodded to the dining room. "Can I get a table?"

"No." Lille pointed to a sign on the wall. "The sign says I can refuse service to anyone, and I'm going to do that. Get out of my diner and don't come back."

I bit my lip, trying not to smile, but man, Lille had him on the ropes. I was mad at him, don't get me wrong, but Lille was steaming.

"But Lille, can't we just shake hands and be friends?" Homer held out a hand. I watched, just in case I had to rush him to the hospital once Lille bit it off.

"You need some help leaving?" She called back to the kitchen, "Sam, come out here and escort our guest out, please."

Sam, the cook for the shift, must have been six-five and a good two hundred fifty pounds or so. Any way you looked at it, the man wasn't tiny. He took off his apron and looked around. "Who do I need to kick out?"

Homer held up his hands and backed out of the doorway. Lille jerked her head back into the kitchen, and Sam grabbed his apron and disappeared with the grace of a retreating troll.

Lille stared at me. "You're still here?"

I thought about asking Lille whom Michael had been sleeping with, for about 1.2 seconds, then I decided to leave with my dining privileges intact. Besides, I had to go break the news to Aunt Jackie.

"Not anymore." I weaved through the line waiting to be seated and disappeared.

I lucked out when I arrived at the apartment. Aunt Jackie wasn't home. I dialed her cell and when no one answered, left a voice mail. "Hey, call me. I've got some news on the food truck."

I left it at that, hoping she wouldn't think it was good news. Then I decided to stop in to see Greg.

Esmeralda sat at the station's reception desk. "Jill, I haven't seen you in forever. What's been going on over at your house? I see all kinds of activity."

"I'm remodeling an upstairs bedroom." I stretched my neck and groaned. "I'll be glad when the house is completely done. My body is rebelling against me."

Her eyes glittered as she appraised me. "Somehow I doubt that. But let's not compare aches and pains. I suppose you're here to see Greg?"

"See, you really are a fortune-teller," I teased. "I just popped in, so if he's busy?"

"He is busy, but that's not why you can't see him." She looked down at the display when the phone rang and ignored the call.

"Go ahead. If you have to get it, I can wait."

She pointed down to the display. "It's on the mayor's line. I'm not required to pick up personal calls, and all business-related calls are supposed to run through the main number. So, no worries." She turned down the ringer volume as the phone continued to chirp. "Anyway, Greg's not here. He left for Bakerstown early this morning and hasn't returned."

"Oh well, I'll catch him after work. See you later." I waved and started to turn.

"Hold on a moment." Esmeralda dug through the pink messages she had scattered all over her desk. "This is one you can take. She said if Greg didn't call her back, she'd call you. Something about a cruise refund?"

I took the pink sheet and glanced at the name scribbled on the slip. Rachel. I nodded. "I'll handle this."

"Jill, be careful," Esmeralda called as I left through the side door.

Aunt Jackie had said there was no way I'd see a refund from a cruise no matter when it was cancelled, but especially with the short notice we'd given Rachel. Now I had an opportunity to talk to her about a completely innocent subject while I tried to find out if she was Michael's little on-the-side girl. Checking my phone, by the time I walked back to the house, got the Jeep, and drove in to Bakerstown, Rachel's travel agency would be closed.

I'd go tomorrow in between my double shift and take my aunt with me. Maybe she could charm the information out of Rachel. I lacked the charm gene, but my aunt had perfected it to a science.

If Rachel Fleur was seeing the used-to-be-married Michael Ashford, my aunt would find out before the woman knew she was spilling her most treasured secret.

Or she'd be mad enough to kick us out of her agency and rip up Greg's refund check.

I pondered the two outcomes as I walked home. The first was probable, but if the second happened, I'd be in real trouble with Greg.

I tried to give myself a third option: Go pick up the check and ignore the Michael connection, but somehow, that path wasn't setting well with the rest of my body, which was screaming that I needed to find the truth.

No doubt about it, I was addicted to the hunt.

# CHAPTER 21

On my way into South Cove for my first shift after my so-called vacation, I decided to check in with Harrold. Now that Adam had admitted to vandalizing the store, I wanted to make sure Harrold was up on all the latest developments on the case.

Okay, fine, I wanted to see if Greg had dropped any information to the owner of The Train Station that he didn't think I needed to know.

Even though it was early, I peeked into the shiny new front show-room window. Harrold stood at the counter, looking at a magazine. I tried the door, thinking it would be locked, but the handle turned eas-ily and the bell over the door hooted with a quick train whistle when I entered.

"Hey, Jill, you on your way to the salt mines?" Harrold's aged, lined face lit up when he saw me. "Coming in to visit an old man? I'm going to have to tell that guy of yours he has some competition."

I wandered up to the counter, noticing that the miniature South Cove village was already back in order. Harrold didn't mess around. If it needed done, he did it. "I'm just checking in to see if you're all right. Did Greg come by and tell you about Adam and his deal with Sandra?"

Harrold closed his train magazine and leaned on his forearms on the glass counter. "He did. Very bad business, don't you think? I just don't know what I ever did to anger that woman."

"I'm not sure you did anything." I decided to jump and tell him what I knew. "She was friends with Lille. I'm not saying Lille asked her to do this," I added quickly.

Harrold sank into a chair and ran his age-spotted hand through his thinning gray hair. "Now I understand."

"What do you mean?" I watched as tears filled his gray eyes. He wiped the back of his hand across his face.

"Last night, Lille brought me dinner. A fried chicken basket, complete with apple pie. The pie was just like Agnes used to make . . . but I'm wandering. So, when I asked her why, she said she felt bad about the things that had been happening at the shop." He shrugged. "I thought she was just being kind."

"Instead, you think she felt responsible for what happened." I finished his sentence.

"Exactly." He quickly lifted his head and stared at me. "She said she never wanted anything like this to happen."

"So, she probably didn't know Sandra had set this in motion." I shook my head. "You may never know why the shop was vandalized, I mean, not really."

"I believe you just told me. A friend thought she was doing a favor for another. Just because it was a bad idea doesn't mean the friend didn't think they were doing the right thing."

"You're awfully philosophical about this." I stared at Harrold, amazed at his compassion and ready forgiveness.

He stood and walked around the counter to stand near me. "If you hold anger in your heart, it just turns to evil. You have to be able to see the good in people, even those people in whom you think there isn't even a speck of good left. Lille has said her 'I'm sorry.' Now it's time for me to accept the gesture."

I left The Train Station with two things. One, a commitment from Harrold's grandson to talk at the Business-to-Business meeting. And two, a deeper understanding of the meaning of forgiveness. Harrold made me want to be a better person.

My phone rang just as I arrived at Coffee, Books, and More. "Jill Gardner." I turned the key in the lock and flipped on the lights, holding the phone to my ear with my shoulder.

"You called and left a message on my machine yesterday? You need promotional assistance?" The man on the other end of the line was friendly, and you could hear the smile in his voice.

"Actually, I'm calling about Promote Your Event? I understand you're purchasing the company?" I hurried to the counter, where I set my purse and light jacket down. I leaned against the edge and hoped.

"I guess it's not a secret anymore since Michael and I signed the papers yesterday. I am blending the agency with my own to make a more rounded-out service for my customers." His voice was wary, but I could tell he didn't want to be rude, just in case I could be a potential customer.

"So, your initial contact was with Michael?" Now I was totally confused. That wasn't what Lille had said at all.

"No, Sandra came to me with the initial offer and all the paperwork was in her name. When I asked Michael about the sale, once I heard of Sandra's untimely death, he seemed shocked. A few days later, he called and agreed to the deal."

I heard papers rustling over the phone line. The man was moving on to his next call. "Thanks for clarifying that. Promote Your Event did some work for a charity event we hosted, and now that I know that you're taking over the company, I'll keep you in mind for our next event."

"I'll send you over a brochure outlining our services and charges." He paused. "Give me your mailing address."

I rattled off the shop's address and then said good-bye. The phone call had matched up with Lille's story. Sandra had been making preparations for skipping town. And skipping out on her marriage. Now all I needed to find was the person who, besides the very well-alibied Michael, would benefit from Sandra's death.

I had an idea, and if I was right, I would know the last clue this afternoon when Aunt Jackie and I visited Bakerstown. I started the first pot of coffee and waited for my commuter customers to start drifting into the shop. Six hours and I'd be on the road. I glanced at the clock, willing the hands to move faster.

Aunt Jackie had been waiting in the shop for Toby to relieve me for a good half hour. I'd called her around ten to fill her in on my phone call from the PR guy and ask if she wanted to be my wingman on the trip to Rachel's to pick up the refund check. Oh, and to ask her if she was Michael's secret mistress. But maybe that term was a redundancy. Maybe all mistresses were secret, or they wouldn't be mistresses? My mind played with the thought, but customers kept me too busy to check out the actual definition of the word.

Toby arrived a few minutes after his official start time. As he washed his hands in the sink, he filled me in. "Sorry, boss. The transport for Adam didn't arrive until just a few minutes ago, and Greg wanted two of us on site for the transfer. I guess this guy can charm his way out of most situations."

"Greg was afraid Adam would talk his way out?" I cleaned the espresso machine as we chatted. "Doesn't sound like him."

"Nah, I don't think he was concerned, but the other guys coming from out of town made the request that we have two people on staff 'round the clock for this guy." Toby slipped on his apron and started restacking the cups on the other side of the machine. "The mayor's going to go bonkers when he sees this month's overtime. I might just be able to make a dent in my student loan with this next check."

"Are we done socializing? I've got things to do. It is my day off, you know." Aunt Jackie checked her hair in a compact mirror, then clicked it shut. Loudly.

"Where are you two going?" Toby slid open the dessert display, checking on the inventory. "Or do I want to know?"

"Nothing bad. We're going to Bakerstown to pick up the refund check from Rachel at the travel agency. Aunt Jackie wanted to talk to her about a trip next fall." I grabbed my purse from under the counter and motioned to my aunt to follow me. "I'll be back at four to relieve you."

"I never doubted it." Toby grinned and followed us into the back room. When he noticed me watching, he pointed to the freezer. "I need to grab another one of those lemon cheesecakes. I sold a ton of that stuff yesterday."

As we left the building and stepped into the bright sunlight, Aunt Jackie slipped on a pair of oversized and overpriced sunglasses. In the Jeep, she turned toward me. "You don't think she'll figure out what we're really asking her, do you? I mean, saying you're the little something on the side is a lot different from admitting you killed the woman standing in the way of your happiness."

"We don't know that Rachel was either one of those things. That's why I'm not taking this crazy theory to Greg until we at least verify she and Michael were having an affair. Then Greg can check her alibi and we'll be out of the sleuthing business." I backed out of my parking spot and turned left onto the road, taking the long way out of town.

"And that's why you're not driving by the police station on the way out of town? Because Greg finding out about what we're doing wouldn't be a problem?" My aunt watched me as I drove the speed limit out of town.

"We're not doing anything wrong," I muttered as we finally reached the highway.

My aunt settled into the passenger seat. "Keep telling yourself that."

The ride to Bakerstown was quiet, which I didn't mind. I'd rather deal with my own issues of keeping things from Greg without the interference or unrequested wisdom from my aunt. By the time we reached the travel agency and pulled into the parking lot, the energy in the car was electric.

Aunt Jackie stared at the little cottage. "You have a plan?"

I shook my head. "Not really. I thought I'd start the conversation and you could ask who she's been dating lately in your typical charming manner."

"And what if she won't tell me?" my aunt pressed. "How far do you want me to take this phony trip story?"

Crap, I hadn't thought of that. What if Rachel wasn't going to be Chatty Cathy about her love life? "Then we get the refund, and I call Greg and tell him what I, what we, think."

She considered this answer, then nodded. "Okay, then. Project Secret Mistress is in full force." She frowned at me. "What are you waiting for? Christmas?"

I climbed out of the Jeep and waited for my aunt to join me. I clicked the lock on the Jeep's key fob. Cathy Addy was peeking out from her yarn shop window. I waved and she disappeared back into the building. "Not very friendly today," I said as we walked into the travel agency.

"Who are you talking about?" Aunt Jackie turned, trying to see around me.

I motioned her into the lobby. "Don't worry about it."

The bell had announced our entrance, and Rachel appeared from the back room. "Hey, my favorite South Cove customers."

I thought we were probably her only South Cove customers, but I didn't point this out. "I'm glad we caught you. Esmeralda said you had a check for Greg? I thought since I was going to be in town today, I'd just grab it on my way."

"I do. I almost never get refunds on cruises, but this particular company is very customer-service oriented. Let me grab it out of the safe." She turned back to the room she'd just left, and a few minutes later, she returned with an envelope. Rachel handed it to me. "There you go. I'd say let me know when you're ready to go again, but actually, I'm closing the agency."

My aunt let out a tiny gasp. "No. I came with Jill today to talk to you about another trip next fall. I adore taking senior hostel trips, especially those that happen on college campuses. I was hoping you could help me find one in New England. I so wanted to see the leaves change."

Rachel sank on the stool near her desk. "I know. I went to school back East, and I've missed the fall change more than I realized." She dug through her desk drawer. "Here's the name and number of a guy who runs an agency out of the city. He's very good, and if you tell him I sent you, he'll give you a good deal."

Aunt Jackie took the card and slipped it into her purse. "I appreciate the referral. So, tell me about your leaving? Are you going back East?"

Rachel's face froze. "Why would you think that?"

"You said you went to school there. Are you trying to rekindle a lost love? Or are you moving because of someone?" My aunt studied a brochure for an all-inclusive island retreat that was on the counter. "I swear, I can't count the number of times my dear husband moved us across the country just because of his job."

I felt my chin drop, but caught it before my surprise at the lie was apparent to Rachel. Aunt Jackie was good. She played her part well. I leaned against the wall, watching Rachel, hoping she was buying our fake girls' talk. "I've never moved for a man. Well, I moved to get away from a man. Maybe you are, too?"

"You've caught me." Rachel stood. "I'm running away with my mystery man. Come here, I want to show you what he bought for me."

We watched as Rachel moved down the hall. She hadn't mentioned Michael yet, but maybe the gift was a picture of the two of them or a clue to where they were moving. I took my aunt's arm and led her, with me following Rachel.

She pushed a door open, then motioned for us to go in first. The room was bare. No furniture, no gift, no clues. I spun around, to see Rachel holding a gun on us. "I don't know exactly what your game is, but I don't have time to play."

"You can't keep us here." I pushed my aunt behind me, hoping Rachel wouldn't actually use the weapon.

Rachel smiled. "Oh, but I can. At least long enough to give Michael and me time to get out of this town. He's already picked up the check from the sale of the business. Now all we have to do is go enjoy the fruits of Sandra's labor. I can't believe that woman was trying to skip town and leave Michael penniless." She leaned against the door frame. "I'm a good sport and all, but I have my standards."

"So, you found out about the sale of the business and killed her before she could leave." I looked at Rachel's hand where she held the gun. She noticed my attention and raised it back so it pointed right at my chest.

"Please don't make me do something stupid." She motioned me back a few steps. "That's better. I didn't mean to kill her. I was just going to talk, but then she went all *crazy* on me and took off walking down the road. I would have just hit her the one time, but she kept moving. In for a penny, my mom always said."

"You're just going to leave us here?" If we were locked in the room, at least I could call for help with my cell. Apparently that idea occurred to Rachel, too.

She motioned with her hand. "Throw your purses out into the hall. That way you won't be tempted to do anything stupid. Once we're in Nevada, I'll call the police station and let them know where you are. Or, if you were smart, someone knows where you are and they may come looking for you sooner."

We did as she asked, then Rachel moved to shut the door but paused. "Oh, one more thing? Tell Greg not to cash that check. There isn't any money in that account. I'd hate for him to think badly of me for writing him a rubber check."

Then she shut and locked the door from the outside. I ran to the window to see if I could open it, but no luck. The window looked out over an open field. We didn't even luck out to be in a room across from the nosy neighbor.

Aunt Jackie dusted off a patch of floor in the corner and sank down. "Come sit. All we have to do is wait until four and Toby will place a call to Greg, who will call the Bakerstown Police, who will rescue us in"—she paused to look at her watch—"three hours, give or take."

I jiggled the door handle, which was solidly locked.

"Jill, come sit down," my aunt repeated. "Besides, even if you get out right now, she's still in the building. She could shoot you."

I hadn't thought of that. Maybe regrouping for a few minutes was for the best. Besides, I didn't want my aunt to be harmed because I was being stupid. I sat down beside her. "Sorry I got you into this."

My aunt patted my hand. "Believe me, if you had come by yourself, I would have been so mad at you. I enjoy our little escapades."

I leaned my head back against the wall. I'd always thought if I had gotten into trouble and arrested, Amy would be the friend sitting beside me saying what fun we had. Now I realized it would probably always have been Aunt Jackie. I really had to stop getting her involved in my foolhardy antics. "I've put you in danger."

"We're only locked in a room. It's not like she's shooting at us or the place is on fire." My aunt closed her eyes. "Maybe I'll take a little nap. I'll have to put my trip into the city for the new gallery opening off until next weekend."

I was too wound up to sleep. And now that she'd mentioned fire, I swore I could smell smoke. I rubbed my face. I was so suggestible. I stared at the door. Then glanced at my watch. Five minutes had passed. I heard a car start up and I stood to look out the window, but I couldn't see the parking lot. I figured that we were alone in the building. I tried opening the window. No luck. Something was nagging at me. Why would Rachel admit to killing Sandra? Unless they were leaving the country today and she was pretty sure we wouldn't be rescued for a while. Still, something felt off.

I glanced at my watch again. Six minutes. This was going to be the longest three hours I'd ever spent. I settled back down next to my aunt and closed my eyes. The smell of smoke got stronger. Shaking my head to try to stop my crazy thoughts, I opened my eyes and saw a thin line of smoke coming into the room from the hallway. Now I knew why Rachel felt comfortable telling us everything. I slipped off my jacket and ran to the door, shoving the cloth between the wood and the floor. I felt the door. It was hot. "Aunt Jackie, get up. The place is on fire. The crazy woman set her own building on fire." My lungs burned, and I felt like I was going to pass out. *Think, Jill, think.*

"What are you talking about?" my aunt grumbled, then sniffed and opened her eyes wide. "The room smells like smoke."

"That's because the house is on fire," I repeated. "Look around, what can we do?"

There was nothing of use in the room, but in the closet, an old cash box was stashed on the top shelf. I pulled it down and took it over to the window. The drop to the ground was too far for Aunt Jackie: she'd break a hip or both when she landed. I, on the other hand, might just break an ankle. As long as it wasn't two, I could crawl to the Jeep and make a call using the OnStar system.

Except I'd locked the doors of the vehicle. I felt my jeans pockets. The key fob was there. I hadn't slipped it in my purse. I pushed the button to set off the alarm and prayed that I was in range for it to work.

No alarm blared.

I stepped near the window and pressed it again. This time I could hear my horn going off. Now at least Cathy next door should notice the alarm and hopefully the fire. I coughed. Even with my coat to block the opening, the smoke was getting stronger in the room. I had to get the window open.

I hit the window with the metal cash box. Nothing. I hit it over and over, nothing. Finally I sank down on my knees to rest and breathe some cleaner air. No way we'd last until four, or probably even until the car alarm clued the neighbor in to calling the police. We were going to die, and it was all my fault.

My aunt pulled me to my feet. "Let me help. Maybe with both of us swinging the box, we can get the glass to break."

We stood on both sides of the window. "One, two, three," I counted out and this time, when the box hit the window, a tiny crack appeared. "It's working." I focused on my aunt, who was getting a little fuzzy from the smoke in the room. "Again. One, two, three."

This time the glass broke, and I felt the cool air pouring into the room. I pushed Aunt Jackie away. "Turn away, I'm going to break this glass out so I can climb out."

My aunt came closer and looked down. "It's too far to the ground."

"Just trust me." I turned her away from the window and started breaking out the glass. Once the bottom pane was cleared, I looked at my aunt. "Give me that jacket."

"There's no way it will fit you, my dear. Besides, it's not cold in here." She leaned out and over the open window. "I still don't think you can jump that. You never were the most coordinated child."

"I'm not going to wear your jacket." I ignored her jab at my physical prowess. I looked at the wooden window frame.

"Dear, you can't be serious." She rubbed the arms of her suit. "This is Chanel. Classic Chanel."

I borrowed and butchered a line from one of the action movies Greg kept making me watch. "Give me the jacket if you want to live." I may have been overpromising.

She looked over at the locked door, where smoke was now billowing into the room, all around the edges of the door. "Fine, but you're replacing the entire suit as soon as I can find one available."

Taking the jacket, I looked closely to see if there were any jagged glass pieces left on the frame or ledge. When I was satisfied it was clear, I laid the jacket over the ledge and lifted my leg out the window. I settled, half in and half out, looking at my aunt. "Wish me luck."

Before I could lift the other leg, I heard a scream from below.

"Don't jump! We'll save you." Cathy Addy stood next to her walker staring in horror at me. I grabbed hold of the ledge. She was blocking my fall spot, and I didn't think landing on an elderly woman would look good in the local papers. Especially if I killed her.

"Move back. I've got to get help." I waved her off, but she just shook her head. "Seriously, you need to move. We can't stay in this room much longer."

My aunt poked her head out the window and took a deep breath of cool air. "What's the holdup?"

Then a fireman came around the building after Cathy. "Lady, you need to go back to the parking lot and away from the house. It's not safe."

She shrugged and pointed at me. "You really need to save those women before you lose them."

The man's gaze followed her arm, and when he saw me, he grabbed the microphone on his uniform. "Get a ladder back here." He put his hand up to hold me back from jumping. "Don't move, ma'am. We'll get you down. Is there anyone else in there with you?"

My aunt poked her head out again. "Me. Please save me." I swear the woman batted her eyes at the man.

He blushed and nodded. "We'll be right there. Don't worry, you're safe now."

I glanced over at my aunt. "Do you *have* to flirt?"

She prepped her hair and faced me. "Do I look okay?"

"For a rescue? You look amazing." I wanted to rest my back on the window frame, but I didn't know if I'd gotten all of the glass out or not. "For a rescue by a *fireman*." My aunt shook her head. "You are so clueless. No wonder you're not married."

I started to tell her that not only had I been married, I was in a serious relationship with no need to flirt with first responders, but before I could speak, a ladder hit the wall of the shop. I glanced down. The lone fireman had been joined by several others. "Can you climb down, or do you need me to assist?"

I swung my leg over to the ladder, then lifted the second to meet the first. I jerked once and wondered if I would end up falling on my butt or worse, even with the fire brigade assistance. But I righted myself quickly and felt my aunt's hand on my shoulder.

"Be careful," she whispered.

I touched her arm and smiled at her. "Back at you."

By the time they'd gotten Aunt Jackie out and the fire mostly contained, Greg had arrived from South Cove. He came over to the ambulance where I was sitting with Aunt Jackie. They'd insisted we use some oxygen to clear out the smoke from our lungs. I felt fine, but I knew if I balked, my aunt would follow suit. Besides, she was having so much fun with the EMTs, I didn't want to disturb her.

"I can't leave you alone for a minute, can I?" Greg stood in front of me, his gaze taking in my appearance. "Are you hurt?"

I stood. "Not even a scratch. Which is amazing since the window shattered into shards of glass. You would have thought—"

My next words were lost as he pulled me close to him and kissed me hard. He didn't let go until I relaxed into him. Tears filled my eyes, and I swallowed them away.

"I thought I'd lost you when the call came in." He looked into my face and pushed my hair back behind my ears. "What were you doing here?"

"Picking up a check from Rachel." Crap, I'd forgotten about Rachel. "Hold up, you need to know this. Rachel killed Sandra because she was going to leave Michael without any money. So, they are taking off with the money and probably to a country that doesn't extradite."

He put his hand up to stop my ramblings. "Don't worry about Rachel. We've got lookouts at the local airports and a BOLO out on her car."

"But I didn't tell anyone. How did you know?"

A voice came from behind Greg. "I told them. I had come into the shop to see if Rachel wanted me to water her plants while she was gone and I heard her telling you all about what she did." Cathy Addy shook her head. "I backed out of the house as quickly as possible and headed back to my house to call the cops. Good thing I talked her into installing the ramps on the building or the two of you might not have made it."

Thank God for nosy—wait, make that concerned—neighbors, I thought. "Thank you, Mrs. Addy."

The woman blushed. "Not a problem, my dear, not a problem at all. But I guess I won't be watering her plants now. I think the fire killed them all."

# CHAPTER 22

The Business-to Business meeting started on time that next week. We had a special speaker, and without Sasha even calling the regular members to check on their attendance, we had a full house. Christopher Snider, Harrold's grandson, was presenting on "10 Reasons You Need a Website." I'd asked Toby to come in to help with refreshments as Sasha was actually going to be sitting at the table, representing Coffee, Books, and More. I had added the website design and upkeep to her list of duties.

Sadie slipped into a seat next to Dustin Austin, and I watched with humor as he looked over at her. Austin looked totally smitten with my friend. I tapped her on the shoulder in greeting, then went to sit next to Sasha. Amy was on my other side.

"We on for shopping on Sunday?" she asked, keeping an eye on Bill Sullivan to see when he was actually going to call the meeting to order.

"I still need a rug and a quilt, so if you're available, I'm game." I'd had a busy week since being rescued from the fire at Rachel's travel agency. Greg had been even busier and hadn't been able to make this meeting. Rachel and Michael were in custody, and each was pointing the finger at the other as the ringleader for their plot to murder Sandra. Tomorrow, Allison Delaine was meeting me at the shop to talk about hosting joint ventures between South Cove and Bakerstown's committees.

Frank Gleason had shown up yesterday at the house to take pictures of the wall and explain that the California Mission Society had misspoken when they said what he was now calling the South Cove Mission site had been approved. The wall had been moved up to a formal study process. Frank thought it was a good step. I was thinking the wall should be either on the list or not within the next twenty years or so.

Of course the Society still wanted us to host a race next year. I told them to call Darla. She could make that decision.

"You look tired." Amy rubbed the back of my neck. "Maybe you need a vacation from your vacation."

A month later, we were finally on a beach at an all-inclusive resort. Greg and I sat side by side in loungers, drinking the fruity umbrella drink of the day. I had just finished a historical fiction book about Jack the Ripper's wife and was thinking about going to the hotel room to switch out to a new book.

"You guys up for snorkeling?" Amy sat down on my lounger. "Justin and I are dying to get in the water."

"Sounds good to me." Greg stood up and put his hands out. "You done reading for a bit?"

"Researching," I countered automatically.

Greg laughed and pulled me up. "Then you are done. Researching is work, and this is a no-work zone."

Greg and Justin sprinted to the shed to grab the snorkel gear. Amy sat down in Greg's chair. "Too bad Jackie and Josh couldn't make it. She would love this beach."

I shook my head. "I'm kind of glad they stayed behind. I mean, really, could you picture Josh in a bathing suit?"

"You're so bad." Amy laughed and shook her shoulders. "Great, now I can't get that image out of my mind."

"Exactly." My phone rang and I reached to answer. The caller ID didn't show a name. "Hello?"

Amy shook her head and whispered, "You're on vacation. You should have let it go to voice mail." I watched as she stood to go join the men.

"Jill, is that you?" a tear-choked Sadie asked.

Fear gripped me. "What's wrong, Sadie? Is it Aunt Jackie? The shop? Oh no, did something happen to Nick?"

I heard her blow her nose and waited. "What? No. Everyone's fine."

"Then why do you sound like you're crying?"

Sadie sniffed. "Austin broke up with me. He's going back to his wife."

*Dustin Austin has a wife?* Greg was waving at me to come over to the shed. I held up a finger and grabbed my tote bag, filling it with the stuff we'd brought out to the beach from the room. "I'm so sorry. I didn't know he was married."

"Believe me, I didn't, either." Sadie paused a moment. "The worst thing is, they are opening a food truck selling gluten-free desserts. And they're parking it in front of Austin's shop. He told me all about the plan. Then he . . ." A fresh wave of sobs filled the phone.

"He what, Sadie?" I wished I was home so I could go over to the bike shop and give this creep a piece of my mind for hurting my friend.

"He asked for my Summer Lemon Surprise Cheesecake recipe."

After I'd calmed Sadie down and promised to call later that afternoon to talk more, I rejoined the group getting ready to snorkel.

"So, what's going on?" Greg nodded to the phone, which I slipped into my tote and then handed to the guy manning the counter for safekeeping while we were out.

I told them Sadie's sad news and then told them about the food truck. "The weird thing is, I think that's the truck Lille and I were trying to buy a couple of months ago. Which means Austin has been planning on breaking up with Sadie for a while now."

"You don't think he was dating her for access to her recipes, do you?" Amy shook her head. "He can't be that conniving of a person."

All I knew was that one of my friends was hurting. And Dustin Austin was the cause. We walked to the shore and slipped into the water, where, for a couple of hours, I forgot everything but watching the life that happened under the waves.

I couldn't help but compare my day with Sadie's that evening when we were sitting around a fire. You never really knew what was going on underneath until you took the time to look.

When I got back to town, finding out all about Dustin Austin was going to be my first project.

"Earth to Jill." Greg stroked my hand, and I looked up from staring at the flames. "You want a beer?"

I pulled him down into a kiss, then nodded. As he walked away, I blessed the hand that had put the four of us together as friends. And then, I let my worries go.

Time to recharge.

Don't Miss Any of
The Tourist Trap Mysteries!
Available now from
Lyrical Press

**In the gentle coastal town of South Cove, California, all
Jill Gardner wants is to keep her store—Coffee, Books,
and More—open and running. So, why is she caught up
in the business of murder?**

### *Guidebook to Murder*

When Jill's elderly friend, Miss Emily, calls her in a fit of pique,
she already knows the city council is trying to force Emily to sell
her dilapidated old house. But Emily's gumption goes for naught
when she dies unexpectedly and leaves the house to Jill—along with
all of her problems . . . *and* her enemies. Convinced her friend was
murdered, Jill is finding the list of suspects longer than the list of
repairs needed on the house. But Jill is determined to uncover the
culprit—especially if it gets her closer to South Cove's finest,
Detective Greg King. Problem is, the killer knows she's on the
case—and is determined to close the book on Jill *permanently* . . .

### *Mission to Murder*

Jill Gardner, proprietor of Coffee, Books, and More, has
discovered that the old stone wall on her property might be a
centuries-old mission worthy of being declared a landmark. But
Craig Morgan, the obnoxious owner of South Cove's most popular
tourist spot, The Castle, makes it his business to contest her claim.
When Morgan is found murdered at The Castle shortly after a
heated argument with Jill, even her detective boyfriend has to ask
her for an alibi. Jill decides she must find the real murderer to clear
her name. But when the killer comes for her, she'll need to jump
from historic preservation to self-preservation . . .

## *If the Shoe Kills*

As owner of Coffee, Books, and More, Jill Gardner looks forward to the hustle and bustle of holiday shoppers. But when the mayor ropes her into being liaison for a new work program, 'tis the season to be wary. Local businesses are afraid the interns will be delinquents, punks, or worse. For Jill, no one's worse than Ted Hendricks—the jerk who runs the program. After a few run-ins, Jill's ready to kill the guy. That, however, turns out to be unnecessary when she finds Ted in his car—dead as a doornail. Detective Greg King assumes it's a suicide. Jill thinks it's murder. And if the holidays weren't stressful enough, a spoiled blonde wants to sue the city for breaking her heel. Jill has to act fast to solve this mess—before the other shoe drops . . .

## *Dressed to Kill*

Of course everyone is expecting a "dead" body at the dress rehearsal . . . but this one isn't acting! It turns out the main suspect is the late actor's conniving girlfriend, Sherry . . . who also happens to be the ex-wife of Jill's main squeeze. Sherry is definitely a master manipulator . . . but is she a killer? Jill may discover the truth only when the curtain comes up on the final act . . . and by then, it may be far too late.

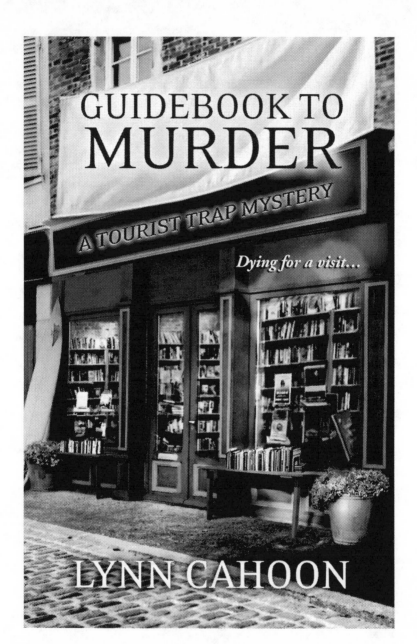

# GUIDEBOOK TO
# MURDER

## A TOURIST TRAP MYSTERY

*Dying for a visit...*

# LYNN CAHOON

MISSION TO
MURDER
A TOURIST TRAP MYSTERY
Don't miss the
deadly landmark…
ANTIQUES
THOMAS
CASTLE TOURS
NEW YORK TIMES BESTSELLING AUTHOR
LYNN CAHOON

# IF THE SHOE
# KILLS

## A TOURIST TRAP MYSTERY

The Glass Slipper

*NEW YORK TIMES* BESTSELLING AUTHOR
# LYNN CAHOON

# DRESSED TO KILL

## A TOURIST TRAP MYSTERY

*What you see is not what you get...*

# LYNN CAHOON

Angela Brewer Armstrong

*USA Today* and *New York Times* best-selling author Lynn Cahoon is an Idaho native. If you visited the town where she grew up, you'd understand why her mystery and romance novels focus around the depth and experience of small town life. Currently, she's living in a small historic town on the banks of the Mississippi River, where her imagination tends to wander. She lives with her husband and two fur babies.

Printed in the United States
by Baker & Taylor Publisher Services